From the day the H-bombs rained, to the establishment of the Reconstituted United Nations, to the conversion of Venus, Poul Anderson has outlined herein the major events in the history of Terrestrial Man. So glory once again in the triumphs of our ancestors—those men and women of Planet Earth who, primitives though they were, won for us first the Solar System and then the stars themselves, under the hegemony of—

The Psychotechnic League...

POUL ANDERSON

The Psycho-Technic League

A TOM DOHERTY
ASSOCIATES BOOK

TOR
science
fiction

PINNACLE BOOKS
NEW YORK

THE PSYCHOTECHNIC LEAGUE

A Pinnacle/Tor Book, published in association with Tom Doherty Associates Books.

First printing, June 1981

ISBN: 0-523-48502-6

Cover illustration by Vincent DiFate

Printed in the United States of America

PINNACLE BOOKS, INC.
1430 Broadway
New York, New York 10018

Acknowledgements

Material original to this edition copyright © 1981 by Poul Anderson. The short story and three novellas (short novels) included in Book I of the History of the Psychotechnic League were first published as follows: Marius, Astounding, June 1957; Un-Man, Astounding, January, 1953; The Sensitive Man, Fantastic Universe, November, 1953; The Big Rain, Astounding, October, 1954.

The Psychotechnic League

POUL ANDERSON

With a Foreword and
interstitial material by
Sandra Miesel

CONTENTS

THE PSYCHOTECHNIC LEAGUE

1958, the year the H-bombs fell, set human history careening in a new direction. So obvious is this nexus, an entire genre of fantastic fiction asks the question "What if World War III had not happened?" Although romantics prefer to imagine alternate twentieth centuries as lost paradises of peace and plenty, the opposite is likelier to be true.

We modern historians generally regard World War III as a mitigated catastrophe. Regrettable as its megadeaths and global devastation were, it drove humanity to establish effective world government and to colonize the solar system decades sooner than these objectives might otherwise have been achieved. More importantly, in strictly pragmatic terms, the early atomic era was the best time to resolve East-West rivalry; the crude weapons of that day could not sterilize Earth. From the standpoint of our mature integrated culture, World War III was a painful childhood illness of our race.

Conflict was inevitable once Eisenhower's death from surgical complications elevated Nixon to the U.S. presidency in June, 1956. Cold War paranoia distorted Nixon's reactions to unrest within the Communist bloc in the autumn of that year. Covert U.S. aid to the Hungarian rebels so enraged the Soviet Union that it backed Egypt past the limits of prudence during the Suez Crisis. The savage Mideast war that followed left Socialism dominant throughout the region and the U.S.S.R. in possession of northern Iran.

The assassination of Tito shortly afterwards enabled the Soviets to bring Yugoslavia back under their control. Political strife among Krushchev, Bulganin, and Zhukov made Soviet policy too erratic for American analysts to predict. International tensions built during 1958. When the U.S.S.R. threatened a new Berlin blockade and the People's Republic of China seized the Nationalist-held islands of Quemoy and Matsu, Nixon took adamant stands on two fronts at once. The East responded with a pre-emptive strike at the West on Christmas Eve, 1958.

These first bombs destroyed prime U.S. targets at home and abroad. The Philippines and Australia's major ports were immobilized. NATO countries lost their capitals and military bases but most of their territory was spared pending future conquest. However, U.S. counter-strikes carried by missiles and the Strategic Air Command inflicted proportionately more damage on enemy targets simply because there were fewer significant ones to be hit.

The Soviets crossed the Rhine, but with their industrial base virtually gone and internal communications cut, they could not resupply their armies adequately, even for conventional warfare. Satellite troops mutinied rather than support a losing cause—their nationalism overpowered their Marxism. Europe liberated itself through a bitter war of attrition. Meanwhile, American and British Commonwealth forces futilely campaigned on the Asian mainland from Indochina to Manchuria.

Behind the lines, anti-Party revolutions shattered the Communist world to bloody bits. The trauma of bombardment exposed hatreds formerly hidden by the blandness of prewar American society. Racial and social clashes erupted throughout the country. Newly freed Europe faced a swarm of civil wars as each ethnic group sought to exploit the general chaos to its own advantage. Worldwide economic collapse ruined those colonies and non-aligned nations that had escaped military attack.

By the fall of 1964, the fires of international conflict had sunk to a few sullen embers. Whether these would die to ashes or burst into fresh flame depended on a single man. . . .

MARIUS

It was raining again, with a bite in the air as the planet spun toward winter. They hadn't yet restored the street lights, and an early dusk seeped up between ruined walls and hid the tattered people who dwelt in caves grubbed out of rubble. Etienne Fourre, chief of the Maquisard Brotherhood and therefore representative of France in the Supreme Council of United Free Europe, stubbed his toe on a cobblestone. Pain struck through a worn-out boot, and he swore with tired expertise. The fifty guards ringing him in, hairy men in a patchwork of clothes—looted from the uniforms of a dozen armies, their own insignia merely a hand-sewn Tricolor brassard—tensed. That was an automatic reaction, the bristling of a wolf at any unawaited noise, long ago drilled into them.

"*Eh, bien,*" said Fourre. "Perhaps Rouget de l'Isle stumbled on the same rock while composing the 'Marseillaise.' "

One-eyed Astier shrugged, an almost invisible gesture in the dark. "When is the next grain shipment due?" he asked. It was hard to think of anything but food above the noise of a shrunken belly, and the Liberators had shucked military formalities during the desperate years.

"Tomorrow, I think, or the next day, if the barges aren't waylaid by river pirates," said Fourre. "And I don't believe they will be, so close to Strasbourg." He tried to smile. "Be of good cheer, my old. Next year should give an ample harvest. The Americans are shipping us a new blight-preventive."

"Always next year," grumbled Astier. "Why don't they send us something to eat now?"

"The blights hit them, too. This is the best they can do for us. Had it not been for them, we would still be skulking in the woods sniping at Russians."

"We had a little something to do with winning."

"More than a little, thanks to Professor Valti. I do not think any of our side could have won without all the others."

"If you call this victory." Astier's soured voice faded into silence. They were passing the broken cathedral, where child-packs often hid. The little wild ones had sometimes attacked armed men with their jagged bottles and rusty bayonets. But fifty soldiers were too many, of course. Fourre thought he heard a scuttering among the stones; but that might only have been the rats. Never had he dreamed there could be so many rats.

The thin, sad rain blew into his face and weighted his beard. Night rolled out of the east, like a message from Soviet lands plunged into chaos and murder. *But we are rebuilding,* he told himself defensively. Each week the authority of the Strasbourg Council reached a civilizing hand farther into the smashed countries of Europe. In ten years, five perhaps—automation was so fantastically productive, if only you could get hold of the machines in the first place—the men of the West would again be peaceful farmers and shopkeepers, their culture again a going concern.

If the multinational Councillors made the right decisions. And they had not been making them. Valti had finally convinced Fourre of that. Therefore he walked through the rain, hugging an old bicycle poncho to his sleazy jacket, and men in barracks were quietly estimating how many jumps it would take to reach their racked weapons. For they must overpower those who did not agree.

A wry notion, that the feudal principle of personal loyalty to a chief should have to be invoked to enforce the decrees of a new mathematics that only some thousand minds in the world understood. But you wouldn't expect the Norman peasant Astier or the Parisian apache Renault to bend the scanty spare time of a year to learning the operations of symbolic sociology. You would merely say, "Come," and they would come because they loved you.

The streets resounded hollow under his feet. It was a world without logic, this one. Only the accidents of survival had made the village apothecary Étienne Fourre into the *de facto* commander of Free France. He could have wished those accidents had taken him and spared Jeanette, but at least he had two sons living, and someday, if they hadn't gotten too much radiation, there would be grandchildren. God was not altogether revengeful.

"There we are, up ahead," said Astier.

Fourre did not bother to reply. He had never been under the common human necessity of forever mouthing words.

Strasbourg was the seat of the Council because of location and because it was not too badly hit. Only a conventional battle with chemical explosives had rolled through here eighteen months ago. The University was almost unscathed, and so became the headquarters of Jacques Reinach. His men prowled about on guard; one wondered what Goethe would have thought could he have returned to the scene of his student days. And yet it was men such as this, with dirty hands and clean weapons, who were civilization. It was their kind who had harried the wounded Russian colossus out of the West and who would restore law and liberty and wind-rippled fields of grain. Someday. Perhaps.

A machine-gun nest stood at the first checkpoint. The sergeant in charge recognized Fourre and gave a sloppy salute. (Still, the fact that Reinach had imposed so much discipline on his horde spoke for the man's personality.)

"Your escort must wait here, my general," he said, half-apologizing. "A new regulation."

"I know," said Fourre. Not all of his guards did, and he must shush a snarling. "I have an appointment with the Commandant."

"Yes, sir. Please stay to the lighted paths. Otherwise you might be shot by mistake for a looter."

Fourre nodded and walked through, in among the buildings. His body wanted to get in out of the rain, but he went slowly, delaying the moment. Jacques Reinach was not just his countryman but his friend. Fourre was nowhere near as close to, say, Helgesen of the Nordic Alliance, or the Italian Totti, or Rojansky of Poland, and he positively disliked the German Auerbach.

But Valti's matrices were not concerned with a man's heart. They simply told you that given such and such conditions, this and that would probably happen. It was a cold knowledge to bear.

The structure housing the main offices was a loom of darkness, but a few windows glowed at Fourre. Reinach had had an electric generator installed—and rightly, to be sure, when his tired staff and his tired self must often work around the clock.

A sentry admitted Fourre to an outer room. There half a dozen men picked their teeth and diced for cartridges while a tubercular secretary coughed over files written on old laundry bills, flyleaves, any scrap of paper that came to hand. The lot of them stood up, and Fourre told them he had come to see the Commandant, chairman of the Council.

"Yes, sir." The officer was still in his teens, fuzzy face already shriveled into old age, and spoke very bad French. "Check your guns with us and go on in."

Fourre unbuckled his pistols, reflecting that this latest requirement, the disarming of commanders before they could meet Chairman Reinach, was what had driven Álvarez into fury and the conspiracy. Yet the decree was not unreasonable; Reinach must know of gathering opposition, and everyone had grown far too used to settling disputes violently. Ah, well, Álvarez was no philosopher, but he was boss of the Iberian Irregulars, and you had to use what human material was available.

The officer frisked him, and that was a wholly new indignity, which heated Fourre's own skin. He choked his anger, thinking that Valti had predicted as much.

Down a corridor then, which smelled moldy in the autumnal dankness, and to a door where one more sentry was posted. Fourre nodded at him and opened the door.

"Good evening, Étienne. What can I do for you?"

The big blond man looked up from his desk and smiled. It was a curiously shy, almost a young smile, and something wrenched within Fourre.

This had been a professor's office before the war. Dust lay thick on the books that lined the walls. Really, they should take more care of books, even if it meant giving less attention to famine and plague and banditry. At the rear was a closed window, with a dark wash of rain flowing across miraculously intact glass. Reinach sat with a lamp by his side and his back to the night.

Fourre lowered himself. The visitor's chair creaked under a gaunt-fleshed but heavy-boned weight. "Can't you guess, Jacques?" he asked.

The handsome Alsatian face, one of the few clean-shaven faces left in the world, turned to study him for a while. "I wasn't sure you were against me, too," said Reinach. "Helgesen, Totti, Alexios . . . yes, that gang . . . but you? We have been friends for many years, Étienne. I didn't expect you would turn on me."

"Not on you." Fourre sighed and wished for a cigarette, but tobacco was a remote memory. "Never you, Jacques. Only your policies. I am here, speaking for all of us—"

"Not quite all," said Reinach. His tone was quiet and unaccusing. "Now I realize how cleverly you maneuvered my firm supporters out of town. Brevoort flying off to Ukrainia to establish relations with the revolutionary government; Ferenczi down in Genoa to collect those ships for our merchant marine; Janosek talked into leading an expedition against the bandits in Schlewswig. Yes, yes, you plotted this carefully, didn't you? But what do you think they will have to say on their return?"

"They will accept a *fait accompli*," answered Fourre. "This generation has had a gutful of war. But I said I was here to speak to you on behalf of my associates. We hoped you would listen to reason from me, at least."

"If it is reason." Reinach leaned back in his chair, cat-comfortable, one palm resting on a revolver butt. "We have threshed out the arguments in council. If you start them again—"

"—it is because I must." Fourre sat looking at the scarred, bony hands in his lap. "We do understand, Jacques, that the chairman of the Council must have supreme power for the duration of the emergency. We agreed to give you the final word. But not the *only* word."

A paleness of anger flicked across the blue eyes. "I have been maligned enough," said Reinach coldly. "They think I want to make myself a dictator. Étienne, after the Second War was over and you went off and became a snug civilian, why do you think I elected to make the Army my career? Not because I had any taste for militarism. But I foresaw our land would again be in danger, within my own lifetime, and I wanted to hold myself ready. Does that sound like . . . like some new kind of Hitler?"

"No, of course not, my friend. You did nothing but follow the example of de Gaulle. And when we chose you to lead our combined forces, we could not have chosen better. Without you—and Valti—there would still be war on the eastern front. We . . . I . . . we think of you as our deliverer, just as if we were the littlest peasant given back his own plot of earth. But you have not been *right*."

"Everyone makes mistakes." Reinach actually smiled. "I admit my own. I bungled badly in cleaning out those Communists at—"

Fourre shook his head stubbornly. "You don't understand, Jacques. It isn't that kind of mistake I mean. Your great error is that you have not realized we are at peace. The war is over."

Reinach lifted a sardonic brow. "Not a barge goes along the Rhine, not a kilometer of railroad track is relaid, but we have to fight bandits, local warlords, half-crazed fanatics of a hundred new breeds. Does that sound like peacetime?"

"It is a difference of . . . of objectives," said Fourre. "And man is such an animal that it is the end, not the means, which makes the difference. War is morally simple: one purpose, to impose your will on the enemy. Not to surrender to an inferior force. But a policeman? He is protecting an entire society, of which the criminal is also a part. A politician? He has to make compromises, even with small groups and with people he despises. You think like a solider, Jacques, and we no longer want or need a soldier commanding us."

"Now you're quoting that senile fool Valti," snapped Reinach.

"If we hadn't had Professor Valti and his sociosymbolic logic to plan our strategy for us, we would still be locked with the Russians. There was no way for us to be liberated from the outside this time. The Anglo-Saxon countries had little strength to spare, after the exchange of missiles, and that little had to go to Asia. They could not invade a Europe occupied by a Red Army whose back was against the wall of its own wrecked homeland. We had to liberate ourselves, with ragged men and bicycle cavalry and aircraft patched together out of wrecks. Had it not been for Valti's plans—and, to be sure, your execution of them—we could never have done so." Fourre shook his head again. He would *not* get angry with Jacques. "I think such a record entitles the professor to respect."

"True . . . then." Reinach's tone lifted and grew rapid. "But he's senile now, I tell you. Babbling of the future, of long-range trends—Can we eat the future? People are dying of plague and starvation and anarchy now!"

"He has convinced me," said Fourre. "I thought much the same as you, myself, a year ago. But he instructed me in the elements of his science, and he showed me the way we are heading. He is an old man, Eino Valti, but a brain still lives under that bald pate."

Reinach relaxed. Warmth and tolerance played across his lips. "Very well, Étienne," he asked "what way are we heading?"

Fourre looked past him into night. "Toward war," he said quite softly. "Another nuclear war, some fifty years hence. It isn't certain the human race can survive that."

Rain stammered on the windowpanes, falling hard now, and wind hooted in the empty streets. Fourre glanced at his watch. Scant time was left. He fingered the police whistle hung about his neck.

Reinach had started. But gradually he eased back. "If I thought that were so," he replied, "I would resign this minute."

"I know you would," mumbled Fourre. "That is what makes my task so hard for me."

"However, it isn't so." Reinach's hands waved as if to brush away a nightmare. "People have had such a grim lesson that—"

"People, in the mass, don't learn," Fourre told him. "Did Germany learn from the Hundred Years' War, or we from Hiroshima? The only way to prevent future wars is to establish a world peace authority: to reconstitute the United Nations and give it some muscles, as well as a charter which favors civilization above any fiction of 'equality.' And Europe is crucial to that enterprise. North of the Himalayas and east of the Don is nothing anymore—howling cannibals. It will take too long to civilize them again. We, ourselves, must speak for the whole Eurasian continent."

"Very good, very good," said Reinach, impatiently. "Granted. But what am I doing that is wrong?"

"A great many things, Jacques. You have heard about

them in the Council. Need I repeat the long list?"
Fourre's head turned slowly, as if it creaked on its neck-
bones, and locked eyes with the man behind the desk. "It
is one thing to improvise in wartime. But you are im-
provising the peace. You forced the decision to send only
two men to represent our combined nations at the conference planned in Rio. Why? Because we're short on transportation, clerical help, paper, even on decent clothes!
The problem should have been studied. It may be all
right to treat Europe as a unit—or it may not; perhaps
this will actually exacerbate nationalism. You made the
decision in one minute when the question was raised, and
would not hear debate."

"Of course not," said Reinach harshly. "If you remember, that was the day we learned of the neofascist coup in
Corsica."

"Corsica could have waited awhile. The place would
have been more difficult to win back, yes, if we hadn't
struck at once. But this business of our U. N. representa-
tion could decide the entire future of—"

"I know, I know. Valti and his theory about the 'pivotal
decision.' Bah!"

"The theory happens to work, my old."

"Within proper limits. I'm a hardhead, Étienne, I admit that." Reinach leaned across the desk, chuckling.
"Don't you think the times demand a hard head? When
hell is romping loose, it's no time to spin fine philosophies
. . . or try to elect a parliament, which I understand is
another of the postponements Dr. Valti holds against
me."

"It is," said Fourre. "Do you like roses?"

"Why, why . . . yes." Reinach blinked. "To look at,
anyway." Wistfulness crossed his eyes. "Now that you
mention it, it's been many years since I last saw a rose."

"But you don't like gardening. I remember that from,
from old days." The curious tenderness of man for man,
which no one has ever quite explained, tugged at Fourre.
He cast it aside, not daring to do otherwise, and said im-

personally: "And you like democratic government, too, but were never interested in the grubby work of maintaining it. There is a time to plant seeds. If we delay, we will be too late; a strong-arm rule will have become too ingrained a habit."

"There is also a time to keep alive. Just to keep alive, nothing else."

"Jacques, I don't accuse you of hardheartedness. You are a sentimentalist: you see a child with belly bloated from hunger, a house marked with a cross to show that the Black Death has walked in — and you feel too much pity to be able to think. It is . . . Valti, myself, the rest of us . . . who are cold-blooded, who are prepared to sacrifice a few thousand more lives now by neglecting the immediately necessary, for the sake of saving all humankind fifty years hence."

"You may be right," said Reinach. "About your cold souls, I mean." His voice was so low that the rain nearly drowned it.

Fourre stole another look at this watch. This was taking longer than expected. He said in a slurred, hurried tone: "What touched off tonight's affair was the Pappas business."

"I thought so," Reinach agreed evenly. "I don't like it either. I know as well as you do that Pappas is a murderous crypto-Communist scoundrel whose own people hate him. But curse it, man, don't you know rats do worse than steal food and gnaw the faces of sleeping children? Don't you know they spread plague? And Pappas has offered us the services of the only efficient rat-exterminating force in Eurasia. He asks nothing in return except that we recognize his Macedonian Free State and give him a seat on the Council."

"Too high a price," said Fourre. "In two or three years we can bring the rats under control ourselves."

"And meanwhile?"

"Meanwhile, we must hope that nobody we love is taken sick."

Reinach grinned without mirth. "It won't do," he said. "I can't agree to that. If Pappas' squads help us, we can save a year of reconstruction, a hundred thousand lives—"

"And throw away lives by the hundred millions in the future."

"Oh, come now. One little province like Macedonia?"

"One very big precedent," said Fourre. "We will not merely be conceding a petty warlord the right to his loot. We will be conceding"—he lifted furry hands and counted off on the fingers—"the right of any ideological dictatorship, anywhere, to exist: which right, if yielded, means war and war and war again; the fatally outmoded principle of unlimited national sovereignty; the friendship of an outraged Greece, which is sure to invoke that same principle in retaliation; the inevitable political repercussions throughout the Near East, which is already turbulent enough; therefore war between us and the Arabs, because we *must* have oil; a seat on the Council to a clever and ruthless man who, frankly, Jacques, can think rings around you—No!"

"You are theorizing about tomorrow," said Reinach. "The rats are already here. What would you have me do instead?"

"Refuse the offer. Let me take a brigade down there. We can knock Pappas to hell . . . unless we let him get too strong first."

Reinach shook his head goodnaturedly. "Who's the warmonger now?" he said with a laugh.

"I never denied we still have a great deal of fighting ahead of us," Fourre said. Sadness tinged his voice; he had seen too many men spilling their guts on the ground and screaming. "I only want to be sure it will serve the final purpose, that there shall never again be a world war. That my children and grandchildren will not have to fight at all."

"And Valti's equations show the way to achieve that?" Reinach asked quietly.

"Well, they show how to make the outcome reasonably probable."

"I'm sorry, Étienne." Reinach shook his head. "I simply cannot believe that. Turning human society into a . . . what's the word? . . . a potential field, and operating on it with symbolic logic: it's too remote. I am here, in the flesh—such of it as is left, on our diet—not in a set of scribbles made by some band of long-haired theorists."

A similar band discovered atomic energy," said Fourre. "Yes, Valti's science is young. But within admitted limitations, it works. If you would just study—"

"I have too much else on hand." Reinach shrugged. A blankness drew across his face. "We've wasted more time than I can afford already. What does your group of generals want me to do?"

Fourre gave it to him as he knew his comrade would wish it, hard and straight like a bayonet thrust. "We ask for your resignation. Naturally, you'll keep a seat on the Council, but Professor Valti will assume the chairmanship and set about making the reforms we want. We will issue a formal promise to hold a constitutional convention in the spring and dissolve the military government within one year."

He bent his head and looked at the time. A minute and half remained.

"No," said Reinach.

"But—"

"Be still!" The Alsatian stood up. The single lamp threw his shadow grotesque and enormous across the dusty books. "Do you think I didn't see this coming? Why do you imagine I let only one man at a time in here, and disarm him? The devil with your generals! The common people know me, they know I stand for them first—and hell take your misty futures! We'll meet the future when it gets here."

"That is what man has always done," said Fourre. He spoke like a beggar. "And that is why the race has always blundered from one catastrophe to the next. This may be our last chance to change the pattern."

Reinach began pacing back and forth behind his desk. "Do you think I like this miserable job?" he retorted. "It simply happens that no one else can do it."

"So now you are the indispensable man," whispered Fourre. "I had hoped you would escape that."

"Go on home, Étienne." Reinach halted, and kindness returned to him. "Go back and tell them I won't hold this against them personally. You had a right to make your demand. Well, it has been made and refused." He nodded to himself thoughtfully. "We will have to make some change in our organization, though. I don't want to be a dictator, but—"

Zero hour. Fourre felt very tired.

He had been denied, and so he had not blown the whistle that would stop the rebels, and matters were out of his hands now.

"Sit down," he said. "Sit down, Marius, and let us talk about old times for a while."

Reinach looked surprised. "Marius? What do you mean?"

"Oh . . . an example from history which Professor Valti gave me." Fourre considered the floor. There was a cracked board by his left foot. Cracked and crazy, a tottering wreck of a civilization, how had the same race built Chartres and the hydrogren bomb?

His words dragged out of him: "In the second century before Christ, the Cimbri and their allies, Teutonic barbarians, came down out of the north. For a generation they wandered about, ripping Europe apart. They chopped to pieces the Roman armies sent to stop them. Finally they invaded Italy. It did not look as if they could be halted before they took Rome herself. But one general by the name of Marius rallied his men. He met the barbarians and annihilated them."

"Why, thank you." Reinach sat down, puzzled.

"But—"

"Never mind." Fourre's lips twisted into a smile. "Let us take a few minutes free and just talk. Do you remember that night soon after the Second War, we were boys, freshly out of the Maquis, and we tumbled around the streets of Paris and toasted the sunrise from Sacre Coeur?"

"Yes. To be sure. That was a wild night!" Reinach laughed. "How long ago it seems. What was your girl's name? I've forgotten."

"Marie. And you had Simone. A beautiful little baggage, Simone. I wonder whatever became of her."

"I don't know. The last I heard—No. Remember how bewildered the waiter was when—"

A shot cracked through the rain, and then the wrathful clatter of machine guns awoke. Reinach was on his feet in one tiger bound, pistol in hand, crouched by the window. Fourre stayed seated.

The noise lifted, louder and closer. Reinach spun about. His gun muzzle glared emptily at Fourre.

"Yes, Jacques."

"Mutiny!"

"We had to." Fourre discovered that he could again meet Reinach's eyes. "The situation was that crucial. If you had yielded . . . if you had even been willing to discuss the question . . . I would have blown the whistle and nothing would have happened. Now we're too late, unless you want to surrender. If you do, our offer still stands. We still want you to work with us."

A grenade blasted somewhere nearby.

"You—"

"Go on and shoot. It doesn't matter very much."

"No." The pistol wavered. "Not unless you—Stay where you are! Don't move!" The hand Reinach passed across his forehead shuddered. "You know how well this place is guarded. You know the people will rise to my side."

"I think not. They worship you, yes, but they are tired and starved. Just in case, though, we staged this for the nighttime. By tomorrow morning the business will be over." Fourre spoke like a rusty engine. "The barracks have already been seized. Those more distant noises are the artillery being captured. The University is surrounded and cannot stand against an attack."

"This building can."

"So you won't quit, Jacques?"

"If I could do that," said Reinach, "I wouldn't be here tonight."

The window broke open. Reinach whirled. The man who was vaulting through shot first.

The sentry outside the door looked in. His rifle was poised, but he died before he could use it. Men with black clothes and blackened faces swarmed across the sill.

Fourre knelt beside Reinach. A bullet through the head had been quick, at least. But if it had struck farther down, perhaps Reinach's life could have been saved. Fourre wanted to weep, but he had forgotten how.

The big man who had killed Reinach ignored his commandos to stoop over the body with Fourre. "I'm sorry, sir," he whispered. It was hard to tell whom he spoke to.

"Not your fault, Stefan." Fourre's voice jerked.

"We had to run through the shadows, get under the wall. I got a boost through this window. Didn't have time to take aim. I didn't realize who he was till—"

"It's all right, I said. Go on, now, take charge of your party, get this building cleaned out. Once we hold it, the rest of his partisans should yield pretty soon."

The big man nodded and went out into the corridor.

Fourre crouched by Jacques Reinach while a sleet of bullets drummed on the outer walls. He heard them only dimly. Most of him was wondering if this hadn't been the best ending. Now they could give their chief a funeral with full military honors, and later they would build a monument to the man who saved the West, and—

And it might not be quite that easy to bribe a ghost. But you had to try.

"I didn't tell you the whole story, Jacques," he said. His hands were like a stranger's, using his jacket to wipe off the blood, and his words ran on of themselves. "I wish I had. Maybe you would have understood . . . and maybe not. Marius went into politics afterward, you see. He had the prestige of his victory behind him, he was the most powerful man in Rome, his intentions were noble, but he did not understand politics. There followed a witch's dance of corruption, murder, civil war, fifty years of it, the final extinction of the Republic. Caesarism merely gave a name to what had already been done.

"I would like to think that I helped spare Jacques Reinach the name of Marius."

Rain slanted in through the broken window. Fourre reached out and closed the darkened eyes. He wondered if he would ever be able to close them within himself.

The cost of heroism is cruelly high. What Fourre had slain was part of himself. His childhood faith perished with Reinach. Yet Stefan Rostomily, the actual killer kept his innocence and later provided Fourre with his finest weapon in the struggle against Chaos.

Famine, plague, want, and radioactivity were slowly conquered. The Years of Hunger gave way to the Years of Madness—it takes very little surplus to fuel new mass mischief. These in turn yielded to quieter times, thanks to the revitalized United Nations organized by the First Conference of Rio. Global peace restored prosperity by the last decades of the century. Space exploration opened a new external frontier while the Psychotechnic Institute that grew out of Professor Valti's theories probed an old internal one. Unfortunately, these happy developments were not to everyone's liking.

UN-MAN

I

They were gone, their boat whispering into the sky with all six of them aboard. Donner had watched them from his balcony—he had chosen the apartment carefully with a view to such features—as they walked out on the landing flange and entered the shell. Now their place was vacant and it was time for him to get busy.

For a moment hesitation was in him. He had waited many days for this chance, but a man does not willingly enter a potential trap. His eyes strayed to the picture on his desk. The darkly beautiful young woman and the children in her arms seemed to be looking at him, her lips were parted as if she were about to speak. He wanted to press the button that animated the film, but didn't quite dare. Gently, his fingers stroked the glass over her cheek.

"Jeanne," he whispered. "Jeanne, honey."

He got to work. His colorful lounging pajamas were exchanged for a gray outfit that would be inconspicuous against the walls of the building. An ordinary featureless mask, its sheen carefully dulled to non-reflection, covered his face. He clipped a flat box of tools to his belt and painted his fingertips with collodion. Picking up a reel of cord in one hand, he returned to the balcony.

From here, two hundred and thirty-four stories up, he had a wide view of the Illinois plain. As far as he could see, the land rolled green with corn, hazing into a far horizon out of which the great sky lifted. Here and there, a clump of trees had been planted, and the white streak of an old highway crossed the field, but otherwise it was one immensity of growth. The holdings of Midwest Agricultural reached beyond sight.

On either hand, the apartment building lifted sheer from the trees and gardens of its park. Two miles long, a city in its own right, a mountain of walls and windows, the unit dominated the plain, sweeping heavenward in a magnificent arrogance that ended sixty-six stories above Donner's flat. Through the light prairie wind that fluttered his garments, the man could hear a low unending hum, muted pulsing of machines and life—the building—itself like a giant organism.

There were no other humans in sight. The balconies were so designed as to screen the users from view of neighbors on the same level, and anyone in the park would find his upward glance blocked by trees. A few brilliant points of light in the sky were airboats, but that didn't matter.

Donner fastened his reel to the edge of the balcony and took the end of the cord in his fingers. For still another moment he stood, letting the sunlight and wind pour over him, filling his eyes with the reaching plains and the high, white-clouded heaven.

He was a tall man, his apparent height reduced by the width of shoulders and chest, a curious rippling grace in his movements. His naturally yellow hair had been dyed brown and contact lenses made his blue eyes dark, but otherwise there hadn't been much done to his face—the broad forehead, high cheekbones, square jaw, and jutting nose were the same. He smiled wryly behind the blank mask, took a deep breath, and swung himself over the balcony rail.

The cord unwound noiselessly, bearing him down past level after level. There was a risk involved in this daylight burglary—someone might happen to glance around the side wall of a balcony and spot him, and even the custom of privacy would hardly keep them from notifying the unit police. But the six he was after didn't time their simultaneous departures for his convenience.

The looming facade slid past, blurred a little by the speed of his descent. One, two, three— He counted as he went by, and at the eighth story down tugged the cord with his free hand. The reel braked and he hung in mid-air.

A long and empty way down— He grinned and began to swing himself back and forth, increasing the amplitude of each arc until his soles were touching the unit face. On the way back, he grasped the balcony rail, just beyond the screening side wall, with his free hand. His body jerked to a stop, the impact like a blow in his muscles.

Still clinging to the cord, he pulled himself one-armed past the screen, over the rail, and onto the balcony floor. Under the gray tunic and the sweating skin, his sinews felt as if they were about to crack. He grunted with relief when he stood freely, tied the cord to the rail, and unclipped his tool case.

The needle of his electronic detector flickered. So there was an alarm hooked to the door leading in from the balcony. Donner traced it with care, located a wire, and cut it. Pulling a small torch from his kit, he approached the door. Beyond its transparent plastic, the rooms lay quiet: a conventional arrangement of furniture, but with a waiting quality over it.

Imagination, thought Donner impatiently, and cut the lock from the door. As he entered, the autocleaner sensed his presence and its dust-sucking wind whined to silence.

The man forced the lock of a desk and riffled through the papers within. One or two in code he slipped into his pocket, the rest were uninteresting. There must be more, though. Curse it, this was their regional headquarters!

His metal detector helped him about the apartment,

looking for hidden safes. When he found a large mass buried in a wall, he didn't trouble with searching for the button to open it, but cut the plastic facing away. The gang would know their place had been raided, and would want to move. If they took another flat in the same building, Donner's arrangement with the superintendent would come into effect; they'd get a vacancy which had been thoughtfully provided with all the spy apparatus he could install. The man grinned again.

Steel gleamed at him through the scorched and melted wall. It was a good safe, and he hadn't time to diddle with it. He plugged in his electric drill, and the diamond head gnawed a small hole in the lock. With a hypodermic he inserted a few cubic centimeters of levinite, and touched it off by a UHF beam. The lock jangled to ruin, and Donner opened the door.

He had only time to see the stet-gun within, and grasp the terrible fact of its existence. Then it spat three needles into his chest, and he whirled down into darkness.

II

Once or twice he had begun to waken, stirring dimly toward light, and the jab of a needle had thrust him back. Now, as his head slowly cleared, they let him alone. And that was worse.

Donner retched and tried to move. His body sagged against straps that held him fast in his chair. Vision blurred in a huge nauseous ache; the six who stood watching him were a ripple of fever-dream against an unquiet shadow.

"He's coming around," said the thin man unnecessarily.

The heavy-set, gray-haired man in the conservative

blue tunic glanced at his timepiece. "Pretty fast, considering how he was dosed. Healthy specimen."

Donner mumbled. The taste of vomit was bitter in his mouth. "Give him some water," said the bearded man.

"Like hell!" The thin man's voice was a snarl. His face was dead white against the shifting, blurring murk of the room, and there was a fever in his eyes. "He doesn't rate it, the—Un-man!"

"Get him some water," said the gray-haired one quietly. The skeletal younger man slouched sulkily over to a chipped basin with an old-fashioned tap and drew a glassful.

Donner swallowed it greedily, letting it quench some of the dry fire in his throat and belly. The bearded man approached with a hypo.

"Stimulant," he explained. "Bring you around faster." It bit into Donner's arm and he felt his heartbeat quicken. His head was still a keen pulsing pain, but his eyes steadied and he looked at the others with returning clarity.

"We weren't altogether careless," said the heavy-set man. "That stet-gun was set to needle anybody who opened the safe without pressing the right button first. And, of course, a radio signal was emitted which brought us back in a hurry. We've kept you unconscious till now."

Donner looked around him. The room was bare, thick with the dust and cobwebs of many years, a few pieces of old-style wooden furniture crouched in ugliness against the cracked plaster walls. There was a single window, its broken glass panes stuffed with rags, dirt so thick on it that he could not be sure if there was daylight outside. But the hour was probably after dark. The only illumination within was from a single fluoro in a stand on the table.

He must be in Chicago, Donner decided through a wave of sickness. One of the vast moldering regions that encompassed the inhabited parts of the dying

city—deserted, not worth destroying as yet, the lair of
rats and decay. Sooner or later, some agricultural outfit
would buy up the nominal title from the government
which had condemned the place and raze what had been
spared by fire and rot. But it hadn't happened yet, and
the empty slum was a good hideaway for anybody.

Donner thought of those miles of ruinous buildings,
wrapped in night, looming hollow against a vacant
sky—dulled echoes in the cracked and grass-grown
streets, the weary creak of a joist, the swift patter of feet
and glare of eyes from the thick dark, menace and loneliness for further than he could run.

Alone, alone. He was more alone here than in the
outermost reaches of space. He knew starkly that he was
going to die.

Jeanne. O Jeanne, my darling.

"You were registered at the unit as Mark Roberts," said
the woman crisply. She was thin, almost as thin as the
bitter-eyed young man beside her. The face was sharp
and hungry, the hair close cropped, the voice harsh with
purpose. "But your ID tattoo is a fake—it's a dye that
comes off with acid. We got your thumbprint and that
number on a check and called the bank central like in an
ordinary verification, and the robofile said yes, that was
Mark Roberts and the account was all right." She leaned
forward, her face straining against the blur of night, and
spat it at him. "Who are you really? Only a secret service
man could get by with that kind of fake. Whose service
are you in?"

"It's obvious, isn't it?" snapped the thin man. "He's not
American Security. We know that. So he must be an Un-
man."

The way he said the last word made it an ugly, in-
human sound. "*The* Un-man!" he repeated.

"Our great enemy," said the heavy-set one thoughtfully. "*The* Un-man—not just an ordinary operative,
with human limitations, but the great and secret one
who's made so much trouble for us."

He cocked his gray head and stared at Donner. "It fits what fragmentary descriptions we have," he went on. "But then, the U.N. boys can do a lot with surgery and cosmetics, can't they? And *the* Un-Man has been killed several times. An operator was bagged in Hong Kong only last month which the killer swore must be our enemy—he said nobody else could have led them such a chase."

That was most likely Weinberger, thought Donner. An immense weariness settled on him. They were so few, so desperately few, and one by one the Brothers went down into darkness. He was next, and after him—

"What I can't understand," said a fifth man—Donner recognized him as Colonel Samsey of the American Guard—"is why, if the U. N. Secret Services does have a corps of—uh—supermen, it should bother to disguise them to look all alike. So that we'll think we're dealing with an immortal?" He chuckled grimly. "Surely they don't expect us to be rattled by that!"

"Not supermen," said the gray-haired one. "Enormously able, yes, but the Un-men aren't infallible. As witness this one." He stood before Donner, his legs spread and his hands on his hips. "Suppose you start talking. Tell us about yourself."

"I can tell you about your own selves," answered Donner. His tongue felt thick and dry, but the acceptance of death made him, all at once, immensely steady. "You are Roger Wade, president of Brain Tools, Incorporated, and a prominent supporter of the Americanist Party." To the woman: "You are Marta Jennings, worker for the Party on a full-time basis. Your secretary, Mr. Wade—" his eyes roved to the gaunt young man—"is Rodney Borrow, Exogene Number—"

"Don't call me that!" Cursing, Borrow lunged at Donner. He clawed like a woman. When Samsey and the bearded man dragged him away, his face was death-white and he dribbled at the mouth.

"And the experiment was a failure," taunted Donner

cruelly.

"Enough!" Wade slapped the prisoner, a ringing open-handed buffet. "We want to know something new, and there isn't much time. You are, of course, immunized against truth drugs—Dr. Lewin's tests have already confirmed that—but I assume you can still feel pain."

After a moment, he added quietly. "We aren't fiends. You know that we're patriots." *Working with the nationalists of a dozen other countries!* thought Donner. "We don't want to hurt or kill unnecessarily."

"But first we want your real identity," said the bearded man, Lewin. "Then your background of information about us, the future plans of your chief, and so on. However, it will be sufficient for now if you answer a few questions pertaining to yourself, residence and so on."

Oh, yes, thought Donner, the weariness like a weight on his soul. *That'll do. Because then they'll find Jeanne and Jimmy, and bring them here, and—*

Lewin wheeled forth a lie detector. "Naturally, we don't want our time wasted by false leads," he said.

"It won't be," replied Donner. "I'm not going to say anything."

Lewin nodded, unsurprised, and brought out another machine. "This one generates low-frequency, low-voltage current," he remarked. "Quite painful. I don't think your will can hold out very long. If it does, we can always try prefrontal lobotomy; you won't have inhibitions then. But we'll give you a chance with this first."

He adjusted the electrodes on Donner's skin. Borrow licked his lips with a dreadful hunger.

Donner tried to smile, but his mouth felt stiff. The sixth man, who looked like a foreigner somehow, went out of the room.

There was a tiny receiver in Donner's skull, behind the right mastoid. It could only pick up messages of a special wave form, but it had its silencing uses too. After all, electric torture is a common form of inquisition, and very hard to bear.

He thought of Jeanne, and of Jimmy, and of the Brotherhood. He wished that the last air he was to breathe weren't stale and dusty.

The current tore him with a convulsive anguish. His muscles jerked against the straps and he cried out. Then the sensitized communicator blew up, releasing a small puff of fluorine.

The image Donner carried into death was that of Jeanne, smiling and bidding him welcome home.

III

Barney Rosenberg drove along a dim, rutted trail toward the sheer loom of the escarpment. Around its corner lay Drygulch. But he wasn't hurrying. As he got closer, he eased the throttle of his sandcat and the engine's purr became almost inaudible.

Leaning back in his seat, he looked through the tiny plastiglass cab at the Martian landscape. It was hard to understand that he would never see it again.

Even here, five miles or so from the colony, there was no trace of man save himself and his engine and the blurred track through sand and bush. Men had come to Mars on wings of fire, they had hammered out their cities with a clangorous brawl of life, mined and smelted and begun their ranches, trekked in sandcats and airsuits from the polar bogs to the equatorial scrubwoods — and still they had left no real sign of their passing. Not yet. Here a tin can or broken tool, there a mummified corpse in the wreck of a burst sealtent, but sand and loneliness drifted over them, night and cold and forgetfulness. Mars was too old and strange for thirty years of man to matter.

The desert stretched away to Rosenberg's left, tumbling in steep drifts of sand from the naked painted hills. Off to the sharply curving horizon the desert marched, an iron barrenness of red and brown and tawny yellow, knife-edged shadows and a weird vicious shimmer of pale sunlight. Here and there a crag lifted, harsh with mineral color, worn by the passing of ages and thin wind to a fluted fantasy. A sandstorm was blowing a few miles off, a scud of dust hissing over stone, stirring the low gray-green brush to a sibilant murmur. On his right the hills rose bare and steep, streaked with blue and green of copper ores, gashed and scored and murmurous with wind. He saw life, the dusty thorn-bushes and the high gaunt cactoids and a flicker of movement as a tiny leaper fled. In one of the precipices, a series of carved, time-blurred steps went up to the ruin of a cliff dwelling abandoned—how long ago?

Overhead the sky was enormous, a reaching immensity of deep greenish blue-violet, incredibly high and cold and remote. The stars glittered faintly in its abyss, the tiny hurtling speck of a moon less bright than they. A shrunken sun stood in a living glory of corona and zodiacal light, the winged disc of royal Egypt lifting over Mars. Near the horizon a thin layer of ice crystals caught the luminescence in a chilly sparkle. There was wind, Rosenberg knew, a whimpering ghost of wind blowing through the bitter remnant of atmosphere, but he couldn't hear it through the heavy plastiglass and somehow he felt that fact as a deeper isolation.

It was a cruel world, this Mars, a world of cold and ruin and soaring scornful emptiness, a world that broke men's hearts and drained their lives from them—rainless, oceanless, heatless, kindless, where the great wheel of the stars swung through a desert of millennia, where the days cried with wind and the nights rang and groaned with frost. It was a world of waste and mystery, a niggard world where a man ate starvation and drank thirst and finally went down in darkness. Men trudged through unending miles, toil and loneliness and quiet creeping fear, sweated and gasped, cursed the planet and wept for the

dead and snatched at warmth and life in the drab colony
towns. *It's all right when you find yourself talking to the
sandbuggers—but when they start talking back, it's time
to go home.*

And yet—and yet— The sweep of the polar moons,
thin faint swirl of wind, sunlight shattered to a million
diamond shards on the hoarfrost cap; the cloven
tremendousness of Rasmussen Gorge, a tumbling, sculp-
tured wilderness of fairy stone, uncounted shifting hues of
color and fleeting shadow; the high cold night of stars,
fantastically brilliant constellations marching over a
crystal heaven, a silence so great you thought you could
hear God speaking over the universe; the delicate day-
flowers of the Syrtis forests, loveliness blooming with the
bitter dawn and dying in the swift sunset; traveling and
searching, rare triumph and much defeat, but always the
quest and the comradeship. Oh, yes, Mars was savage to
her lovers, but she gave them of her strange beauty and
they would not forget her while they lived.

Maybe Stef was the lucky one, thought Rosenberg. *He
died here.*

He guided the sandcat over a razorback ridge. For a
moment he paused, looking at the broad valley beyond.
He hadn't been to Drygulch for a couple of years; that'd
be almost four Earth years, he remembered.

The town, half underground below its domed roof,
hadn't changed much outwardly, but the plantations had
doubled their area. The genetic engineers were doing
good work, adapting terrestrial food plants to Mars and
Martian plants to the needs of humans. The colonies were
already self-supporting with regard to essentials, as they
had to be considering the expense of freight from Earth.
But they still hadn't developed a decent meal animal;
that part of the diet had to come from yeast-culture
factories in the towns and nobody saw a beefsteak on
Mars. *But we'll have that too, one of these years.*

A worn-out world, stern and bitter and grudging, but

it was being tamed. Already the new generation was
being born. There wasn't much fresh immigration from
Earth these days, but man was unshakably rooted here.
Someday he'd get around to modifying the atmosphere
and weather till humans could walk free and unclothed
over the rusty hills — but that wouldn't happen till he,
Rosenberg, was dead, and in an obscure way he was glad
of it.

The cat's supercharging pumps roared, supplementing
tanked oxygen with Martian air for the hungry Diesel as
the man steered it along the precarious trail. It was
terribly thin, that air, but its oxygen was mostly ozone
and that helped. Passing a thorium mine, Rosenberg
scowled. The existence of fissionables was the main
reason for planting colonies here in the first place, but
they should be saved for Mars.

*Well, I'm not really a Martian any longer. I'll be an
Earthman again soon. You have to die on Mars, like Stef,
and give your body back to the Martian land, before you
altogether belong here.*

The trail from the mine became broad and hard-
packed enough to be called a road. There was other
traffic now, streaming from all corners — a loaded ore-
car, a farmer coming in with a truckful of harvested
crops, a survey expedition returning with maps and
specimens. Rosenberg waved to the drivers. They were of
many nationalities, but except for the Pilgrims that
didn't matter. Here they were simply humans. He hoped
the U.N. would get around to internationalizing the
planets soon.

There was a flag on a tall staff outside the town, the
Stars and Stripes stiff against an alien sky. It was of
metal — it had to be in that murderous corroding
atmosphere — and Rosenberg imagined that they had to
repaint it pretty often. He steered past it, down a long
ramp leading under the dome. He had to wait his turn at
the airlock, and wondered when somebody would invent

a better system of oxygen conservation. These new experiments in submolar mechanics offered a promising lead.

He left his cat in the underground garage, with word to the attendant that another man, its purchaser, would pick it up later. There was an odd stinging in his eyes and he patted its scarred flanks. Then he took an elevator and a slideway to the housing office and arranged for a room; he had a couple of days before the *Phobos* left. A shower and a change of clothes were sheer luxury and he reveled in them. He didn't feel much desire for the cooperative taverns and pleasure joints, so he called up Doc Fieri instead.

The physician's round face beamed at him in the plate. "Barney, you old sandbugger! When'd you get in?"

"Just now. Can I come up?"

"Yeah, sure. Nothing doing at the office—that is, I've got company, but he won't stay long. Come right on over."

Rosenberg took a remembered route through crowded hallways and elevators till he reached the door he wanted. He knocked: Drygulch's imports and its own manufactories needed other things more urgently than call and recorder circuits. "Come in!" bawled the voice.

Rosenberg entered the cluttered room, a small leathery man with gray-sprinkled hair and a beaky nose, and Fieri pumped his hand enthusiastically. The guest stood rigid in the background, a lean ascetic figure in black—a Pilgrim. Rosenberg stiffened inwardly. He didn't like that sort, Puritan fanatics from the Years of Madness who'd gone to Mars so they could be unhappy in freedom. Rosenberg didn't care what a man's religion was, but nobody on Mars had a right to be so clannish and to deny cooperation as much as New Jerusalem. However, he shook hands politely, relishing the Pilgrim's ill-concealed distaste—they were anti-Semitic too.

"This is Dr. Morton," explained Fieri. "He heard of my research and came around to inquire about it."

"Most interesting," said the stranger. "And most promising, too. It will mean a great deal to Martian colonization."

"And surgery and biological research everywhere," put in Fieri. Pride was bursting from him.

"What is it, Doc?" asked Rosenberg, as expected.

"Suspended animation," said Fieri.

"Hm?"

"Uh-huh. You see, in what little spare time I have, I've puttered around with Martian biochemistry. Fascinating subject, and unearthly in two meanings of the word. We've nothing like it at home—don't need it. Hibernation and estivation approximate it, of course."

"Ummm . . . yes." Rosenberg rubbed his chin. "I know what you mean. Everybody does. The way so many plants and animals needing heat for their metabolisms can curl up and 'sleep' through the nights, or even through the whole winter. Or they can survive prolonged droughts that way." He chuckled. "Comparative matter, of course. Mars is in a state of permanent drought, by Earthly standards."

"And you say, Dr. Fieri, that the natives can do it also?" asked Morton.

"Yes. Even they, with a quite highly developed nervous system, can apparently 'sleep' through such spells of cold or famine. I had to rely on explorers' fragmentary reports for that datum. There are so few natives left, and they're so shy and secretive. But last year I did finally get a look at one in such a condition. It was incredible—respiration was indetectable, the heartbeat almost so, the encephalograph showed only a very slow, steady pulse. But I got blood and tissue samples, and was able to analyze and compare them with secretions from other life forms in suspension."

"I thought even Martians' blood would freeze in a winter night," said Rosenberg.

"It does. The freezing point is much lower than with

human blood, but not so low that it can't freeze at all.
However, in suspension, there's a whole series of enzymes
released. One of them, dissolved in the bloodstream,
changes the characteristics of the plasma. When ice
crystals form, they're *more* dense than the liquid, therefore cell walls aren't ruptured and the organism survives.
Moreover, a slow circulation of oxygen-bearing radicals
and nutrient solutions takes place even through the ice,
apparently by some process analogous to ion exchange.
Not much, but enough to keep the organism alive and
undamaged. Heat, a sufficient temperature, causes the
breakdown of these secretions and the animal or plant
revives. In the case of suspension to escape thirst or
famine, the process is somewhat different, of course,
though the same basic enzymes are involved."

Fieri laughed triumphantly and slapped a heap of
papers on his desk. "Here are my notes. The work isn't
complete yet. I'm not quite ready to publish, but it's more
or less a matter of detail now." A Nobel Prize glittered in
his eye.

Morton skimmed through the manuscript. "*Very*
interesting," he murmured. His lean, close-cropped head
bent over a structural formula. "The physical chemistry
of this material must be weird."

"It is, Morton, it is." Fieri grinned.

"Hmmmm—do you mind if I borrow this to read? As I
mentioned earlier, I believe my lab at New Jerusalem
could carry out some of these analyses for you."

"That'll be fine. Tell you what, I'll make up a stat of
this whole mess for you. I'll have it ready by tomorrow."

"Thank you." Morton smiled, though it seemed to hurt
his face. "This will be quite a surprise, I'll warrant. You
haven't told anyone else?"

"Oh, I've mentioned it around, of course, but you're
the first person who's asked for the technical details.
Everybody's too busy with their own work on Mars. But
it'll knock their eyes out back on Earth. They've been

looking for something like this ever since—since the Sleeping Beauty story—and here's the first way to achieve it."

"I'd like to read this too, Doc," said Rosenberg.

"Are you a biochemist?" asked Morton.

'Well, I know enough biology and chemistry to get by, and I'll have leisure to wade through this before my ship blasts."

"Sure, Barney," said Fieri. "And do me a favor, will you? When you get home, tell old Summers at Cambridge—England, that is—about it. He's their big biochemist, and he always said I was one of his brighter pupils and shouldn't have switched over to medicine. I'm a hell of a modest cuss, huh? But damn it all, it's not everybody who grabs onto something as big as this!"

Morton's pale eyes lifted to Rosenberg's. "So you are returning to Earth?" he asked.

"Yeah. The *Phobos.*" He felt he had to explain, that he didn't want the Pilgrim to think he was running out. "More or less doctor's orders, you understand. My helmet cracked open in a fall last year, and before I could slap a patch on I had a beautiful case of the bends, plus the low pressure and the cold and the ozone raising the very devil with my lungs." Rosenberg shrugged, and his smile was bitter. "I suppose I'm fortunate to be alive. At least I have enough credit saved to retire. But I'm just not strong enough to continue working on Mars, and it's not the sort of place where you can loaf and remain sane."

"I see. It is a shame. When will you be on Earth, then?"

"Couple of months. The *Phobos* goes orbital most of the way—do I look like I could afford an acceleration passage?" Rosenberg turned to Fieri. "Doc, will there be any other old sanders coming home this trip?"

" 'Fraid not. You know there are darn few who retire from Mars to Earth. They die first. You're one of the lucky ones."

"A lonesome trip, then. Well, I suppose I'll survive it."

Morton made his excuses and left. Fieri stared after him. "Odd fellow. But then, all these Pilgrims are. They're anti almost everything. He's competent, though, and I'm glad he can tackle some of those analyses for me." He slapped Rosenberg's shoulder. "But forget it, old man! Cheer up and come along with me for a beer. Once you're stretched out on those warm white Florida sands, with blue sky and blue sea and luscious blondes walking by, I guarantee you won't miss Mars."

"Maybe not." Rosenberg looked unhappily at the floor. "It's never been the same since Stef died. I didn't realize how much he'd meant to me till I'd buried him and gone on by myself."

"He meant a lot to everyone, Barney. He was one of those people who seem to fill the world with life, wherever they are. Let's see—he was about sixty when he died, wasn't he? I saw him shortly before, and he could still drink any two men under the table, and all the girls were still adoring him."

"Yeah. He was my best friend, I suppose. We tramped Earth and the planets together for fifteen years." Rosenberg smiled. "Funny thing, friendship. Stef and I didn't even talk much. It wasn't needed. The last five years have been pretty empty without him."

"He died in a cave-in, didn't he?"

"Yes. We were exploring up near the Sawtooths, hunting a uranium lode. Our diggings collapsed, he held that toppling roof up with his shoulders and yelled at me to scramble out—then before he could get clear, it came down and burst his helmet open. I buried him on a hill, under a cairn, looking out over the desert. He was always a friend of high places."

"Mmmmmm—yes— Well, thinking about Stefan Rostomily won't help him or us now. Let's go get that beer, shall we?"

IV

The shrilling within his head brought Robert Naysmith to full awareness with a savage force. His arm jerked, and the brush streaked a yellow line across his canvas.

"Naysmith!" The voice rattled harshly in his skull. "Report to Prior at Frisco Unit. Urgent. Martin Donner has disappeared, presumed dead. You're on his job now. Hop to it, boy."

For a moment Naysmith didn't grasp the name. He'd never met anyone called Donner. Then—yes, that was on the list, Donner was one of the Brotherhood. And dead now.

Dead— He had never seen Martin Donner, and yet he knew the man with an intimacy no two humans had realized before the Brothers came. Sharp in his mind rose the picture of the dead man, smiling a characteristic slow smile, sprawled back in a relaxer with a glass of Scotch in one strong blunt-fingered hand. The Brothers were all partial to Scotch, thought Naysmith with a twisting sadness. And Donner had been a mech-volley fan, and had played good chess, read a lot and sometimes quoted Shakespeare, tinkered with machinery, probably had a small collection of guns—

Dead. Sprawled sightlessly somewhere on the turning planet, his muscles stiff, his body already devouring itself in proteolysis, his brain darkened, withdrawn into the great night, and leaving an irreparable gap in the tight-drawn line of the Brotherhood.

"You might pick up a newscast on your way," said the voice in his head conversationally. "It's hot stuff."

Naysmith's eyes focused on his painting. It was shaping up to be a good one. He had been experimenting with techniques, and this latest caught the wide sunlit dazzle of California beach, the long creaming swell of waves, the hot cloudless sky and the thin harsh grass and the tawny-skinned woman who sprawled on the sand. Why did they have to call him just now?

"Okay, Sofie," he said with resignation. "That's all. I've got to get back."

The sun-browned woman rolled over on one elbow and looked at him. "What the devil?" she asked. "We've only been here three hours. The day's hardly begun."

"It's gone far enough, I'm afraid." Naysmith began putting away his brushes. "Home to civilization."

"But I don't want to!"

"What has that got to do with it?" He folded his easel.

"But why?" she cried, half getting up.

"I have an appointment this afternoon." Naysmith strode down the beach toward the trail. After a moment, Sofie followed.

"You didn't tell me that," she protested.

"You didn't ask me," he said. He added a "Sorry" that was no apology at all.

There weren't many others on the beach, and the parking lot was relatively uncluttered. Naysmith palmed the door of his boat and it opened for him. He slipped on tunic, slacks, and sandals, put a beret rakishly atop his sun-bleached yellow hair, and entered the boat. Sofie followed, not bothering to don her own clothes.

The ovoid shell slipped skyward on murmuring jets. "I'll drop you off at your place," said Naysmith. "Some other time, huh?"

She remained sulkily silent. They had met accidentally a week before, in a bar. Naysmith was officially a cybernetic epistemologist on vacation, Sofie an engineer on the Pacific Colony project, off for a holiday from her job and her free-marriage group. It had been a pleasant interlude, and Naysmith regretted it mildly.

Still—the rising urgent pulse of excitement tensed his body and cleared the last mists of artistic preoccupation from his brain. You lived on a knife edge in the Service, you drew breath and looked at the sun and grasped after the real world with a desperate awareness of little time. None of the Brotherhood were members of the Hedonists, they were all too well-balanced for that, but inevitably they were epicureans.

When you were trained from—well, from birth, even the sharpness of nearing death could be a kind of pleasure. *Besides,* thought Naysmith, *I might be one of the survivors.*

"You are a rat, you know," said Sofie.

"Squeak," said Naysmith. His face—the strange strong face of level fair brows and wide-set blue eyes, broad across the high cheekbones and in the mouth, square-jawed and crag-nosed—split in a grin that laughed with her while it laughed at her. He looked older than his twenty-five years. And she, thought Sofie with sudden tiredness, looked younger than her forty. Her people had been well off even during the Years of Hunger; she'd always been exposed to the best available biomedical techniques, and if she claimed thirty few would call her a liar. But—

Naysmith fiddled with the radio. Presently a voice came out of it; he didn't bother to focus the TV.

"— —the thorough investigation demanded by finance minister Arnold Besser has been promised by President Lopez. In a prepared statement, the President said: "The rest of the ministry, like myself, are frankly inclined to discredit this accusation and believe that the Chinese government is mistaken. However, its serious nature—' "

"Lopez, eh? The U.N. President himself," murmured Naysmith. "That means the accusation has been made officially now."

"What accusation?" asked the woman. "I haven't heard a 'cast for a week."

"The Chinese government was going to lodge charges that the assassination of Kwang-ti was done by U.N. secret agents," said Naysmith.

"Why, that's ridiculous!" she gasped. "The *U.N.?*" She shook her dark head. "They haven't the—right. The U.N. agents, I mean. Kwang-ti was a menace, yes, but assassination! I don't believe it."

"Just think what the anti-U.N. factions all over the Solar System, including our own Americanists, are going to make of this," said Naysmith. "Right on top of charges of corruption comes one of murder!"

"Turn it off," she said. "It's too horrible."

"These are horrible times, Sofie."

"I thought they were getting better." She shuddered. "I remember the tail-end of the Years of Hunger, and then the Years of Madness, and the Socialist Depression—people in rags, starving; you could see their bones—and a riot once, and the marching uniforms, and the great craters—No! The U.N.'s like a dam against all that hell. It *can't* break!"

Naysmith put the boat on automatic and comforted her. After all, anyone loyal to the U.N. deserved a little consideration.

Especially in view of the suppressed fact that the Chinese charge was absolutely true.

He dropped the woman off at her house, a small prefab in one of the colonies, and made vague promises about looking her up again. Then he opened the jets fully and streaked north toward Frisco Unit.

V

There was a lot of traffic around the great building, and his autopilot was kept busy bringing him in. Naysmith slipped a mantle over his tunic and a conventional half-mask over his face, the latter less from politeness than as a disguise. He didn't think he was being watched, but you were never sure. American Security was damnably efficient.

If ever wheels turned within wheels, he thought sardonically, modern American politics did the spinning. The government was officially Labor and pro-U.N., and was gradually being taken over by its sociotynamicists, who were even more in favor of world federation. However, the conservatives of all stripes, from the mildly socialist Republicans to the extreme Americanists, had enough seats in Congress and enough power generally to exert a potent influence. Among other things, the conservative coalition had prevented the abrogation of the Department of Security, and Hessling, its chief was known to have Americanist leanings. So there were at least a goodly number of S-men out after "foreign agents"—which included Un-men.

Fourre had his own agents in American Security, of course. It was largely due to their efforts that the American Brothers had false IDs and that the whole tremendous fact of the Brotherhood had remained secret. But some day, thought Naysmith, the story would come out—and then the heavens would fall.

So thin a knife edge, so deep an abyss of chaos and ruin— Society was mad, humanity was a race of insane, and the few who strove to build stability were working against shattering odds. *Sofie was right. The U.N. is a dike, holding back a sea of radioactive blood from the lands of men. And I*, thought Naysmith wryly, *seem to be the little boy with his finger in the dike.*

His boat landed on the downward ramp and rolled into the echoing vastness of the unit garage. He didn't quite dare land on Prior's flange. A mechanic tagged the vehicle, gave Naysmith a receipt, and guided him toward an elevator. It was an express, bearing him swiftly past the lower levels of shops, offices, service establishments, and places of education and entertainment, up to the residential stories. Naysmith waited for his stop. No one spoke to anyone else, the custom of privacy had become too ingrained. He was just as glad of that.

On Prior's level, the hundred and seventh, he stepped onto the slideway going east, transferred to a northbound strip at the second corner, and rode half a mile before he came to the alcove he wanted. He got off, the rubbery floor absorbing the very slight shock, and entered the recess. When he pressed the door button, the recorded voice said: "I am sorry, Mr. Prior is not at home. Do you wish to record a message?"

"Shut up and let me in," said Naysmith.

The code sentence activated the door, which opened for him. He stepped into a simply furnished vestibule as the door chimed. Prior's voice came over the intercom: "Naysmith?"

"The same."

"Come on in, then. Living room."

Naysmith hung up his mask and mantle, slipped off his sandals, and went down the hall. The floor was warm and resilient under his bare feet, like living flesh. Beyond another door that swung aside was the living room, also furnished with a bachelor austerity. Prior was a lone wolf by nature, belonging to no clubs and not even the loosest free-marriage group. His official job was semantic analyst for a large trading outfit; it gave him a lot of free time for his U.N. activities, plus a good excuse for traveling anywhere in the Solar System.

Naysmith's eyes flickered over the dark negroid face of his co-worker—Prior was not a Brother, though he knew of the band—and rested on the man who lay in the adjoining relaxer. "Are *you* here, chief?" He whistled. "Then it must be really big."

"Take off your clothes and get some sun-lamp," invited Prior, waving his eternal cigaret at a relaxer. "I'll try to scare up some Scotch for you."

"Why the devil does the Brotherhood always have to drink Scotch?" grumbled Etienne Fourre. "Your padded expense accounts eat up half my budget. Or drink it up, I should say."

He was squat and square and powerful, and at eighty was still more alive than most boys. Small black eyes glistened in a face that seemed carved from scarred and pitted brown rock; his voice was a bass rumble from the shaggy chest, its English hardly accented. Geriatrics could only account for some of the vitality that lay like a coiled spring in him, for the entire battery of diet, exercise, and chemistry has to be applied from birth to give maximum effect and his youth antedated the science. *But he'll probably outlive us all*, thought Naysmith.

There was something of the fanatic about Etienne Fourre. He was a child of war whose most relentless battle had become one against war itself. As a young man he had been in the French Resistance of World War II. Later he had been high in the Western liaison with the European undergrounds of World War III, entering the occupied and devastated lands himself on his dark missions. He had fought with the liberals against the neo-fascists in the Years of Hunger and with the gendarmerie against the atomists in the Years of Madness and with U.N. troops in the Near East where his spy system had been a major factor in suppressing the Great Jehad. He had accepted the head of the secret service division of the U.N. Inspectorate after the Conference of Rio revised the charter and had proceeded quietly to engineer the coup which overthrew the anti-U.N. government of Argentina. Later his men had put the finger on Kwang-ti's faked revolution in the Republic of Mongolia, thus ending that conquest-from-within scheme; and he was ultimately the one responsible for the Chinese dictator's assassination. The Brotherhood was his idea from the beginning, his child and his instrument.

Such a man, thought Naysmith, would in earlier days have stood behind the stake and lash of an Inquisition, would have marched at Cromwell's side and carried out the Irish massacres, would have helped set up world-wide Communism—a sternly religious man, for all his mordant atheism, a living sword which needed a war. *Thank God he's on our side!*

"All right, what's the story?" asked the Un-man aloud.

"How long since you were on a Service job?" countered Fourre.

"About a year. Schumacher and I were investigating the *Arbeitspartei* in Germany. The other German Brothers were tied up in that Austrian business, you remember, and I speak the language well enough to pass for a Rhinelander when I'm in Prussia."

"Yes, I recall. You have been loafing long enough, my friend." Fourre took the glass of wine offered him by Prior, sipped it, and grimaced. *Merde!* Won't these Californians ever give up trying?" Swinging back to Naysmith: "I am calling in the whole Brotherhood on this. I shall have to get back to Rio fast, the devil is running loose down there with those Chinese charges and I will be lucky to save our collective necks. But I have slipped up to North America to get you people organized and under way. I am pretty damn sure that the leadership of our great unknown enemy is down in Rio—probably with Besser, who is at least involved in it but has taken some very excellent precautions against assassination—and it would do no good to kill him only to have someone else take over. At any rate, the United States is still a most important focus of anti-U.N. activity, and Donner's capture means a rapid deterioration of things here. Prior, who was Donner's contact man tells me that he was apparently closer to spying out the enemy headquarters for this continent than any other operative. Now that Donner is gone, Prior has recommended you to succeed in his assignment."

"Which was what?"

"I will come to that. Donner was an engineer by

training. You are a cybernetic analyst, *hein?*"

"Yes, officially," said Naysmith. "My degrees are in epistemology and communications theory, and my supposed job is basic-theoretical consultant. Trouble-shooter in the realm of ideas." He grinned. "When I get stuck, I can always refer the problem to Prior here."

"Ah, so. You are then necessarily something of a lin-guist too, eh? Good. Understand, I am not choosing you for your specialty, but rather for your un-specialty. You are too old to have had the benefit of Synthesis training. Some of the younger Brothers are getting it, of course—there is a lad in Mexico, Peter Christian, whose call numbers you had better get from Prior in case you need such help."

"Meanwhile, an epistemologist or semanticist is the closest available thing to an integrating synthesist. By your knowledge of language, psychology, and the general sciences, you should be well equipped to fit together whatever information you can obtain and derive a larger picture from them. I don't know." Fourre lit a cigar and puffed ferociously.

"Well, I can start anytime. I'm on extended leave of absence from my nominal job already," said Naysmith. "But what about this Donner? How far had he gotten, what happened to him, and so on?"

"I'll give you the background, because you'll need it," said Prior. "Martin Donner was officially adopted in Canada, and, as I said, received a mechanical engineering degree there. About four years ago we had reason to think the enemy was learning that he wasn't all he seemed, so we transferred him to the States, flanged up an American ID for him and so on. Recently he was put to work investigating the Americanists. His leads were simple: he got a job with Brain Tools, Inc., which is known to be lousy with Party members. He didn't try to infiltrate the Party—we already have men in it, of course, though they haven't gotten very high—but he did snoop around, gather data, and finally put the snatch on a certain man and pumped him full of truth drug." Naysmith didn't ask what had happened to the victim; the struggle was utterly ruthless, with all history at stake. "That gave him news about the midwestern headquarters of the conspiracy, so he went there. It was one of the big units in Illinois. He got himself an apartment and—disappeared. That was almost two weeks ago." Prior shrugged. "He's quite certainly dead by now. If they didn't kill him themselves, he'll have found a way to suicide."

"You can give me the dossier on what Donner learned and communicated to you?" asked Naysmith.

"Yes, of course, though I don't think it'll help you much." Prior looked moodily at his glass. "You'll be pretty much on your own. I needn't add that anything goes, from privacy violation to murder, but that with the Service in such bad odor right now you'd better not leave any evidence. Your first job, though, is to approach Donner's family. You see, he was married."

"Oh?"

"I don't mean free-married, or group-married, or trial-married, or any other version," snapped Prior impatiently. "I mean *married*. Old style. One kid."

"Hmmmm—that's not so good, is it?"

"No. Un-men really have no business marrying that way, and most especially the Brothers don't. However—you see the difficulties, don't you? *If* Donner is still alive, somehow, and the gang traces his ID and grabs the wife and kid, they've got a hold on him that may make him spill all he knows; if by some chance he is still alive. No sane man is infinitely loyal to a cause."

"Well, I suppose you provided Donner with a midwestern ID."

"Sure. Or rather, he used the one we already had set up—name, fingerprints, number, the data registered at Midwest Central. Praise Allah, we've got friends in the

registry bureau! But Donner's case is bad. In previous
instances where we lost a Brother, we've been able to
recover the corpse or were at least sure that it was safely
destroyed. Now the enemy has one complete Brother
body, ready for fingerprinting, retinals, bloodtyping,
Bertillon measurements, autopsy, and everything else
they can think of. We can expect them to check that set
of physical data against every ID office in the country.
And when they find the same identification under
different names and numbers in each and every file—all
hell is going to let out for noon."

"It will take time, of course," said Fourre. "We have
put in duplicate sets of non-Brother data too, as you
know; that will give them extra work to do. Nor can they
be sure which set corresponds to Donner's real identity."

In spite of himself, Naysmith grinned again. "Real
identity" was an incongruous term as applied to the
Brotherhood. However—

"Nevertheless," went on Fourre, "there is going to be
an investigation in every country on Earth and perhaps
the Moon and planets. The Brotherhood is going to have
to go underground, in this country at least. And just now
when I have to be fighting for my service's continued existence down in Rio!"

*They're closing in. We always knew, deep in our
brains, that this day would come, and now it is upon us.*

"Even assuming Donner is dead, which is more likely,"
said Prior, "his widow would make a valuable captive for
the gang. Probably she knows very little about her husband's Service activities, but she undoubtedly has a vast
amount of information buried in her subconscious—faces, snatches of overheard conversation,
perhaps merely the exact dates Donner was absent on this
or that mission. A skilled man could get it out of her, you
know—thereby presenting the enemy detectives with any
number of leads—some of which would go straight to our
most cherished secrets."

"Haven't you tried to spirit her away?" asked Naysmith.

"She won't spirit," said Prior. "We sent an accredited agent to warn her she was in danger and advise her to come away with him. She refused flat. After all, how can she be sure our agent isn't the creature of the enemy? Furthermore, she took some very intelligent precautions, such as consulting the local police, leaving notes in her bankbox to be opened if she disappears without warning, and so on, which have in effect made it impossibly difficult for us to remove her against her will. If nothing else, we couldn't stand the publicity. All we've been able to do is put a couple of men to watching her—and one of these was picked up by the cops the other day and we had hell's own time springing him."

"She's got backbone," said Naysmith.

"Too much," replied Prior. "Well, you know your first assignment. Get her to go off willingly with you, hide her and the kid away somewhere, and then go underground yourself. After that, it's more or less up to you, boy."

"But how'll I persuade her to—"

"Isn't it obvious?" snapped Fourre.

It was. Naysmith grimaced. "What kind of skunk do you take me for?" he protested feebly. "Isn't it enough that I do your murders and robberies for you?"

VI

Brigham City, Utah was not officially a colony, having existed long before the postwar resettlements. But it had always been a lovely town, and had converted itself almost entirely to modern layout and architecture. Naysmith had not been there before, but he felt his heart warming to it—*the same as Donner, who is dead now.*

He opened all jets and screamed at his habitual speed low above the crumbling highway. Hills and orchards lay green about him under a high clear heaven, a great oasis lifted from the wastelands by the hands of men. They had come across many-miled emptiness, those men of another day, trudging dustily by their creaking, bumping, battered wagons on the way to the Promised Land. He, today, sat on plastic-foam cushions in a metal shell, howling at a thousand miles an hour till the echoes thundered, but was himself fleeing the persecutors.

Local traffic control took over as he intersected the radio beam. He relaxed as much as possible, puffing a nervous cigaret while the autopilot brought him in. When the boat grounded in a side lane, he slipped a full mask over his head and resumed, manually, driving.

The houses nestled in their screens of lawn and trees, the low half-underground homes of small families. Men and women, some in laboring clothes, were about on the slideways, and there were more children in sight, small bright flashes of color laughing and shouting, than was common elsewhere. The Mormon influence, Naysmith supposed; free-marriage and the rest hadn't ever been very fashionable in Utah. Most of the fruit-raising plantations were still privately owned small-holdings too, using cooperation to compete with the giant government-regulated agricultural combines. But there would nevertheless be a high proportion of men and women here who commuted to outside jobs by airbus—workers on the Pacific Colony project, for instance.

He reviewed Prior's file on Donner, passing the scanty items through his memory. The Brothers were always on call, but outside their own circle they were as jealous of their privacy as anyone else. It had, however, been plain that Jeanne Donner worked at home as a mail-consultant semantic linguist—correcting manuscript of various kinds—and gave an unusual amount of personal attention to her husband and child.

Naysmith felt inwardly cold.

Here was the address. He brought the boat to a silent halt and started up the walk toward the house. Its severe modern lines and curves were softened by a great rush of morning glory, and it lay in the rustling shade of trees, and there was a broad garden behind it. That was undoubtedly Jeanne's work; Donner would have hated gardening.

Instinctively, Naysmith glanced about for Prior's watchman. Nowhere in sight. But then, a good operative wouldn't be. Perhaps that old man, white-bearded and patriarchal, on the slideway; or the delivery boy whipping down the street on his biwheel; or even the little girl skipping rope in the park across the way. She might not be what she seemed: the biological laboratories could do strange things, and Fourre had built up his own secret shops—

The door was in front of him, shaded by a small vine-draped portico. He thumbed the button, and the voice informed him that no one was at home. Which was doubtless a lie, but— *Poor kid! Poor girl, huddled in there against fear, against the night which swallowed her man—waiting for his return, for a dead man's return.* Naysmith shook his head, swallowing a gorge of bitterness, and spoke into the recorder: "Hello, honey, aren't you being sort of inhospitable?"

She must have activated the playback at once, because it was only a moment before the door swung open. Naysmith caught her in his arms as he stepped into the vestibule.

"Marty, Marty, Marty!" She was sobbing and laughing, straining against him, pulling his face down to hers. The long black hair blinded his stinging eyes. "Oh, Marty, take off that blasted mask. It's been so long—"

She was of medium height, lithe and slim in his grasp, the face strong under its elfish lines, the eyes dark and lustrous and very faintly slanted, and the feel and the

shaking voice of her made him realize his own loneliness
with a sudden desolation. He lifted the mask, letting its
helmet-shaped hollowness thud on the floor, and kissed
her with hunger. *God damn it*, he thought savagely,
*Donner would have to pick the kind I'm a sucker for! But
then, he'd be bound to do so, wouldn't he?*

"No time, sweetheart," he said urgently, while she
ruffled his hair. "Get some clothes and a mask—Jimmy
too, of course. Never mind packing anything. Just call up
the police and tell 'em you're leaving of your own accord.
We've got to get out of here fast."

She stepped back a pace and looked at him with
puzzlement. "What's happened, Marty?" she whispered.

"Fast, I said!" He brushed past her into the living
room. "I'll explain later."

She nodded and was gone into one of the bedrooms,
bending over a crib and picking up a small sleepy figure.
Naysmith lit another cigaret while his eyes prowled the
room.

It was a typical prefab house, but Martin Donner, this
other self who was now locked in darkness, had left his
personality here. None of the mass-produced featureless
gimmickry of today's floaters: this was the home of people
who had meant to stay. Naysmith thought of the succes-
sion of apartments and hotel rooms which had been his
life, and the loneliness deepened in him.

Yes—just as it should be. Donner had probably built
that stone fireplace himself, not because it was needed
but because the flicker of burning logs was good to look
on. There was an antique musket hanging above the
mantle, which bore a few objects: old marble clock,
wrought-brass candlesticks, a flashing bit of Lunar
crystal. The desk was a mahogany anachronism among
relaxers. There were some animated films on the walls,
but there were a couple of reproductions too—a Rem-
brandt rabbi and a Constable landscape—and a few en-
gravings. There was an expensive console with a wide

selection of music wires. The bookshelves held their share of microprint rolls, but there were a lot of old-style volumes too, carefully rebound. Naysmith smiled as his eye fell on the well-thumbed set of Shakespeare.

The Donners had not been live-in-the-past cranks, but they had not been rootless either. Naysmith sighed and recalled his anthropology. Western society had been based on the family as an economic and social unit; the first *raison d'être* had gone out with technology, the second had followed in the last war and the postwar upheavals. Modern life was an impersonal thing. Marriage—permanent marriage—came late when both parties were tired of chasing and was a loose contract at best; the crèche, the school, the public entertainment, made children a shadowy part of the home. And all of this reacted on the human self. From a creature of strong, highly focused emotional life, with a personality made complex by the interaction of environment and ego, Western man was changing to something like the old Samoan aborigines; easy-going, well-adjusted, close friendship and romantic love sliding into limbo. You couldn't say that it was good or bad, one way or the other; but you wondered what it would do to society.

But what could be done about it? You couldn't go back again, you couldn't support today's population with medieval technology even if the population had been willing to try. But that meant accepting the philosophical basis of science, exchanging the cozy medieval cosmos for a bewildering grid of impersonal relationships and abandoning the old cry of man shaking his fist at an empty heaven. *Why?* If you wanted to control population and disease, (and the first, at least, was still a hideously urgent need) you accepted chemical contraceptives and antibiotic tablets and educated people to carry them in their pockets; but then it followed that the traditional relationships between the sexes became something else. Modern technology had no use for the pick-and-shovel laborer or for the routine intellectual; so you were faced with a huge class of people not fit for anything else, and what were you going to do about it? What your great, unbelievably complex civilization-machine needed, what it *had* to have in appalling quantity, was the trained man, trained to the limit of his capacity. But then education had to start early and, being free as long as you could pass exams, be ruthlessly selective. Which meant that your first classes, Ph.D.'s at twenty or younger, looked down on the Second schools, who took out their frustration on the Thirds—intellectual snobbishness, social friction, but how to escape it?

And it was, after all, a world of fantastic anachronisms. It had grown too fast and too unevenly. Hindu peasants scratched in their tiny fields and lived in mud huts while each big Chinese collective was getting its own powerplant. Murderers lurked in the slums around Manhattan Crater while a technician could buy a house and furniture for six months' pay. Floating colonies were being established in the oceans, cities rose on Mars and Venus and the Moon, while Congo natives drummed at the rain-clouds. Reconciliation—*how?*

Most people looked at the surface of things. They saw that the great upheavals, the World Wars and the Years of Hunger and the Years of Madness and the economic breakdowns, had been accompanied by the dissolution of traditional social modes, and they thought that the first was the cause of the second. "Give us a chance and we'll bring back the good old days." They couldn't see that those good old days had carried the seeds of death within them, that the change in technology had brought a change in human nature itself which would have deeper effects than any ephemeral transition period. War, depression, the waves of manic perversity, the hungry men and the marching men and the doomed men, were not causes, they were effects—symptoms. The world was changing and you can't go home again.

The psychodynamicists thought they were beginning to understand the process, with their semantic epistemology, games theory, least effort principle, communications theory—maybe so. It was too early to tell. The Scientific Synthesis was still more a dream than an achievement, and there would have to be at least one generation of Synthesis-trained citizens before the effects could be noticed. Meanwhile, the combination of geriatrics and birth control, necessary as both were, was stiffening the population with the inevitable intellectual rigidity of advancing years, just at the moment when original thought was more desperately needed than ever before in history. The powers of chaos were gathering, and those who saw the truth and fought for it were so terribly few. *Are you absolutely sure you're right? Can you really justify your battle?*

"Daddy!"

Naysmith turned and held out his arms to the boy. A two-year-old, a sturdy lad with light hair and his mother's dark eyes, still half misted with sleep, was calling him. *My son—Donner's son, damn it!*" "Hullo, Jimmy." His voice shook a little.

Jeanne picked the child up. She was masked and voluminously cloaked, and her tones were steadier than his. "All right, shall we go?"

Naysmith noddd and went to the front door. He was not quite there when the bell chimed.

"Who's that?" His ragged bark and the leap in his breast told him how strained his nerves were.

"I don't know. I've been staying indoors since—" Jeanne strode swiftly to one of the bay windows and lifted a curtain, peering out. "Two men. Strangers."

Naysmith fitted the mask on his own head and thumbed the playback switch. The voice was hard and sharp. "This is the Federal police. We know you are in, Mrs. Donner. Open at once."

"S-men!" Her whisper shuddered.

Naysmith nodded grimly. "They've tracked you down so soon, eh? Run and see if there are any behind the house."

Her feet pattered across the floor. "Four in the garden," she called.

"All right." Naysmith caught himself just before asking if she could shoot. He pulled the small flat stet-pistol from his tunic and gave it to her as she returned. He'd have to assume her training; the needler was recoilless anyway. " 'Once more unto the breach, dear friends—' We're getting out of here. Keep close behind me and shoot at their faces or hands. They may have breastplates under the clothes."

His own magnum automatic was cold and heavy in his hand. It was no gentle sleepy-gas weapon. At short range it would blow a hole in a man big enough to put your arm through, and a splinter from its bursting slug killed by hydrostatic shock. The rapping on the door grew thunderous.

She was all at once as cool as he. "Trouble with the law?" she asked crisply.

"The wrong kind of law," he answered. "We've still got cops on our side, though, if that's any consolation."

They couldn't be agents of Fourre's or they would have given him the code sentence. That meant they were sent by the same power which had murdered Martin Donner. He felt no special compunctions about replying in kind. The trick was to escape.

Naysmith stepped back into the living room and picked up a light table, holding it before his body as a shield against needles. Returning to the hall he crowded himself in front of Jeanne and pressed the door switch.

As the barrier swung open, Naysmith fired, a muted hiss and a dull thump of lead in flesh. That terrible impact sent the S-man off the porch and tumbling to the lawn in blood. His companion shot as if by instinct, a needle thunking into the table. Naysmith gunned him down even as he cried out.

Now—outside—to the boat and fast! Sprinting across the grass, Naysmith felt the wicked hum of a missile fan his cheek. Jeanne whirled, encumbered by Jimmy, and sprayed the approaching troop with needles as they burst around the corner of the house.

Naysmith was already at the opening door of his jet. He fired once again while his free hand started the motor.

The S-men were using needles. They wanted the quarry alive. Jeanne stumbled, a dart in her arm, letting Jimmy slide to earth. Naysmith sprang back from the boat. A needle splintered on his mask and he caught a whiff that made his head swoop.

The detectives spread out, approaching from two sides as they ran. Naysmith was shielded on one side by the boat, on the other by Jeanne's unstirring form as he picked her up. He crammed her and the child into the seat and wriggled across them. Slamming the door, he grabbed for the controls.

The whole performance had taken less than a minute. As the jet stood on its tail and screamed illegally skyward, Naysmith realized for the thousandth time that no ordinary human would have been fast enough and sure enough to carry off that escape. The S-men were good but they had simply been outclassed.

They'd check the house, inch by inch and find his recent fingerprints, and those would be the same as the stray ones left here and there throughout the world by certain Un-man operatives—the same as Donner's. It was *the* Un-man, the hated and feared shadow who could strike in a dozen places at once, swifter and deadlier than flesh had a right to be, and who had now risen from his grave to harry them again. He, Naysmith, had just added another chapter to a legend.

Only—the S-men didn't believe in ghosts. They'd look for an answer. And if they found the right answer, that was the end of every dream.

And meanwhile the hunt was after him. Radio beams, license numbers, air-traffic analysis, broadcast alarms,

ID files — all the resources of a great and desperate power would be hounding him across the world, and nowhere could he rest.

VII

Jimmy was weeping in fright, and Naysmith comforted him as well as possible while ripping through the sky. It was hard to be gay, laugh with the boy and tickle him and convince him it was all an exciting game, while Jeanne slumped motionless in the seat and the earth blurred below. But terror at such an early age could have devastating psychic effects and had to be allayed at once. *It's all I can do for you, son. The Brotherhood owes you that much, after the dirty trick it played in bringing you into this world as the child of one of us.*

When Jimmy was at ease again, placed in the back seat to watch a television robotshow, Naysmith surveyed his situation. The boat had more legs than the law permitted, which was one good aspect. He had taken it five miles up, well above the lanes of controlled traffic, and was running northward in a circuitous course. His hungry engines gulped oil at a frightening rate; he'd have to stop for a refill two or three times. Fortunately, he had plenty of cash along. The routine identification of a thumbprint check would leave a written invitation to the pursuers, whereas they might never stumble on the isolated fuel stations where he meant to buy.

Jeanne came awake, stirring and gasping. He held her close to him until the spasm of returning consciousness had passed and her eyes were clear again. Then he lit a cigaret for her and one for himself, and leaned back against the cushions.

"I suppose you're wondering what this is all about," he said.

"Uh-huh." Her smile was uncertain. "How much can you tell me?"

"As much as is safe for you to know," he answered. *Damn it, how much does she already know. I can't give myself away yet! She must be aware that her husband is—was—an Un-man, that his nominal job was a camouflage, but the details?*

"Where are we going?" she asked.

"I've got a hiding place for you and the kid, up in the Canadian Rockies. Not too comfortable, I'm afraid, but reasonably safe. If we can get there without being intercepted. It—"

"We interrupt this program to bring you an urgent announcement. A dangerous criminal is at large in an Airflyte numbered USA-1349-U-7683 Repeat, USA-1349-U-7683. This man is believed to be accompanied by a woman and child. If you see the boat, call the nearest police headquarters or Security office at once. The man is wanted for murder and kidnaping, and is thought to be the agent of a foreign power. Further announcements with complete description will follow as soon as possible."

The harsh voice faded and the robotshow came back on. "Man, oh man, oh man," breathed Naysmith. "They don't waste any time, do they?"

Jeanne's face was white, but her only words were: "How about painting this boat's number over?"

"Can't stop for that now or they'd catch us sure." Naysmith scanned the heavens. "Better strap yourself and Jimmy in, though. If a police boat tracks us, I've got machine guns in this one. We'll blast them."

She fought back the tears with a heart-wrenching gallantry. "Mind explaining a little?"

"I'll have to begin at the beginning," he said cautiously. "To get it all in order, I'll have to tell you a lot of things you already know. But I want to give you the complete pattern. I want to break away from the dirty names like spy and traitor, and show you what we're really trying to do."

"*We?*" She caressed the pronoun. No sane human likes to stand utterly alone.

"Listen," said Naysmith. "I'm an Un-man. But a rather special kind. I'm not in the Inspectorate, allowed by charter and treaty to carry out investigations and report violations of things like disarmament agreements to the council. I'm in the U.N. Secret Service—the *secret* Secret Service—and our standing is only quasi-legal. Officially we're an auxiliary to the Inspectorate; in practice we do a hell of a lot more. The Inspectorate is supposed to tell the U.N. Moon bases where to plant their rocket bombs; the Service tries to make bombardment unnecessary by forestalling hostile action."

"By assassinating Kwang-ti?" she challenged.

"Kwang-ti was a menace. He'd taken China out of the U.N. and was building up her armies. He'd made one attempt to take over Mongolia by sponsoring a phony revolt, and nearly succeeded. I'm not saying that he was knocked off by a Chinese Un-man, in spite of his successor government's charges. I'm just saying it was a good thing he died."

"He did a lot for China."

"Sure. And Hitler did a lot for Germany and Stalin did a lot for Russia, all of which was nullified, along with a lot of innocent people, when those countries went to war. Never forget that the U.N. exists first, last, and all the time to keep the peace. Everything else is secondary."

Jeanne lit another cigaret from the previous one. "Tell me more," she said in a voice that suggested she had known this for a long time.

"Look," said Naysmith, "the enemies the U.N. has faced in the past were as nothing to what endangers it now. Because before the enmity has always been more or less open. In the Second War, the U.N. got started as a military alliance against the fascist powers. In the Third War it became, in effect, a military alliance against its own dissident and excommunicated members. After Rio

it existed partly as an instrument of multilateral
negotiation but still primarily as an alliance of a great
many states, not merely Western, to prevent or suppress
wars anywhere in the world. Oh, I don't want to play
down its legal and cultural and humanitarian and
scientific activities, but the essence of the U.N. was force,
men and machines it could call on from all its member
states—even against a member of itself, if that nation was
found guilty by a majority vote in the Council. It wasn't
quite as large of the United States as you think to turn its
Lunar bases over to the U.N. It thought it could still
control the Council as it had done in the past, but matters
didn't work out that way. Which is all the to the good.
We need a truly international body."

"Anyway, the principle of intervention to stop all wars,
invited or not, led to things like the Great Jehad and the
Brazil-Argentine affair. Small-scale war fought to
prevent large-scale war. Then when the Russian government appealed for help against its nationalist insurgents,
and got it, the precedent of active intervention within a
country's own boundaries was set—much to the good and
much to the distaste of almost every government, including the American. The conservatives were in power
here about that time, you remember, trying unsuccess-
fully to patch up the Socialist Depression, and they nearly
walked us out of membership. Not quite, though. And
those other international functions, research and trade
regulation and so on, have been growing apace."

"You see where this is leading? I've told you many times
before—" a safe guess, that—"but I'll tell you again. The
U.N. is in the process of becoming a federal world
government. Already it has its own Inspectorate, its own
small police force, and its Lunar Guard. Slowly, grudg-
ingly, the nations are being induced to disarm—we
abolished our own draft ten years or so back, remember?
There's a movement afoot to internationalize the planets
and the ocean developments, put them under direct U.N.

authority. We've had international currency stabilization for a long time now; sooner or later, we'll adopt one money unit for the world. Tariffs are virtually extinct. Oh, I could go on all day."

"Previous proposals to make a world government of the U.N. were voted down. Nations were too short-sighted. But it is nevertheless happening, slowly, piece by piece, so that the final official unification of man will be only a formality. Understand? Of course you do. It's obvious. The trouble is, our enemies have begun to understand it too."

Naysmith lit a cigaret for himself and scowled at the blue cloud swirling from his nostrils. "There are so many who would like to break the U.N. There are nationalists and militarists of every kind, every country, men who would rise to power if the old anarchy returned. The need for power is a physical hunger in that sort. There are big men of industry, finance and politics, who'd like to cut their enterprises loose from regulation. There are labor leaders who want a return of the old strife which means power and profit for them. There are religionists of a dozen sorts who don't like our population-control campaigns and the quiet subversion of anti-contraceptive creeds. There are cranks and fanatics who seek a chance to impose their own beliefs, everyone from Syndics to Neocommunists, Pilgrims to Hedonists. There are those who were hurt by some or other U.N. action; perhaps they lost a son in one of our campaigns, perhaps a new development or policy wiped out their business. They want revenge. Oh, there are a thousand kind of them, and if once the U.N. collapses they'll all be free to go fishing in troubled waters."

"Tell me something new," said Jeanne impatiently.

"I have to lead up to it, darling. I have to explain what this latest threat is. You see, these enemies of ours are getting together. All over the world, they're shelving their many quarrels and uniting into a great secret organization whose one purpose is to weaken and destroy the U.N. You wouldn't think fanatical nationalists of different countries could cooperate? Well, they can, because it's the only way they'll ever have a chance later on to attack each other. The leadership of this organization, which we Un-men somewhat inelegantly refer to as the gang, is brilliant; a lot of big men are members and the whole thing is beautifully set up. Such entities as the Americanist Party have become fronts for the gang. Whole governments are backing them, governments which are reluctant U.N. members only because of public opinion at home and the pressure that can be brought to bear on non-members. Kwang-ti's successors brought China back in, I'm sure, only to ruin us from within. U.N. Councillors are among their creatures, and I know not how many U.N. employees."

Naysmith smiled humorlessly. "Even now, the great bulk of people throughout the world are pro-U.N., looking on it as a deliverer from the hell they've survived. So one way the enemy has to destroy us is by sabotage from inside. Corruption, arrogance, inefficiency, illegal actions—perpetrated by their own agents in the U.N. and becoming matters of public knowledge. You've heard a lot of that, and you'll hear still more in the months to come if this is allowed to go on. Another way is to ferret out some of our darker secrets—secrets which every government necessarily has—and make them known to the right people. All right, let's face it: Kwang-ti *was* assassinated by an Un-man. We thought the job had been passed off as the work of democratic conspirators, but apparently there's been a leak somewhere and the Chinese accusation is shaking the whole frail edifice of international cooperation. The Council will stall as long as possible, but eventually it'll have to disown the Service's action and heads will roll. Valuable heads."

"Now if at the proper moment, with the U.N. badly weakened, whole nations walking out again, public con-

fidence trembling, there should be military revolutions
within key nations—and the Moon bases seized by ground
troops from a nearby colony— Do you see it? Do you see
the return of international anarchy, dictatorship,
war—and every Un-man in the Solar System hunted to
his death?"

VIII

By a roundabout course avoiding the major towns and
colonies, it was many hours even at the airboat's speed to
Naysmith's goal. He found his powers of invention
somewhat taxed enroute. First he had to give Jeanne a
half true account of his whereabouts in the past weeks.
Then Jimmy, precociously articulate—as he should be,
with both parents well into the genius class—felt dis-
turbed by the gravity of his elders and the imminent re-
disappearance of a father whom he obviously wor-
shipped, and could only be comforted by Naysmith's long
impromptu saga of Crock O'Dile, a green Irish alligator
who worked at the Gideon Kleinmein Home for Helpless
and Houseless Horses. Finally there were others to
contend with, a couple of filling station operators and the
clerk in a sporting goods store where he purchased
supplies: they had to be convinced in an unobtrusive way
that these were dull everyday customers to be forgotten
as soon as they were gone. It all seemed to go off easily
enough, but Naysmith was cold with the tension of
wondering whether any of these people had heard the
broadcast alarms. Obviously not, so far. But when they
got home and, inevitably, were informed, would they
remember well enough?

He zigzagged over Washington, crossing into British
Columbia above an empty stretch of forest. There was no

official reason for an American to stop, but the border was a logical place for the S-men to watch.

"Will the Canadian police cooperate in hunting us?" asked Jeanne.

"I don't know," said Naysmith. "It depends. You see, American Security, with its broad independent powers, has an anti-U.N. head. On the other hand, the President is pro-U.N. as everybody knows, and Fourre will doubtless see to it that he learns who this wanted criminal is. He can't actually countermand the chase without putting himself in an untenable position, but he can obstruct it in many ways and can perhaps tip off the Canadian government. All on the Q.T., of course."

The boat swung east until it was following the mighty spine of the Rockies, an immensity of stone and forest and snow turning gold with sunset. Naysmith had spent several vacations here, camping and painting, and knew where he was headed. It was after dark when he slanted the boat downward, feeling his way with the radar.

There was an abandoned uranium-hunting base here, one of the shacks still habitable. Naysmith bounced the boat to a halt on the edge of a steep cliff, cut the engines, and yawned hugely. "End of the line," he said.

They climbed out, burdened with equipment, food, and the sleeping child. Naysmith wheeled the vehicle under a tall pine and led the way up a slope. Jeanne drew a lungful of the sharp moonlit air and sighed. "Martin, it's beautiful! Why didn't you ever take me here before?"

He didn't answer. His flashlight picked out the crumbling face of the shack, its bare wood and metal blurred with many years. The door creaked open on darkness. Inside, it was bare, the flooring rotted away to a soft black mould, a few sticks of broken furniture scattered like bones. Taking a purchased ax, he went into the woods after spruce boughs, heaping them under the sleeping bags which Jeanne had laid out. Jimmy whimpered a little in his dreams, but they didn't wake him to eat.

Naysmith's watch showed midnight before the cabin was in order. He strolled out for a final cigaret and Jeanne followed to stand beside him. Her fingers closed about his.

The Moon was nearly full, rising over a peak whose heights were one glitter of snow. Stars wheeled enormously overhead, flashing and flashing in the keen cold air. The forests growing up the slant of this mountain soughed with wind, tall and dark and heady-scented, filled with night and mystery. Down in the gorge there was a river, a long gleam of broken moonlight, the fresh wild noise of its passage drifting up to them. Somewhere an owl hooted.

Jeanne shivered in the chill breeze and crept against Naysmith. He drew his mantle about both of them, holding her close. The little red eye of his cigaret waxed and waned in the dark.

"It's so lovely here," she whispered. "Do you have to go tomorrow?"

"Yes." His answer came harshly out of his throat. "You've supplies enough for a month. If anyone chances by, then you're of course just a camper on vacation. But I doubt they will, this is an isolated spot. If I'm not back within three weeks, though, follow the river down. There's a small colony about fifty miles from here. Or I may send one of our agents to get you. He'll have a password—let's see—'The crocodiles grow green in Ireland.' Okay?"

Her laugh was muted and wistful.

"I'm sorry to lay such a burden on you, darling," he said contritely.

"It's nothing—except that you'll be away, a hunted man, and I won't know—" She bit her lip. Her face was white in the streaming moon-glow. "This is a terrible world we live in."

"No, Jeanne. It's a—a potentially lovely world. My job

is to help keep it that way." He chucked her under the chin, fighting to smile. "Don't let it worry you. Good-night, sweet princess."

She kissed him with yearning. For an instant Naysmith hung back. *Should I tell her? She's safely away now—she has a right to know I'm not her husband—*

"What's wrong, Marty? You seem so strange."

I don't dare. I can't tell her—not while the enemy is abroad, not while there's a chance of their catching her. And a little longer in her fool's paradise—I can drop out of sight, let someone else give her the news— You crawling coward!

He surrendered. But it was a cruel thing to know, that she was really clasping a dead man to her.

They walked slowly back to the cabin.

Colonel Samsey woke with an animal swiftness and sat up in bed. Sleep drained from him as he saw the tall figure etched black against his open balcony door. He grabbed for the gun under his pillow.

"I wouldn't try that, friend." The voice was soft. Moon-light streamed in to glitter on the pistol in the intruder's hand.

"Who are you?" Samsey gasped it out, hardly aware of the incredible fact yet. Why—he was a hundred and fifty stories up. His front entrance was guarded, and no copter could so silently have put this masked figure on his balcony.

"Out of bed, boy. Fast! Okay, now clasp your hands on top of your head."

Samsey felt the night wind cold on his naked body. It was a helplessness, this standing unclothed and alone, out of his uniform and pistol belt, looking down the muzzle of a stranger's gun. His close-cropped scalp felt stubbly under his palms.

"How did you get in?" he whispered.

Naysmith didn't feel it necessary to explain the process.

He had walked from the old highway on which he had landed his jet and used vacuum shoes and gloves to climb the sheer face of Denver Unit. "Better ask why I came," he said.

"All right, blast you! Why? This is a gross violation of privacy, plus menace and—" Samsey closed his mouth with a snap. Legality had plainly gone by the board.

"I want some information." Naysmith seated himself half-way on a table, one leg swinging easily, the gun steady in his right hand while his left fumbled in a belt pouch. "And you, as a high-ranking officer in the American Guard and a well-known associate of Roger Wade, seemed likeliest to have it."

"You're crazy! This is— We're just a patriotic society. You know that. Or should. We—"

"Cram it, Samsey," said Naysmith wearily. "The American Guard has ranks, uniforms, weapons, and drills. Every member belongs to the Americanist Party. You're a private army, Nazi style, and you've done the murders, robberies, and beatings of the Party for the past five years. As soon as the government is able to prove that in court, you'll all go to the Antarctic mines and you know it. Your hope is that your faction can be in power before there's a case against you."

"Libel! We're a patriotic social group—"

"I regret my approach," said Naysmith sardonically. And he did. Direct attack of this sort was not only unlawful, it was crude and of very limited value. But he hadn't much choice. He *had* to get some kind of line on the enemy's plans, and the outlawing of the Brotherhood and the general suspicion cast on the Service meant that standard detective approaches were pretty well eliminated for the time being. Half a loaf— "Nevertheless, I want certain information. The big objective right now is to overthrow the U.N. How do you intend to accomplish that? Specifically, what is your next assignment?"

"You don't expect—"

Samsey recoiled as Naysmith moved. The Un-man's left hand come out of his pouch like a striking snake even as his body hurtled across the floor. The right arm grasped Samsey's biceps, twisting him around in front of the intruder, a knee in his back, while the hypodermic needle plunged into his neck.

Samsey struggled, gasping. The muscles holding him were like steel, cat-lithe, meeting his every wrench with practiced ease. And now the great wave of dizziness came. He lurched and Naysmith supported him, easing him back to the bed.

The hypo had been filled with four cubic centimeters of a neoscopaneurine mixture, very nearly a lethal dose. But it would act fast! Naysmith did not think the colonel had been immunized against such truth drugs. The gang wouldn't trust its lower echelons that much.

Moonlight barred the mindlessly drooling face on the pillow with a streak of icy silver. It was very quiet here, only the man's labored breathing and the sigh of wind blowing the curtains at the balcony door. Naysmith gave his victim a stimulant injection, waited a couple of minutes, and began his interrogation.

Truth drugs have been misnamed. They do not intrinsically force the subject to speak truth; they damp those higher brain centers needed to invent a lie or even to inhibit response. The subject babbles, with a strong tendency to babble on those subjects he has previously been most concerned to keep secret. A skilled psychologist can lead the general direction of the talk.

First, of course, the private nastiness which every human has buried within himself came out, like suppuration from an inflamed wound. Naysmith had been through this before, but he grimaced—Samsey was an especially bad sort. These aggressively manly types often were. Naysmith continued patiently until he got onto more interesting topics.

Samsey didn't know anyone higher in the gang than Wade. Well, that was to be expected. In fact, Naysmith thought scornfully, he, the outsider, knew more about the organization of the enemy than any one member below the very top ranks. But this was a pretty general human characteristic too. A man did his job, for whatever motives of power, profit, or simple existence he might have, and didn't even try to learn where it fitted into the great general pattern. The synthesizing mentality is tragically rare.

But a free society at least permitted its members to learn, and a rational society encouraged them to do so; whereas totalitarianism, from the bossy foreman to the hemispheric dictator, was based on the deliberate suppression of communications. Where there was no feedback, there could be no stability except through the living death of imposed intellectual rigidity.

Back to business! Here came something he had been waiting for, the next task for the American Guard's thugs. The *Phobos* was due in from Mars in a week. Guardsmen were supposed to arrange the death of one Barney Rosenberg, passenger, as soon as possible after his debarkation on Earth. Why? The reason was not given and had not been asked, but a good description of the man was available.

Mars—yes, the Guard was also using a privately owned spaceship to run arms to a secret base in the Thyle II country, where they were picked up by Pilgrims.

So! The Pilgrims were in on the gang. The Service had suspected as much, but here was proof. This might be the biggest break of all, but Naysmith had a hunch that it was incidental. Somehow, the murder of an obscure returnee from Mars impressed him as involving greater issues.

There wasn't more which seemed worth the risk of waiting. Naysmith had a final experiment to try.

Samsey was a rugged specimen, already beginning to

pull out of his daze. Naysmith switched on a lamp, its radiance falling across the distorted face below him. The eyes focused blurrily on his sheening mask. Slowly, he lifted it.

"Who am I, Samsey?" he asked quietly.

A sob rattled in the throat. "Donner—but you're dead. We killed you in Chicago. You died, you're dead."

That settled that. Naysmith replaced his mask. Systemtically, he repaired the alarms he had annulled for his entry and checked the room for traces of his presence. None. Then he took Samsey's gun from beneath the pillow. Silenced, naturally. He folded the lax fingers about the trigger and blew the colonel's brains out.

They'd suspect it wasn't suicide, of course, but they might not think of a biochemical autopsy before the drugs in the bloodstream had broken down beyond analysis. At least there was one less of them. Naysmith felt no qualms. This was not a routine police operation, it was war.

He went back to the balcony, closing the door behind him. Swinging over the edge as he adjusted his vacuum cups, he started the long climb earthward.

The Service could ordinarily have provided Naysmith with an excellent disguise, but the equipment needed was elaborate and he dared not assume that any of the offices which had it were unwatched by Security. Better rely on masks and the feeble observational powers of most citizens to brazen it out.

Calling Prior from a public communibooth, even using the scrambler, was risky too, but it had to be done. The mails were not to be trusted any more, and commmunication was an absolute necessity for accomplishment.

The voice was gray with weariness: "Mars, eh? Nice job, Naysmith. What should we do?"

"Get the word to Fourre, of course, for whatever he can make of it. And a coded radio message to our operatives

on Mars. They can check this Pilgrim business and also
look into Rosenberg's background and associates. Should
be a lot of leads there. However, I'll try to snatch
Rosenberg myself, with a Brother or two to help me,
before the Americanists get him."

"Yeah, you'd better. The Service's hands are pretty
well tied just now while the U.N. investigation of the
Chinese accusations is going on. Furthermore, we can't
be sure of many of our own people. So we, and especially
the Brotherhood, will have to act pretty much independently for the time being. Carry on as well as you
can. However, I can get your information to Rio and
Mars all right."

"Good man. How are things going with you?"

"Don't call me again, Naysmith. I'm being watched,
and my own men can't stop a really all-out assassination
attempt." Prior chuckled dryly. "If they succeed, we can
talk it over in hell."

"To modify what the old *cacique* said about Spaniards
in Heaven, if there are nationalists in hell, I'm not sure if
I want to go there. Okay, then. And good luck!"

It was only the next day that the newscasts carried word
of the murder of one Nathan Prior, semanticist residing
at Frisco Unit. It was believed to be the work of foreign
agents, and S-men had been assigned to aid the local
police.

IX

Most of the Brothers had, of course, been given disguises
early in their careers. Plastic surgery had altered the dis-
tinctive countenance and the exact height, false fingerprints and retinals had been put in their ID records; each
of them had a matching set of transparent plastic "tips"

to put on his own fingers when he made a print for any
official purpose. These men should temporarily be safe,
and there was no justification for calling on their help
yet. They were sitting tight and wary, for if the deadly
efficiency of Hessling's organization came to suspect them
and pull them in, an elementary physical exam would rip
the masquerade wide open.

That left perhaps a hundred undisguised Brothers in
the United States when word came for them to go
underground. Identical physique could be too
useful—for example, in furnishing unshakeable alibis, or
in creating the legend of a superman who was
everywhere—to be removed from all. Some of these
would be able to assume temporary appearances and
move in public for a while. The rest had to cross the
border or hide.

The case of Juho Lampi was especially unfortunate. He
had made enough of a name as a nucleonic engineer in
Finland to be invited to America, and his disguise was
only superficial. When Fourre's warning went out on the
code circuit, he left his apartment in a hurry. A mechanic
at the garage where he hired an airboat recognized the
picture that had been flashed over the entire country.
Lampi read the man's poorly hidden agitation, slugged
him, and stole the boat, but it put the S-men on his trail.
It told them, furthermore, that the identical men were
not only American.

Lampi had been given the name and address of a
woman in Iowa. The Brothers were organized into cells of
half a dozen each, with its own rendezvous and contacts,
and this was to be Lampi's while he was in the States. He
went there after dark and got a room. Somewhat later,
Naysmith showed up. Naysmith, being more nearly a
full-time operative, knew where several cells had their
meeting places. He collected Lampi and decided not to
wait for anyone else. The *Phobos* was coming to Earth in
a matter of hours. Naysmith had gone to Iowa in a self-

driver boat hired from a careless office in Colorado; now, through the woman running the house, the two men rented another and flew back to Robinson field.

"I have my own boat—repainted, new number, and so on—parked near here," said Naysmith. "We'll take off in it. If we get away."

"And then what?" asked Lampi. His English was good, marked with only a trace of accent. The Brothers were natural linguists.

"I don't know. I just don't know." Naysmith looked moodily about him. "We're being hunted as few have ever been hunted." He murmured half to himself:

"I heard myself proclaim'd;
And by the happy hollow of a tree
Escap'd the hunt. No port is free; no place,
That guard and most unusual vigilance
Does not attend my taking."

They were sitting in the Moonjumper, bar and restaurant adjacent to the spaceport. They had chosen a booth near the door, and the transparent wall on this side opened onto the field. Its great pale expanse of concrete stretched under glaring floodlights out toward darkness, a gigantic loom of buildings on three sides of it. Coveralled mechanics were busy around a series of landing cradles. A uniformed policeman strolled by, speaking idly with a technician. Or was it so casual? The technie looked solemn.

"Oh, well," said Lampi. "To get onto a more cheerul subject, have you seen Warschawski's latest exhibition?"

"What's so cheerful about that?" asked Naysmith. "It's awful. Sculpture just doesn't lend itself to abstraction as he seems to think."

Though the Brothers naturally tended to have similar tastes, environment could make a difference. Naysmith and Lampi plunged into a stiff-necked argument about modern art. It was going at a fine pace when they were interrupted.

The curtains of the booth had been drawn. They were twitched aside now and the waitress looked in. She was young and shapely, and the skimpy playsuit might have been painted on. Beyond her, the bar room was a surge of people, a buzz and hum and rumble of voices. In spite of the laboring ventilators, there was a blue haze of smoke in the air.

"Would you like another round?" asked the girl.

"Not just yet, thanks," said Naysmith, turning his masked face toward her. He had dyed his yellow hair a mousey brown at the hideaway, and Lampi's was now black, but that didn't help much; there hadn't been much time to change the wiry texture. He sat stooped, so that she wouldn't see at a casual glance that he was as big as Lampi, and hoped she wasn't very observant.

"Want some company?" she asked. "I can fix it up."

"No thanks," said Naysmith. "We're waiting for the rocket."

"I mean later. Nice girls. You'll like them." She gave him a mechanically meretricious smile.

"Ummmm—well—" Naysmith swapped a glance with Lampi, who nodded. He arranged an assignation for an hour after the landing and slipped her a bill. She left them, swaying her hips.

Lampi chuckled. "It's hardly fair to a couple of hard-working girls," he said. "They will be expecting us."

"Yeah. Probably supporting aged grandmothers, too." Naysmith grinned and lifted the Scotch to the mouth-slit of his mask. "However, it's not the sort of arrangement two fugitives would make."

"What about the American Guardsmen?"

"Probably those burly characters lounging at the bar. Didn't you notice them as we came in? They'll have friends elsewhere who'll—"

"*Your attention, please. The first tender from the Phobos will be cradling in ten minutes, carrying half the passengers from Mars. The second will follow ten minutes later. Repeat, the first—"*

"Which one is Rosenberg on?" asked Lampi.

"How should I know?" Naysmith shrugged. "We'll just have to take our chance. Drink up."

He patted his shoulder-holstered gun and loosened the tunic over it. He and Lampi had obtained breastplates and half-boots at the hideaway; their masks were needle-proof, and arm or groin or thigh was hard to hit when a knee-length cloak flapped around the body. They should be fairly well immunue to stet-guns if they worked fast. Not to bullets-but even the Guardsmen probably wouldn't care to use those in a crowd. The two men went out of the booth and mingled with the people swirling toward the passenger egress. They separated as they neared the gate and hung about on the fringe of the group. There were a couple of big hard-looking men in masks who had shouldered their way up next to the gate. One of them had been in the Moonjumper, Naysmith remembered.

He had no picture of Rosenberg, and Samsey's incoherent description had been of little value. The man was a nonentity who must have been off Earth for years. But presumably the Guardsmen knew what to look for. Which meant that—

There was a red and yellow glare high in the darkened heavens. The far thunder became a howling, bellowing, shaking roar that trembled in the bones and echoed in the skull. Nerves crawled with the nameless half terror of unheard subsonic vibrations. The tender grew to a slim spear-head, backing down with radio control on the landing cradle. Her chemical blasts splashed vividly off the concrete baffles. When she lay still and the rockets cut off, there was a ringing silence.

Endless ceremony—the mechanics wheeled up a stairway, the airlock ground open, a steward emerged, a medical crew stood by to handle space sickness—Naysmith longed for a cigaret. He shifted on his feet and forced his nerves to a thuttering calm.

There came the passengers, half a dozen of them filing toward the gateway. They stopped one by one at the clearance booth to have their papers stamped. The two Guardsmen exchanged a masked glance.

A stocky Oriental came through first. Then there was a woman engineer in Spaceways uniform who held up the line as she gathered two waiting children into her arms. Then—

He was a small bandy-legged man with a hooked nose and a leathery brown skin, shabbily clad, lugging a battered valise. One of the Guardsmen tapped him politely on the arm. He looked up and Naysmith saw his lips moving, the face etched in a harsh white glare. He couldn't hear what was said over the babble of the crowd, but he could imagine it. "Why, yes, I'm Barney Rosenberg. What do you want?"

Some answer was given him; it didn't really matter what. With a look of mild surprise, the little fellow nodded. The other Guardsman pushed over to him, and he went out of the crowd between them. Naysmith drew his stet-gun, holding it under his cloak, and cat-footed after. The Guardsmen didn't escort Rosenberg into the shadows beyond the field, but walked over toward the Moonjumper. There was no reason for Rosenberg to suspect their motives, especially if they stood him a drink.

Naysmith lengthened his stride and fell in beside the right-hand man. He didn't waste time: his gun was ready, its muzzle against the victim's hip. He fired. The Guardsman strangled on a yell.

Lampi was already on the left, but he'd been a trifle slow. That enemy grabbed the Finn's gun wrist with a slashing movement. Naysmith leaned over the first guardsman, who clawed at him as he sagged to his knees, and brought the edge of his left palm down on the second one's neck, just at the base of the skull. The blow cracked numbingly into his own sinews.

"What the blazes—" Rosenberg opened his mouth to shout. There was no time to argue, and Lampi needled him. With a look of utter astonishment, the prospector wilted. Lampi caught him under the arms and hoisted him to one shoulder.

The kidnaping had been seen. People were turning around, staring. Somebody began to scream. Lampi stepped over the two toppled men and followed Naysmith.

Past the door of the bar, out to the street, hurry!

A whistle skirled behind them. They jumped over the slideway and dashed across the avenue. There was a transcontinental Diesel truck bearing down on them, its lights one great glare, the roar of its engine filling the world. Naysmith thought that it brushed him. But its huge bulk was a cover. They plunged over the slideway beyond, ignoring the stares of passersby, and into the shadows of a park.

A siren began to howl. When he had reached the sheltering gloom thrown by a tree, Naysmith looked behind him. Two policemen were coming, but they hadn't spotted the fugitives yet. Naysmith and Lampi ducked through a formal garden, jumping hedges and running down twisted paths. Gravel scrunched underfoot.

Quartering across the park, Naysmith led the way to his airboat. He fumbled the door open and slithered inside. Lampi climbed in with him, tossing Rosenberg into the back seat and slamming the door. The boat slid smoothly out into passing traffic. There were quite a few cars and boats abroad, and Naysmith mingled with them.

Lampi breathed heavily in the gloom. A giant neon sign threw a bloody light over his mask. "Now what?" he sked.

"Now we get the devil out of here," said Naysmith. "Those boys are smart. It won't take them long to alert traffic control and stop all nearby vehicles for search. We have to be in the air before that time."

They left the clustered shops and dwellings, and Naysmith punched the board for permission to take off southbound. The automatic signal flashed him a fourth-lane directive. He climbed to the indicated height and went obediently south on the beam. Passing traffic was a stream of moving stars around him.

The emergency announcement signal blinked an angry red. "Fast is right," said Lampi, swearing in four languages.

"Up we go," said Naysmith.

He climbed vertically, narrowly missing boats in the higher levels, until he was above all lanes. He kept climbing till his vehicle was in the lower stratosphere. Then he turned westward at top speed.

"We'll go out over the Pacific," he explained. "Then we find us a nice uninhabited islet with some trees and lie doggo till tomorrow night. Won't be any too comfortable, but it'll have to be done and I have some food along." He grinned beneath his mask. "I hope you like cold canned beans, Juho."

"And then—?"

"I know another island off the California coast," said Naysmith. "We'll disguise this boat at our first stop, of course, changing the number and recognition signal and so on. Then at the second place we'll refuel and I'll make an important call. You can bet your last mark the enemy knows who pulled this job and will have alerted all fuel station operators this time. But the man where we're going is an absentminded old codger who won't be hard to deceive." He scowled. "That'll take about the last of my cash money, too. Have to get more somehow, if we're to carry on in our present style."

"Where do we go from there?" said Lampi.

"North, I suppose. We have to hide Rosenberg somewhere, and you—" Naysmith shook his head, feeling a dull pain within him. That was the end of the masquerade. Jeanne Donner would know.

At first Barney Rosenberg didn't believe it. He was too shocked. The Guardsmen had simply told him they were representatives of some vaguely identified company which was thinking of developments on Mars and wanted to consult him. He'd been offered a hotel suite and had been told the fee would be nice. Now he looked at his kidnapers with bewildered eyes and challenged them to say who they were.

"Think we'd be fools enough to carry our real IDs around?" snorted Naysmith. "You'll just have to take our word for it that we're U.N. operatives—till later, anyway, when we can safely prove it. I tell you, the devil is loose on Earth and you need protection. Those fellows were after your knowledge, and once they got that you'd have been a corpse."

Rosenberg looked from one masked face to the other. His head felt blurred, the drug was still in him and he couldn't think straight. But those voices—

He thought he remembered the voices. Both of them. Only they were the same.

"I don't know anything," he said weakly. "I tell you, I'm just a prospector, home from Mars."

"You must have information—that's the only possibility," said Lampi. "Something you learned on Mars which is important to them, perhaps to the whole world. What?"

Fieri in Drygulch, and the Pilgrim who had been so eager—

Rosenberg shook his head, trying to clear it. He looked at the two big cloaked figures hemming him in. There was darkness outside the hurtling airboat.

"Who are you?" he whispered.

"I told you we're friends. Un-men. Secret agents." Naysmith laid a hand on Rosenberg's shoulder. "We want to help you, that's all. We want to protect you and whatever it is you know."

Rosenberg looked at the hand—strong, sinewy, blunt-

fingered, with fine gold hairs on the knuckles. But no,
no, no! His heart began thumping till he thought it must
shatter his ribs.

"Let me see your faces," he gasped.

"Well—why not?" Naysmith and Lampi took off their
masks. The dull panel light gleamed off the same
features; broad, strong-boned, blue-eyed. There was a
deep wrinkle above each jutting triangle of nose. The left
ear was faintly bigger than the right. Both men had a
trick of cocking their head a trifle sideways when
listening.

We'll tell him we're twin brothers, thought Naysmith
and Lampi simultaneously.

Rosenberg shrank into the seat. There was a tiny
whimper in his throat.

"Stef," he murmured. "Stefan Rostomily."

X

The newscasts told of crisis in the U.N. Etienne Fourre,
backed by its President, was claiming that the Chinese
government was pressing a fantastic charge to cover up
designs of its own. A full-dress investigation was in order.
Only—as Besser, Minister of International Finance,
pointed out—when the official investigating service was
itself under suspicion, who could be trusted to get at the
facts?

In the United States, Security was after a dangerous spy
and public enemy. Minute descriptions of Donner-
Naysmith-Lampi were on all the screens. Theoretically,
the American President could call off the hunt, but that
would mean an uproar in the delicately balanced Congress; there'd have been a vote of confidence, and if the
President lost that, he and his cabinet would have to

resign—and who would be elected to succeed? But Naysmith and Lampi exchanged grins at the interview statement of the President, that he thought this much-hunted spy was in Chinese pay.

Officially, Canada was cooperating with the United States in chasing the fugitive. Actually, Naysmith was sure it was bluff, a sop to the anti-U.N. elements in the Dominion. Mexico was doing nothing—but that meant the Mexican border was being closely watched.

It couldn't go on. The situation was so unstable that it would have to end, one way or another, in the next several days. If Hessling's men dragged in a Brother—Whether or not Fourre's organization survived, it would have lost its greatest and most secret asset.

But the main thing, Naysmith reflected grimly, was to keep Fourre's own head above water. The whole purpose of this uproar was to discredit the man and his painfully built-up service, and to replace him and his key personnel with nationalist stooges. After that, the enemy would find the next stages of their work simple.

And what can I do?

Naysmith felt a surge of helplessness. Human society had grown too big, too complex and powerful. It was a machine running blind and wild, and he was a fly caught in the gears.

There was one frail governor on the machine, only one, and if it were broken the whole thing would shatter. What to do? What to do?

He shrugged off the despair and concentrated on the next moment. The first thing was to get Rosenberg's information to his own side.

The island was a low sandy swell in an immensity of ocean. There was harsh grass on it, and a few trees gnarled by the great winds, and a tiny village. Naysmith dropped Lampi on the farther side of the island to hide till they came back for him. Rosenberg took the Finn's mask, and the two jetted across to the fuel station. While their boat's tanks were being filled, they entered a public communibooth.

Peter Christian, in Mexico City—Naysmith dialed the number given him by Prior. That seemed the best bet. Wasn't the kid undergoing Synthesis training? His logic might be able to integrate this meaningless flux of data.

No doubt every call across either border was being monitored, illegally but thoroughly. However, the booth had a scrambler unit. Naysmith fed it a coin, but it didn't activate it immediately.

"Could I speak to Peter Christian?" he asked the servant whose face appeared in the screen. "Tell him it's his cousin Joe calling. And give him this message: 'The ragged scoundrel leers merrily, not peddling babies.' "

"*Señor?*" The brown face looked astonished.

"It's a private signal. Write it down, please, so you get it correct." Naysmith dictated slowly. " 'The ragged scoundrel —' "

"Yes, understand. Wait, please, I will call the young gentleman."

Naysmith stood watching the screen for a moment. He could vaguely make out the room beyond, a solid and handsomely furnished place. Then he stabbed at the scrambler buttons. There were eight of them, which could be punched in any order to yield 40,320 possible combinations. The key letters, known to every Brother, were currently MNTSRPBL, and "the ragged scoundrel" had given Christian the order Naysmith was using. When Hessling's men got around to playing back their monitor tapes, the code sentence wouldn't help them unscramble without knowledge of the key. On the other hand, it wouldn't be proof that their quarry had been making the call; such privacy devices were not uncommon.

Naysmith blanked the booth's walls and removed his own and Rosenberg's masks. The little man was in a state of hypnosis, total recall of the Fieri manuscript he had read on Mars. He was already drawing structural formulas of molecules.

The random blur and noise on the screen clicked away as Peter Christian set the scrambler unit at that end. It was his own face grown younger which looked out at Naysmith—a husky blond sixteen-year-old, streaked with sweat and panting a little. He grinned at his Brother.

"Sorry to be so long," he said. "I was working out in the gym. Have a new mech-volley play to develop which looks promising." His English was fluent and Naysmith saw no reason to use a Spanish which, in his own case, had grown a little rusty.

"Who're you the adoptive son of?" asked the man. Privacy customs didn't mean much in the Brotherhood.

"Holger Christian—Danish career diplomat, currently ambassador to Mexico. They're good people, he and his wife."

Yes, thought Naysmith, they would be, if they let their foster child, even with his obvious brilliance, take Synthesis. The multi-ordinal integrating education was so new and untried, and its graduates would have to make their own jobs. But the need was desperate. The sciences had grown too big and complex, like everything else, and there was too much overlap between the specialties. Further progress required the fully trained synthesizing mentality.

And progress itself was no longer something justified only by Victorian prejudice. It was a matter of survival. Some means of creating a stable social and economic order in the face of continuous revolutionary change had to be found. More and more technological development was bitterly essential. Atomic-powered oil synthesis had come barely in time to save a fuel-starved Earth from industrial breakdown. Now new atomic energy fuels had to be evolved before the old ores were depleted. The rising incidence of neurosis and insanity among the intelligent and apathy among the insensitive had to be checked before other Years of Madness came. Heredity damaged by hard radiation had to be unscrambled, somehow, before dangerous recessive traits spread through the entire human population. Communications theory, basic to modern science and sociology, had to be perfected. There had to be. Why enumerate? Man had come too far and too fast. Now he was balanced on a knife edge over the red gulfs of hell.

When Peter Christian's education was complete, he would be one of Earth's most important men—whether he realized it himself or not. Of course, even his foster parents didn't know that one of his Snythesis instructors was an Un-man who was quietly teaching him the fine points of secret service. They most assuredly did not know that their so normal and healthy boy was already initiated into a group whose very existence was an unrecorded secret.

The first Brothers had been raised in families of Un-man technies and operators who had been in on the project from the start. This practice continued on a small scale, but most of the new children were put out for adoption through recognized agencies around the world—having first been provided with a carefully faked background history. Between sterility and the fear of mutation, there was no difficulty in placing a good-looking man child with a superior family. From baby-hood, the Brother was under the influence—a family friend or a pediatrician or instructor or camp counselor or minister, anyone who could get an occasional chance to talk intimately with the boy, would be a sparetime employee of Fourre's and helped incline the growing personality the right way. It had been established that a Brother could accept the truth and keep his secret from the age of twelve, and that he never refused to turn Un-man. From then on, progress was quicker. The Brothers were precocious: Naysmith was only twenty-five, and he had been on his first mission at seventeen; Lampi was an authority in his field at twenty-three. There should be no hesitation in dumping this responsibility on Christian, even if there had been any choice in the matter.

"Listen," said Naysmith. "You know all hell has broken loose and that the American S-men are out to get us. Specifically, I'm the one they think they're hunting. But Lampi, a Finnish Brother, and I have put the snatch on one Barney Rosenberg from Mars. He has certain information the enemy wants." The man knew what the boy must be thinking—in a way, those were his own thoughts—and added swiftly: "No, we haven't let him in on the secret, though the fact that he was a close friend of Rostomily's makes it awkward. But it also makes him trust us. He read the report of a Fieri on Mars, concerning suspended animation techniques. He'll give it to you now. Stand by to record."

"Okay, *ja, sí.*" Christian grinned and flipped a switch. He was still young enough to find this a glorious cloak-and-dagger adventure. Well, he'd learn, and the learning would be a little death within him.

Rosenberg began to talk, softly and very fast, holding up his structural formulas and chemical equations at the appropriate places. It took a little more than an hour. Christian would have been bored if he hadn't been so interested in the material; Naysmith fumed and sweated unhappily. Any moment there might come suspicion, discovery— The booth was hot.

"That's all, I guess," said Naysmith when the prospector had run down. "What do you make of it?"

"Why, it's sensational! It'll jump biology two decades!" Christian's eyes glowed. "Surgery—yes, that's obvious. Research techniques— *Gud Fader i himlen,* what a discovery!"

"And why do you think it's so important to the enemy?" snapped Naysmith.

"Isn't it plain? The military uses, man! You can use a light dose to immunize against terrific accelerations. Or you can pack a spaceship with men in frozen sleep, load 'em in almost like boxes, and have no supply worries enroute. Means you can take a good-sized army from planet to planet. And of course there's the research aspect. With what can be learned with the help of suspension techniques, biological warfare can be put on a wholly new plane."

"I thought as much." Naysmith nodded wearily. It was the same old story, the worn-out tale of hate and death and oppression. The logical end-product of scientific warfare was that *all* data became military secrets—a society without feedback or stability. That was what he fought against. "All right, what can you do about it?"

"I'll unscramble the record—no, better leave it scrambled—and get it to the right people. Hmmm—give me a small lab and I'll undertake to develop certain phases of this myself. In any case, we can't let the enemy have it."

"We've probably already given it to them. Chances are they have monitors on this line. But they can't get around to our recording and to trying all possible unscrambling combinations in less than a few days, especially if we keep them busy." Naysmith leaned forward, his haggard eyes probing into the screen. "Pete, as the son of a diplomat you must have a better than average notion of the overall politico-military picture. What can we do?"

Christian sat still for a moment. There was a curious withdrawn expression on the young face. His trained mind was assembling logic networks in a manner unknown to previous history. Finally he looked back at the man.

"There's about an eighty percent probability that Besser is the head of the gang," he said. "Chief of international finance, you know. That's an estimate of my own; I don't have Fourre's data, but I used a basis of Besser's past history and known character, his country's recent history, the necessary communications for a least-effort anti-U.N. setup on a planetary scale; the—never mind. You already know with high probability that Roger Wade is his chief for North America. I can't predict Besser's actions very closely, since in spite of his prominence he uses privacy as a cover-up for relevant psychological data. If we assume that he acts on a survival axiom, and logically apart from his inadequate ground-ing in modern socio-theory and his personal bias—hm."

"Besser, eh? I had my own suspicions, besides what I've been told. Financial integration has been proceeding rather slowly since he took office. Never mind. We have to strike at his organization. What to do?"

"I need more data. How many American Brothers are underground in the States and can be contacted?"

"How should I know? All that could would try to skip the country. I'm only here because I know enough of the overall situation to act usefully, I hope."

"Well, I can scare up a few in Mexico and South America, I think. We have our own communications. And I can use my 'father's' sealed diplomatic circuit to get in touch with Fourre. You have this Lampi with you, I suppose?" Christian sat in moody stillness for a while. Then:

"I can only suggest—and it's a pretty slim guess—that you two let yourselves be captured."

The man sighed. He had rather expected this.

Naysmith brought the boat whispering down just as the first cold light of sunrise crept skyward. He buzzed the narrow ledge where he had to land, swung back, and lowered the wheels. When they touched, it was a jarring, brutal contact that rattled his teeth together. He cut the motor and there was silence.

If Jeanne was alert, she'd have a gun on him now. He opened the door and called loudly: "The crocodiles grow green in Ireland." Then he stepped out and looked around him.

The mountains were a shadowy looming. Dawn lay like roses on their peaks. The air was fresh and chill, strong with the smell of pines, and there was dew underfoot and alarmed birds clamoring into the sky. Far below him, the river thundered and brawled.

Rosenberg climbed stiffly after him and leaned against the boat. Earth gravity dragged at his muscles, he was cold and hungry and cruelly tired, and these men who were ghosts of his youth would not tell him what the darkness was that lay over the world. Sharply he remembered the thin bitter sunup of Mars, a gaunt desert misting into life and a single crag etched against loneliness. Homesickness was an ache in him.

Only—he had not remembered Earth could be so lovely.

"Martin! Oh, Martin!" The woman came down the trail, running, slipping on the wet needles. Her raven hair was cloudy about the gallantly lifted head, and there was a light in her eyes which Rosenberg had almost forgotten. "Oh, my darling, you're back!"

Naysmith held her close, kissing her with hunger. One minute more, one little minute before Lampi emerged, was that too much?

He hadn't been able to leave the Finn anywhere behind. There was no safe hiding place in all America, not when the S-men were after him. There could be no reliable rendezvous later, and Lampi would be needed. He had to come along.

Of course, the Finn could have stayed masked and mute the entire while he was at the cabin. But Rosenberg would have to be left there, it was the best hideaway for him. The prospector might be trusted to keep secret the fact that two identical men had brought him here—or he might not. He was shrewd; Jeanne's conversation would lead him to some suspicion of the truth, and he might easily decide that she had been the victim of a shabby trick and should be given the facts. Then anything could happen.

Oh, with some precautions Naysmith could probably hide his real nature from the girl a while longer. Rosenberg might very well keep his mouth shut on request. But there was no longer any point in concealing the facts from her—she would not be captured by the gang before they had the Un-man himself. In any case, she must be told sooner or later. The man she thought was her husband was probably going to die, and it was as well that she think little of him and have no fears and sorrows on his account. One death was enough for her.

He laid his hands on the slim shoulders and stood back a bit, looking into her eyes. His own crinkled in the way she must know so well, and they were unnaturally bright in the dawn-glow. When he spoke, it was almost a whisper.

"Jeanne, honey, I've got some bad news for you."

He felt her stiffen beneath his hands, saw the face tighten and heard the little hiss of indrawn breath. There were dark rings about her eyes, she couldn't have slept very well while he was gone.

"This is a matter of absolute secrecy," he went on, tonelessly. "No one, repeat no one, is to have a word of it. But you have a right to the truth."

"Go ahead." There was an edge of harshness in her voice. "I can take it."

"I'm not Martin Donner," he said. "Your husband is dead."

She stood rigid for another heartbeat, and then she pulled wildly free. One hand went to her mouth. The other was half lifted as if to fend him off.

"I had to pretend it, to get you away without any fuss," he went on, looking at the ground. "The enemy would have—tortured you, maybe. Or killed you and Jimmy. I don't know."

Juho Lampi came up behind Naysmith. There was compassion on his face. Jeanne stepped backward, voiceless.

"You'll have to stay here," said Naysmith bleakly. "It's the only safe place. Here is Mr. Rosenberg, whom we're leaving with you. I assure you he's completely innocent of anything that has been done. I can't tell either of you more than this." He took a long step toward her. She stood her ground, unmoving. When he clasped her hands into his, they were cold. "Except that I love you," he whispered.

Then, swinging away, he faced Lampi. "We'll clean up and get some breakfast here," he said. "After that, we're off."

Jeanne did not follow them inside. Jimmy, awakened by their noise, was delighted to have his father back (Lampi had re-assumed a mask) but Naysmith gave him disappointingly little attention. He told Rosenberg that the three of them should stay put here as long as possible before striking out for the village, but that it was hoped to send a boat for them in a few days.

Jeanne's face was cold and bloodless as Naysmith and Lampi went back to the jet. When it was gone, she started to cry. Rosenberg wanted to leave and let her have it out by herself, but she clung to him blindly and he comforted her as well as he could.

XI

There was no difficulty about getting captured. Naysmith merely strolled into a public lavatory at Oregon Unit and took off his mask to wash his face; a man standing nearby went hurriedly out, and when Naysmith emerged he was knocked over by the stet-gun of a Unit policeman. It was what came afterward that was tough.

He woke up, stripped and handcuffed, in a cell, very shortly before a team of S-men arrived to lead him away.

These took the added precaution of binding his ankles before stuffing him into a jet. He had to grin sourly at that, it was a compliment of sorts. Little was said until the jet came down on a secret headquarters which was also a Wyoming ranch.

There they gave him the works. He submitted meekly to every identification procedure he had ever heard of. Fluoroscopes showed nothing hidden within his body except the communicator, and there was some talk of operating it out; but they decided to wait for orders from higher up before attempting that. They questioned him and, since he had killed two or three of their fellows, used methods which cost him a couple of teeth and a sleepless night. He told them his name and address, but little else.

Orders came the following day. Naysmith was bundled into another jet and flown eastward. Near the destination, the jet was traded for an ordinary, inconspicuous airboat. They landed after dark on the grounds of a large new mansion in western Pennsylvania—Naysmith recalled that Roger Wade lived here—and he was led inside. There was a soundproofed room with a full battery of interrogation machines under the residential floors. The prisoner was put into a chair already equipped with straps, fastened down, and left for a while to ponder his situation.

He sighed and attempted to relax, leaning back against the metal of the chair. It was an uncomfortable seat, cold and stiff as it pressed into his naked skin. The room was long and low-ceilinged, barren in the white glare of high-powered fluoros, and the utter stillness of it muffled his breath and heartbeat. The air was cool, but somehow that absorbent quiet choked him. He faced the impassive dials of a lie detector and an electric neurovibrator, and the silence grew and grew.

His head ached, and he longed for a cigaret. His eyelids were sandy with sleeplessness and there was a foul taste in his mouth. Mostly, though, he thought of Jeanne Donner.

Presently, the door at the end of the room opened and a group of people walked slowly toward him. He recognized Wade's massive form in the van. Behind him trailed a bearded man with a lean, sallow face; a young chap thin as a rail, his skin dead white and his hands clenching and unclenching nervously; a gaunt homely woman; and a squat, burly subordinate whom he did not know but assumed to be an S-man in Wade's pay. The others were familiar to Service dossiers: Lewin, Wade's personal physician; Rodney Borrow, his chief secretary; Marta Jennings, Americanist organizer. There was death in their eyes.

Wade proceeded quietly up toward Naysmith. Borrow drew a chair for him and he sat down in it and took out a cigaret. Nobody spoke till he had it lighted. Then he blew the smoke in Naysmith's direction and said gently: "According to the official records, you really are Robert Naysmith of California. But tell me, is that only another false identity?"

Naysmith shrugged. "Identity is a philosophical basic," he answered. "Where does similarity leave off and identity begin?"

"Mmmmmm-hm." Wade nodded slowly. "We've killed you at least once, and I suspect more than once. But are you Martin Doner, or are you his twin? And in the latter case, how does it happen that you two, or you three, four, five, ten thousand—are *completely* identical?"

"Oh, not quite," said Naysmith.

"No-o-o. There are the little scars and peculiarities due to environment—and habits, language, accent, occupation. But for police purposes you and Donner are the same man. How was it done?"

Naysmith smiled. "How much am I offered for that information?" he parried. "As well as other information you know I have?"

"So." Wade's eyes narrowed. "You weren't captured—not really. You gave yourself up."

"Maybe. Have you caught anyone else yet?"

Wade traded a glance with the Security officer. Then, with an air of decision, he said briskly. "An hour ago, I was informed that a man answering your description had been picked up in Minnesota. He admitted to being one Juho Lampi of Finland, and I'm inclined to take his word for it though we haven't checked port-of-entry records yet. How many more of you can we expect to meet?"

"As many as you like," said Naysmith. "Maybe more than that."

"All right. You gave yourself up. You must know that we have no reason to spare your life—or lives. What do you hope to gain?"

"A compromise," answered Naysmith. "Which will, of course, involve our release."

"How much are you willing to tell us now?"

"As little as possible, naturally. We'll have to bargain."

Stall! Stall for time! The message from Rio has got to come soon. It's got to, or we're all dead men.

Borrow leaned over his master's shoulder. His voice was high and cracked, stuttering just a trifle: "How will we know you're telling the truth?"

"How will you know that even if you torture me?" shrugged Naysmith. "Your bird dogs must have reported that I've been immunized to drugs."

"There are still ways," said Lewin. His words fell dull in the muffling silence. "Prefrontal lobotomy is usually effective."

Yes, this is the enemy. These are the men of darkness. These are the men who in other days sent heretics to burning, or fed the furnaces of Belsen, or stuffed the rockets with radioactive death. Now they're opening skulls and slashing brains across. Argue with them! Let them kick and slug and whip you, but don't let them know—

"Our bargain might not be considered valid if you do that."

"The essential element of a bargain," said Wade pompously, "is the free will and desire of both parties. You're not free."

"But I am. You've killed one of me and captured two others. How do you know the number of me which is still running loose, out there in the night?"

Borrow and Jennings flickered uneasy eyes toward the smooth bare walls. The woman shuddered, ever so faintly.

"We needn't be clumsy about this," said Lewin. "There's the lie detector, first of all. Its value is limited, but this man is too old to have had Synthesis training, so he can't fool it much. Then there are instruments that make a man quite anxious to talk. I have a chlorine generator here, Naysmith. How would you like to breathe a few whiffs of chlorine?"

"Or just a vise—applied in the right place," snapped Jennings.

"Hold up a minute," ordered Wade. "Let's find out how much he wants to reveal without such persuasion."

"I said I'd trade information, not give it away," said Naysmith. He wished the sweat weren't running down his face and body for all of them to see. The reek of primitive, uncontrollable fear was sharp in his nostrils; not the fear of death, but of the anguish and mutilation which were worse than oblivion.

"What do *you* want to know?" snapped the Security officer contemptuously.

"Well," said Naysmith, "first off, I'd like to know your organization's purpose."

"What's that?" Wade's heavy face blinked at him, and an angry flush mottled his cheeks. "Let's not play crèche games. You know what we want."

"No, seriously, I'm puzzled." Naysmith forced mildness into his tones. "I realize you don't like the status quo and want to change it. But you're all well off now. What do you hope to gain?"

"What— That will do!" Wade gestured to the officer,

and Naysmith's head rang with a buffet. "We haven't time to listen to your bad jokes."

Naysmith grinned viciously. If he could get them mad, play on those twisted emotions till the unreasoning thalamus controlled them—it would be hard on him, but it would delay their real aims. "Oh, I can guess," he said. "It's personal, isn't it? None of you really know what's driving you to this, except for the stupid jackals who're in with you merely because it pays better than any work they could get on their own merits. Like you, for instance." He glanced at the S-man and sneered deliberately.

"Shut up!" This time the blow was to his jaw. Blood ran out of his mouth, and he sagged a little against the straps that held him. But his voice lifted raggedly.

"Take Miss Jennings, for one. Not that I would, even if you paid me. You're all twisted up inside, aren't you? Too ugly to get a man, too scared of yourself to get a surgical remodeling. You're trying your clumsy damndest to sublimate it into patriotism—and what kind of symbol is a flagpole? I notice it was you who made that highly personal suggestion about torturing me."

She drew back, the rage of a whipped animal in her. The S-man took out a piece of hose, but Wade gestured him away. The leader's face had gone wooden.

"Or Lewin—another case of psychotic frustration." Naysmith smiled, a close-lipped and unpleasant smile of bruised lips, at the doctor. "I warrant you'd work for free if you hadn't been hired. A two-bit sadist has trouble finding outlets these days."

"Now we come to Rodney Borrow."

"Shut up!" cried the thin man. He edged forward. Wade swept him back with a heavy arm.

"Exogene!" Naysmith's smile grew warm, almost pitying. "It's too bad that human exogenesis was developed during the Years of Madness, when moral scruples went to hell and scientists were as fanatical as everyone else. They grew you in a tank, Borrow, and your pre-natal life, which every inherited instinct said should be warm and dark and sheltered, was one hell of study—bright lights, probes, microslides taken of your tissues. They learned a lot about the human fetus, but they should have killed you instead of letting such a pathetic quivering mass of engrammed psychoses walk around alive. If you could call it life, Exogene."

Borrow lunged past Wade. There was slaver running from his lips, and he clawed for Naysmith's eyes. The S-man pulled him back and suddenly he collapsed, weeping hysterically. Naysmith shuddered beneath his skin. *There but for the Grace of God—*

"And how about myself?" asked Wade. "These amateur analyses are most amusing. Please continue."

"Guilt drive. Overcompensation. The Service has investigated your childhood and adolescent background and—"

"And?"

"Come on Roger. It's fun. It won't hurt a bit."

The big man sat stiff as an iron bar. For a long moment there was nothing, no sound except Borrow's sobs; no movement. Wade's face turned gray.

When he spoke, it was as if he were strangling: "I think you'd better start that chlorine generator, Lewin."

"With pleasure!"

Naysmith shook his head. "And you people want to run things," he murmured. "We're supposed to turn over a world slowly recovering its sanity to the likes of you."

The generator began to hiss and bubble at his back. He could have turned his head to watch it, but that would have been a defeat. And he needed every scrap of pride remaining in this ultimate loneliness.

"Let me run the generator," whispered Borrow.

"No," said Lewin. "You might kill him too fast."

"Maybe we should wait till they bring this Lampi here," said Jennings. "Let him watch us working Naysmith over."

Wade shook his head. "Maybe later," he said.

"I notice that you still haven't tried to find out what I'm willing to tell you without compulsion," interjected Naysmith.

"Well, go ahead," said Wade in a flat voice. "We're listening."

A little time, just a little more time, if I can spin them a yarn—

"Etienne Fourre has more resources than you know," declared Naysmith. "A counter blow has been prepared which will cost you dearly. But since it would also put quite a strain on us, we're willing to discuss—if not a permanent compromise, for there can obviously be none, at least an armistice. That's why—"

A chime sounded. "Come in," said Wade loudly. His voice activated the door and a man entered.

"Urgent call for you, Mr. Wade," he reported. "Scrambled."

"All right." The leader got up. "Hold off on that chlorine till I get back, Lewin." He went out.

When the door had closed behind him, Lewin said calmly: "Well, he didn't tell us to refrain from other things, did he?"

They took turns using the hose. Naysmith's mind grew a little hazy with pain. But they dared not inflict real damage, and it didn't last long.

Wade came back. He ignored Lewin, who was hastily pocketing the truncheon, and said curtly: "We're going on a trip. All of us. Now."

The word had come. Naysmith sank bank, breathing hard. Just at that moment, the relief from pain was too great for him to think of anything else. It took him several minutes to start worrying about whether Peter Christian's logic had been correct, and whether the Service could fulfill its part, and even whether the orders that came to Wade had been the right ones.

XII

It was late afternoon before Barney Rosenberg had a chance to talk with Jeanne Donner, and then it was she who sought him out. He had wandered from the cabin after lunch, scrambling along the mountainside and strolling through the tall forest. But Earth gravity tired him, and he returned in a few hours. Even then, he didn't go back to the cabin, but found a log near the rim of the gorge and sat down to think.

So this was Earth.

It was a cool and lovely vision which opened before him. The cliffs tumbled in a sweep of gray and slate blue, down and down into the huge sounding canyon of the river. On the farther side the mountain lifted in a mist of dim purple up to its sun-blazing snow and the skyey vastness beyond. There were bushes growing on the slopes that fell riverward, green blurring the severe rock, here and there a cluster of fire-like berries. Behind Rosenberg and on either side were the trees, looming pine in a cavern of shadow, slim whispering beech, ash with the streaming, blinding raining sunlight snared in its leaves. He had not remembered how much color there was on this planet.

And it was alive with sound. The trees murmured. Mosquitoes buzzed thinly around his ears. A bird was singing—he didn't know what kind of bird, but it had a wistful liquid trill that haunted his thoughts. Another answered in whistles, and somewhere a third was chattering and chirping its gossip. A squirrel darted past like a red comet, and he heard the tiny scrabble of its claws.

And the smells—the infinite living world of odors; pine and mould and wildflowers and the river mist! He had almost forgotten he owned a sense of smell, in the tanked sterility of Mars.

Oh, his muscles ached and he was lonely for the grim bare magnificence of the deserts and he wondered how he would ever fit into this savage world of men against men. But still — Earth was home, and a billion years of evolution could not be denied.

Someday Mars would be a full-grown planet and its people would be rich and free. Rosenberg shook his head, smiling a little. Poor Martians!

There was a light footstep behind him. He turned and saw Jeanne Donner approaching. She had on a light blouse-and-slack outfit which didn't hide the grace of her or the weariness, and the sun gleamed darkly in her hair. Rosenberg stood up with a feeling of awkwardness.

"Please sit down." Her voice was grave, somehow remote. "I'd like to join you for a little while, if I may."

"By all means." Rosenberg lowered himself again to the mossy trunk. It was cool and yielding, a little damp, under his hand. Jeanne sat beside him, elbows on knees. For a moment she was quiet, looking over the sun-flooded land. Then she took out a pack of cigarets and held them toward the man. "Smoke?" she asked.

"Uh — no, thanks. I got out of the habit on Mars. Oxygen's too scarce, usually. We chew instead, if we can afford tobacco at all."

"M-hm." She lit a cigaret for herself and drew hard on it, sucking in her cheeks. He saw how fine the underlying bony structure was. Well — Stef had always picked the best women, and gotten them.

"We'll rig a bed for you," she said. "Cut some spruce boughs and put them under a sleeping bag. Makes a good doss."

"Thanks." They sat without talking for a while. The cigaret smoke blew away in ragged streamers. Rosenberg could hear the wind whistling and piping far up the canyon.

"I'd like to ask you some questions," she said at last, turning her face to him. "If they get too personal, just say so."

"I've nothing to hide—worse luck." He tried to smile. "Anyway, we don't have those privacy notions on Mars. They'd be too hard to maintain under our living conditions."

"They're a recent phenomenon on Earth, anyway," she said. "Go back to the Years of Madness, when there was so much eccentricity of all kinds, a lot of it illegal. Oh, hell!" She threw the cigaret to the ground and stamped it savagely out with one heel. "I'm going to forget my own conditioning too. Ask me anything you think is relevant. We've got to get to the truth of this matter."

"If we can. I'd say it was a well-guarded secret."

"Listen," she said between her teeth. "My husband was Martin Donner. We were married three and a half years—and I mean married. He couldn't tell me much about this work. I knew he was really an Un-man and that his engineering work was only a blind, and that's about all he ever told me. Obviously, he never said a word about having—duplicates. But leaving that aside, we were in love and we got to know each other as well as two people can in that length of time. More than just physical appearance. It was also a matter of personality, reaction-patterns, facial expressions, word-configuration choices, manner of moving and working, the million little things which fit into one big pattern. An overall *getstalt*, understand?"

"Now this man—What did you say his name was?"

"Naysmith. Robert Naysmith. At least, that's what he told me. The other fellow was called Lampi."

"I'm supposed to believe that Martin died and that this—Naysmith—was substituted for him," she went on hurriedly. "They wanted to get me out of the house fast, couldn't stop to argue with me, so they sent in this ringer. Well, I saw him there in the house. He escaped with me and the boy. We had a long and uneasy flight together up here—you know how strain will bring out the most basic characteristics of a person. He stayed here overnight—" A slow flush crept up her cheeks and she looked away.

Then, defiantly, she swung back on Rosenberg. "And he fooled me completely. Everything about him was Martin. *Everything!* Oh, I suppose there were minor variations, but they must have been very minor indeed. You can disguise a man these days, with surgery and cosmetics and whatnot, so that he duplicates almost every detail of physique. But can surgery give him the same funny slow way of smiling, the same choice of phrases, the same sense of humor, the same way of picking up his son and talking to him, the same habit of quoting Shakespeare, and way of taking out a cigaret and lighting it one-handed, and corner-cutting way of piloting an airboat—the same *soul?* Can they do that?"

"I don't know," whispered Rosenberg. "I shouldn't think so."

"I wouldn't really have believed it," she said. "I'd have thought he was trying to tell me a story for some unknown reason. Only there was that other man with him, and except for their hair being dyed I couldn't tell them apart—and you were along too, and seemed to accept the story," She clutched his arm. "Is it true? Is my husband really dead?"

"I don't know," he answered grayly. "I think they were telling the truth, but how can I know?"

"It's more than my own sanity," she said in a tired voice. "I've got to know what to tell Jimmy. I can't say anything now."

Rosenberg looked at the ground. His words came slowly and very soft: "I think your best bet is to sit tight for a while. This is something which is big, maybe the biggest secret in the universe. And it's either very good or very bad. I'd like to believe that it was good."

"But what do you know of it?" She held his eyes with her own, he couldn't look away, and her hand gripped his arm with a blind force. "What can you tell me? What do you think?"

He ran a thin, blue-veined hand through his grizzled

hair and drew a breath. "Well," he said, "I think there probably are a lot of these identical Un-men. We know that there are — were — three, and I got the impression there must be more. Why not? That Lampi was a foreigner; he had an accent; so if they're found all over the world —"

"Un-man." She shivered a little, sitting there in the dappled shade and sunlight. "It's a hideous word. As if they weren't human."

"No," he said gently. "I think you're wrong there. They — well, I knew their prototype, and he was a *man*."

"Their — no!" Almost, she sprang to her feet. With an effort, she controlled herself and sat rigid. *"Who was that?"*

"His name was Stefan Rostomily. He was my best friend for fifteen years."

"I — don't know — never heard of him." Her tones were thick.

"You probably wouldn't have. He was off Earth the whole time. But his name is still a good one out on the planets. You may not know what a Rostomily valve is, but that was his invention. He tinkered it up one week for convenience, sold it for a good sum, and binged that away." Rosenberg chuckled dimly. "It made history, that binge. But the valve meant a lot to Martian colonists."

"Who was he?"

"He never said much about his background. I gathered he was a European, probably Czech or Austrian. He must have done heroic things in the underground and guerrilla fighting during the Third War. But it kind of spoiled him for a settled career. By the time things began to calm a little, he'd matured in chaos and it was too late to do any serious studying. He drifted around Earth for a while, took a hand in some of the fighting that still went on here and there — he was with the U.N. forces that suppressed the Great Jehad, I know. But he got sick of killing, too, as any sane man would. In spite of his background, Mrs.

Donner, he was basically one of the sanest men I ever knew. So at last he bluffed his way onto a spaceship—didn't have a degree, but he learned engineering in a hell of a hurry, and he was good at it. I met him on Venus, when I was prospecting around; I may not look it, but I'm a geologist and mineralogist. We ended up on Mars. Helped build Sandy Landing, helped in some of the plantation development work, prospected, mapped and surveyed and explored—we must've tried everything. He died five years ago. A cave-in. I buried him there on Mars."

The trees about them whispered with wind.

"And these others are—his sons?" she murmured. She was trembling a little now.

Rosenberg shook his head. "Impossible. These men are *him*. Stef in every last feature, come alive and young again. No child could ever be that close to his father."

"No. No, I suppose not."

"Stef was a human being, through and through," said Rosenberg. "But he was also pretty close to being a superman. Think of his handicaps: childhood gone under the Second War and its aftermath, young manhood gone in the Third War, poor, self-educated, uprooted. And still he was balanced and sane, gentle except when violence was called for—then he was a hellcat, I tell you. Men and women loved him; he had that kind of personality. He'd picked up a dozen languages, and he read their literatures with more appreciation and understanding than most professors. He knew music and composed some good songs of his own—rowdy but good. They're still being sung out on Mars. He was an artist, did some fine murals for several buildings, painted the Martian landscape like no camera has ever shown it, though he was good with a camera too. I've already told you about his inventiveness, and he had clever hands that a machine liked. His physique stood up to anything—he was almost sixty when he died and could still match any boy of twenty. He—why go on? He was everything, and good at everything."

"I know," she answered. "Martin was the same way." Her brief smile was wistful. "Believe me, I had the devil's own time hooking him. Real competition there." After a moment she added thoughtfully: "There must be a few such supermen walking around in every generation. It's just a matter of a happy genetic accident, a preponderance of favorable characteristics appearing in the same zygote, a highly intelligent mesomorph. Some of them go down in history. Think of Michelangelo, Vespucci, Raleigh—men who worked at everything: science, politics, war, engineering, exploration, art, literature. Others weren't interested in prominence, or maybe they had bad luck. Like your friend."

"I don't know what the connection is with these Un-men," said Rosenberg. "Stef never said a word to me—but of course, he'd've been sworn to secrecy, or it might even have been done without his knowledge. Only what was done? Matter duplication? I don't think so. If the U.N. had matter duplication, it wouldn't be in the fix it is now. What was done—and *why?*"

Jeanne didn't answer. She was looking away now, across the ravine to the high clear beauty of mountains beyond. It was blurred in her eyes. Suddenly she got up and walked away.

XIII

There was a night of stars and streaming wind about the jet. The Moon was low, throwing a bridge of broken light across the heaving Atlantic immensity. Once, far off, Naysmith saw a single meteoric streak burning upward, a rocket bound for space. Otherwise he sat in darkness and alone.

He had been locked into a tiny compartment in the rear of the jet. Wade and his entourage, together with a pilot and a couple of guards, sat forward; the jet was comfortably furnished, and they were probably catching up on their sleep. Naysmith didn't want a nap, though the weakness of hunger and his injuries was on him. He sat staring out of the port, listening to the mighty rush of wind and trying to estimate where they were.

The middle Atlantic, he guessed, perhaps fifteen degrees north latitude. If Christian's prognosis of Besser's reactions was correct, they were bound for the secret world headquarters of the gang, but Wade and the others hadn't told him anything. They were over the high seas now, the great unrestful wilderness which ran across three-fourths of the planet's turning surface, the last home on Earth of mystery and solitude. Anything could be done out here, and when fish had eaten the bodies who would ever be the wiser?

Naysmith's gaze traveled to the Moon, riding cold above the sea. Up there was the dominion over Earth. Between the space-station observatories and the rocket bases of the Lunar Guard, there should be nothing which the forces of sanity could not smash. The Moon had not rained death since the Third War, but the very threat of that monstrous fist poised in the sky had done much to quell a crazed planet. If the Service could tell the Guard where to shoot —

Only it couldn't. It never could, because this rebellion was not the armed uprising of a nation with cities and factories and mines. It was a virus within the body of all humankind. You wouldn't get anywhere bombing China, except to turn four hundred million innocent victims who had been your friends against you — because it was a small key group in the Chinese government which was conspiring against sanity.

You can blast a sickness from outside, with drugs and

antibiotics and radiation. But the darkness of the human mind can only be helped by a psychiatrist; the cure must come from within itself.

If the U.N. were not brought tumbling down, but slowly eaten away, mutilated and crippled and demoralized, what would there be to shoot at? Sooner or later, official orders would come disbanding its police and Lunar Guard. Or there were other ways to attack those Moon bases. If they didn't have the Secret Service to warn them, it would be no trick for an enemy to smuggle military equipment to the Moon surface itself and blow them apart from there.

And in the end—what? Complete and immediate collapse into the dog-eat-dog madness which had come so close once to ruining civilization? (*Man won't get another chance. We were luckier than we deserved the last time.*) Or a jerry-built world empire of oppression, the stamping out of that keen and critical science whose early dawn-light was just beginning to show man a new path, a thousand-year nightmare of humanity turned into an ant-hill? There was little choice between the two.

Naysmith sighed and shifted on the hard bare seat. They could have had the decency to give him some clothes and a cigaret. A sandwich at the very least. Only, of course, the idea was to break down his morale as far as possible.

He tried again, for the thousandth time, to evaluate the situation, but there were too many unknowns and in-tangibles. It would be stupid to insist that tonight was a crisis point in human history. It could be—then again, if this attempt of the Brotherhood ended in failure, if the Brothers themselves were hunted down, there might come some other chance, some compensating factor. *Might!* But passive reliance on luck was ruin.

And in any case, he thought bleakly, tonight would surely decide the fate of Robert Naysmith.

The jet slanted downward, slowing as it wailed out of

the upper air. Naysmith leaned against the wall, gripping the edge of the port with manacled hands, and peered below. Moonlight washed a great rippling mass of darkness, and in the center of it something which rose like a metal cliff.

A sea station!

I should have guessed it, thought Naysmith wildly. His brain felt hollow and strange. *The most logical place; accessible, mobile, under the very nose of the world but hidden all the same. I imagine the Service has considered this possibility—only how could it check all the sea stations in existence? It isn't even known how many there are.*

This one lay amidst acres of floating weed. Probably one of the specially developed sea plants with which it was hoped to help feed an overcrowded planet; or maybe this place passed itself off as an experiment station working to improve the growth. In either case, ranch or laboratory, Naysmith was sure that its announced activities were really carried out, and there was a completely working staff with all equipment and impeccable dossiers. The gang's headquarters would be underneath, in the submerged bowels of the station.

An organization like this had to parallel its enemy in most respects. Complex and world-wide—no. System-wide, if it really included Pilgrim fanatics who wanted to take over Mars. It would have to keep extensive records, have some kind of communications center. *This is it! By Heaven, this is their brain!*

The shiver of excitement faded into a hard subsurface tingle. A dead man had no way of relaying his knowledge to Fourre.

There was a landing platform at one end of the great floating structure. The pilot brought his jet down to a skillful rest, cut the motors, and let silence fall. Naysmith heard the deep endless voice of the sea, rolling and washing against the walls. He wondered how far it was to the next humanity. Far indeed. Perhaps they were beyond the edge of death.

The door opened and light filtered into the compartment. "All right, Naysmith," said the guard. "Come along."

Obediently, the Un-man went out between his captors to stand on the platform. It was floodlit, cutting off the view of the ocean surging twenty or thirty feet under its rails. The station superstructure, gymbal-mounted and gyro-stabilized above its great caissons, wouldn't roll much even in the heaviest weather. There were two other jets standing nearby. No sign of armament, though Naysmith was sure that missile tubes were here in abundance and that each mechanic carried a gun.

The wind was chill on his body as he was led toward the main cabin. Wade strode ahead of him, cloak flapping wildly in the flowing, murmuring night. To one side, Naysmith saw Borrow's stiff white face and the sunken expressionlessness of Lewin. Perhaps those two would be allowed to work him over.

They entered a short hallway. At the farther end, Wade pressed his hand to a scanner. A panel slid back in front of an elevator cage. "In," grunted one of the S-men.

Naysmith stood quietly, hemmed into a corner by the wary bodies of his guards. He saw that Borrow and Jennings were shivering with nervous tension. A little humorless smile twisted his mouth. Whatever else happened, the Brotherhood had certainly given the enemy a jolt.

The elevator sighed to a halt. Naysmith was led out, down a long corridor lined with doors. One of them stood ajar, and he saw walls covered with micro-file cabinets. Yes, this must be their archive. A besmocked man went the other way, carrying a computer tape. Unaided human brains were no longer enough even for those who would overthrow society. Too big, too big.

At the end of the hall, Naysmith was ushered into a

large room. It was almost as if he were back in Wade's torture chamber—the same bright lights, the same muffling walls, the same instruments of inquisition. His eyes swept its breadth until they rested on the three men who sat behind a rack of neuroanalyzers.

The Brothers could tell each other apart; there were enough subtle environmental differences for that. Naysmith recognized Lampi, who seemed undamaged except for a black eye; he must have been taken directly here on orders. There was also Carlos Martinez of Guatemala, whom he had met before, and a third man whom he didn't recognize but who was probably South American.

They smiled at him, and he smiled back. Four pairs of blue eyes looked out of the same lean muscular faces, four blond heads nodded, four brains flashed the same intangible message: *You too, my Brother? Now we must endure.*

Naysmith was strapped in beside Martinez. He listened to Wade, speaking to Lucientes who had been suspected of being the Argentine sector chief of the rebels: "Besser hasn't come yet?"

"No, he is on the way. He should be very soon."

Besser is the real head, then, the organizing brain—and he is on his way! The four Brothers held themselves rigid, four identical faces staring uncannily ahead, not daring to move or exchange a glance. *Besser is coming!*

Wade took a restless turn about the room. "It's a weird business," he said thinly. "I'm not sure I like the idea of having all four together—in this very place."

"What can they do?" shrugged Lucientes. "My men captured Villareal here in Buenos Aires yesterday. He had been an artist, supposedly, and dropped out of sight when word first came about a fugitive Un-man answering that description. But he made a childish attempt to get back to his apartment and was arrested without difficulty. Martinez was obtained in Panama City with equal ease. If they are that incompetent—"

"But they aren't! They're anything but!" Wade glared at the prisoners. "This was done on purpose, I tell you. Why?"

"I already said—" Naysmith and Villareal spoke almost simultaneously. They stopped, and the Argentine grinned and closed his mouth. "I told you," Naysmith finished. "We wanted to bargain. There was no other quick and expedient way of making the sort of contact we needed."

"Were four of you needed?" snapped Wade. "Four valuable men?"

"Perhaps not so valuable," said Lewin quietly. "Not if there are any number of them still at large."

"They are not supernatural!" protested Lucientes. "They are flesh and blood. They can feel pain, and cannot break handcuffs. I know! Nor are they telepaths or anything equally absurd. They are—" His voice faltered.

"Yes?" challenged Wade. "They are what?"

Naysmith drew into himself. There was a moment of utter stillness. Only the heavy breathing of the captors, the captors half terrified by an unknown, and all the more vicious and deadly because of that, had voice.

The real reason was simple, thought Naysmith—so simple that it defeated those tortuous minds. It had seemed reasonable, and Christian's logic had confirmed the high probability, that one man identical with the agent who had been killed would be unsettling enough, and that four of them, from four different countries, would imply something so enormous that the chief conspirator would want them all together in his own strongest and most secret place, that he himself would want to be there at the questioning.

Only what happened next?

"They aren't human!" Borrow's voice was shrill and

wavering. "They can't be. Not four or five or a thousand identical men. The U.N. has its own laboratories. Fourre could easily have had secret projects carried out."

"So?" Lewin's eyes blinked sardonically at the white face.

"So they're robots—androids, synthetic life—whatever you want to call it. Test-tube monsters!"

Lewin shook his head, grimly. "That's too big a stride forward," he said. "No human science will be able to do that for centuries to come. You don't appreciate the complexity of a living human being—and our best efforts haven't yet synthesized even one functioning cell. I admit these fellows have something—superhuman—about them. They've done incredible things. But they can't be robots. It isn't humanly possible."

"Humanly!" screamed Borrow: "Is man the only scientific race in the universe? How about creatures from the stars? Who's the real power behind the U.N.?"

"That will do," snapped Wade. "We'll find out pretty soon." His look fastened harsh on Naysmith. "Let's forget this stupid talk of bargaining. There can be no compromise until one or the other party is done for."

That's right. The same thought quivered in four living brains.

"I—" Wade stopped and swung toward the door. It opened for two men who entered.

One was Arnold Besser. He was a small man, fine-boned, dark-haired, still graceful at seventy years of age. There was a flame in him that burned past the drab plainness of his features, the eerie light of fanaticism deep within his narrow skull. He nodded curtly to the greetings and stepped briskly forward. His attendant came after, a big and powerful man in chauffeur's uniform, cat-quiet, his face rugged and expressionless.

Only—only—Naysmith's heart leap wildly within him. He looked away from the chauffeur-guard, up into the eyes of Arnold Besser.

"Now, then." The chief stood before his prisoners, hands on hips, staring impersonally at them but with a faint shiver running beneath his pale skin. "I want to know you people's real motive in giving yourselves up. I've studied your 'vised dossiers, such as they are, on the way here, so you needn't repeat the obvious. I want to know everything else."

" 'The quality of mercy is not strained,' " murmured Lampi. Naysmith's mind continued the lovely words. He needed their comfort, for here was death.

"The issues are too large and urgent for sparring," said Besser. There was a chill in his voice as he turned to Lewin. "We have four of them here, and presumably each of them knows what the others know. So we can try four different approaches. Suggestions?"

"Lobotomy on one," answered the physician promptly. "We can remove that explosive detonator at the same time, of course. But it will take a few days before he can be questioned, even under the best conditions, and perhaps there has been some precaution taken so that the subject will die. We can try physical methods immediately on two of them, in the presence of each other. We had better save a fourth—just in case."

"Very well." Besser's gaze went a white-jacketed man behind the prisoners. "You are the surgeon here. Take one away and get to work on his brain."

The doctor nodded and began to wheel Martinez' chair out of the room. Lewin started a chlorine generator. The chauffeur-guard leaned against a table, watching with flat blank eyes.

The end? Goodnight, then, world, sun and moon and wind in the heavens. Goodnight, Jeanne.

A siren hooted. It shrilled up and down a saw-edged scale, ringing in metal and glass and human bones. Besser whirled toward a communicator. Wade stood heavy and paralyzed. Jennings screamed.

The room shivered, and they heard the dull crumping

of an explosion. The door opened and a man stumbled in, shouting something. His words drowned in the rising whistle and bellow of rocket missiles.

Suddenly there was a magnum gun in the chauffeur's hand. It spewed a rain of slugs as he crouched, swinging it around the chamber. Naysmith saw Besser's head explode. Two of the guards had guns halfway out when the chauffeur cut them down.

The communicator chattered up on the wall, screaming something hysterical about an air attack. The chauffeur was already across to the door switch. He closed and locked the barrier, jumped over Wade's body, and grabbed for a surgical saw. It bit at the straps holding Naysmith, drawing a little blood. Lampi, Martinez, and Villareal were whooping aloud.

The chauffeur spoke in rapid Brazilo-Portuguese: "I'll get you free. Then take some weapons and be ready to fight. They may attack us in here, I don't know. But there will be paratroops landing as soon as our air strength has reduced their defenses. We should be able to hold out till then."

It had worked. The incredible, desperate, precarious plan had worked. Besser, in alarm and uncertainty, had gone personally to his secret headquarters. He had been piloted by his trusted gunman as usual. Only—Fourre's office would long have known about that pilot, studied him, prepared a surgically disguised duplicate from a Brazilian Un-man and held this agent in reserve. When Christian's message came, the chauffeur had been taken care of and the Un-man had replaced him—and had been able to slip a radio tracer into Besser's jet—a tracer which the Rio-based U.N. police had followed.

And now they had the base!

Naysmith flung himself out of the chair and snatched a gun off the floor. He exchanged a glance with his rescuer, a brief warm glance of kinship and comradeship and belongingness. Even under the disguise and the carefully learned mannerisms, there had been something intangible which he had known—or was it only the fact that the deliverer had moved with such swift and certain decision?

"Yes," said the Brazilian unnecessarily. "I too am a Brother."

XIV

There was one morning when Naysmith came out of his tent and walked down to the sea. This was in Northwest National Park, the new preserve which included a good stretch of Oregon's coast. He had come for rest and solitude, to do some thinking which seemed to lead nowhere, and had stayed longer than he intended. There was peace here, in the great rocky stretch of land, the sandy nooks between, the loneliness of ocean, and the forest and mountains behind. Not many people were in the park now, and he had pitched his tent remote from the camping grounds anyway.

It was over. The job was finished. With the records of Besser's headquarters for clues and proof, Fourre had been in a position to expose the whole conspiracy. Nobody had cared much about the technical illegality of his raid. Several governments fell—the Chinese had a spectacularly bloody end—and were replaced with men closer to sanity. Agents had been weeded out of every regime. In America, Hessling was in jail and there was talk of disbanding Security altogether. The U.N. had a renewed prestige and power, a firmer allegiance from the peoples of the world. Happy ending?

No. Because it was a job which never really ended. The enemy was old and strong and crafty, it took a million forms and it could never quite be slain. For it was man himself — the madness and sorrow of the human soul, the revolt of a primitive against the unnatural state called civilization and freedom. Somebody would try again. His methods would be different, he might not have the same avowed goal, but he would be the enemy and the watchers would have to break him. *And who shall watch the watchmen?*

Security was a meaningless dream. There was no stability except in death. Peace and happiness were not a reward to be earned, but a state to be maintained with toil and grief.

Naysmith's thinking at the moment concerned personal matters. But there didn't seem to be any answer except the one gray command: Endure.

He crossed the beach, slipping on rocks and swearing at the chill damp wind. His plunge into the water was an icy shock which only faded with violent swimming. But when he came out, he was tingling with wakefulness.

Romeo, he thought, toweling himself vigorously, *was an ass. Psychological troubles are no excuse for losing your appetite. In fact, they should heighten the old reliable pleasures. Mercutio was the real hero of that play.*

He picked his way toward the tent, thinking of bacon and eggs. As he mounted the steep, rocky bank, he paused, scowling. A small airboat had landed next to his own. *Damn! I don't feel like being polite to anybody.* But when he saw the figure which stood beside it, he broke into a run.

Jeanne Donner waited for him, gravely as a child. When he stood before her, she met his gaze steadily, mute, and it was he who looked away.

"How did you find me?" he whispered at last. He thought the fury of his heartbeat must soon break his ribs. "I dropped out of sight pretty thoroughly."

"It wasn't easy," she answered, smiling a little. "After the U.N. pilot took us back to the States, I pestered the life out of everyone concerned. Finally one of them forgot privacy laws and told me—I suppose on the theory that you would take care of the nuisance. I've been landing at every isolated spot in the park for the last two days. I knew you'd want to be alone."

"Rosenberg—?"

"He agreed to accept hypno-conditioning for a nice payment—since he was sure he'd never learn the secret anyway. Now he's forgotten that there ever was another Stefan Rostomily. I refused, of course."

"Well—" His voice trailed off. Finally he looked at her again and said harshly: "Yes, I've played a filthy trick on you. The whole Service has, I guess. Only it's a secret which men have been killed for learning."

She smiled again, looking up at him with a lilting challenge in her eyes. "Go ahead," she invited.

His hands dropped. "No. You've got a right to know this. I should never have—oh, well, skip it. We aren't complete fanatics. An organization which drew the line nowhere in reaching its aims wouldn't be worth having around!"

"Thank you," she breathed.

"Nothing to thank me for. You've probably guessed the basis of the secret already, if you know who Rostomily was."

"And what he was. Yes, I think I know. But tell me."

"They needed a lot of agents for the Service—agents who could meet specifications. Somebody got acquainted with Rostomily while he was still on Earth. He himself wasn't trained, or interested in doing such work, but his heredity was wanted—the pattern of genes and chromosomes. Fourre had organized his secret research laboratories. That wasn't hard to do, in the Years of Madness. Exogenesis of a fertilized ovum was already an accomplished fact. It was only one step further to take a few complete cells from Rostomily and use them as—as a chromosome source.

"We Brothers, all of us, we're completely human. Except that our hereditary pattern is derived entirely from one person instead of from two and, therefore, duplicates its prototype exactly. There are thousands of us by now, scattered around the Solar System. I'm one of the oldest. There are younger ones coming up to carry on."

"Exogenesis—" She couldn't repress a slight shudder.

"It has a bad name, yes. But that was only because of the known experiments which were performed, with their prenatal probing. Naturally that would produce psychotics. *Our* artifical wombs are safer and more serene even than the natural kind."

She nodded then, the dark wings of her hair falling past the ivory planes of her cheeks. "I understand. I see how it must be—you can tell me the details later. And I see why. Fourre needed supermen. The world was too chaotic and violent—it still is—for anything less than a brotherhood of supermen."

"Oh—look now!"

"No, I mean it. You aren't the entire Service, or even a majority of it. But you're the crack agents, the swordhand." Suddenly she smiled, lighting up the whole universe, and gripped his arm. Her fingers were cool and slender against his flesh. "And how wonderful it is! Remember *King Henry the Fifth?*"

The words whispered from him:

"And Crispin Crispian shall ne'er go by,
From this day to the ending of the world,
But we in it shall be remembered,
We few, we happy few, we band of brothers—"

After a long moment, he added wryly: "But we can't look for fame. Not for a long time yet. The first requirement of a secret agent is secrecy, and if it were known that our kind exists half our usefulness would be gone."

"Oh, yes. I understand." She stood quiet for a while. The wind blew her dress and hair about her, fluttering them against the great clean expanse of sea and forest and sky.

"What are you going to do now?" she asked.

"I'm not sure. Naturally, we'll have to kill the story of a wanted murderer answering our description. That won't be hard. We'll announce his death resisting arrest, and after that—well, people forget. In a year or two the memory will be gone. But of course several of us, myself included, will need new identities, have to move to new homes. I've been thinking of New Zealand."

"And it will go on. You work will go on. Aren't you ever lonely?"

He nodded, then tried to grin. "But let's not go on a crying jag. Come on and have breakfast with me. I'm a helluvva good egg frier."

"No, wait." She drew him back and made him face her. "Tell me—I want the truth now. You said, the last time, that you loved me. Was that true?"

"Yes," he said steadily. "But it doesn't matter. I was unusually vulnerable. I'd always been the cat who walks by himself, more so even than most of my Brothers. I'll get over it."

"Maybe I don't want you to get over it," she said.

He stood without motion for a thunderous century. A sea gull went crying overhead.

"You are Martin," she told him. "You aren't the same, not quite, but you're still Martin with another past. And Jimmy needs a father, and I need you."

He couldn't find words, but they weren't called for anyway.

This was but a single battle in the everlasting struggle between growth and decay. Could enemies within and without be held in check long enough for the forces of progress to advance? Since the flaws in human society were the product of flaws in each of its members, fundamental improvement had to begin with the individual. Synthesis training devised by Dr. Michael Tighe of the Psychotechnic Institute seemed a promising means of producing fully-developed persons who could shape history.

But psychodynamics could enslave as well as liberate. Only five years after the Besser conspiracy was broken, a would-be Messiah named Bertrand Meade plotted to subvert the Institute's discoveries.

THE SENSITIVE MAN

I

The Mermaid Tavern had been elaborately decorated: great blocks of hewn coral for pillars and booths, stripers and swordfish on the walls, murals of Neptune and his maid ballet, quite an eye-catcher. But the broad quartz windows showed merely a shifting greenish-blue of seawater, and the only live fish visible were in an aquarium across the bar. Pacific Colony lacked the grotesque loveliness of the Florida and Cuba settlements. Here they were somehow a working city, even in their recreations.

The sensitive man paused for a moment in the foyer, sweeping the big circular room with a hurried glance. Less than half the tables were filled. This was an hour of interregnum, while the twelve-to-eighteen-hundred shift was still at work and the others had long finished their more expensive amusements. There would always be a few around, of course. Dalgetty typed them as he watched.

A party of engineers, probably arguing about the compression strength of the latest submarine tank, to judge from the bored expressions of the three or four rec girls who had joined them. A biochemist, who seemed to have forgotten his plankton and seaweed for the time being and to have focused his mind on the pretty young clerk with him. A couple of hardhanded caissoniers, settling down to some serious drinking.

A maintenance man, a computerman, a tank pilot, a diver, a sea rancher, a bevy of stenographers, a bunch of very obvious tourists, more chemists and metallurgists—the sensitive man dismissed them all. There were others he couldn't classify with any decent probability, but after a second's hesitation he decided to ignore them too. That left only the group with Thomas Bancroft.

They were sitting in one of the coral grottoes, a cave of darkness to ordinary vision. Dalgetty had to squint to see in, and the muted light of the tavern was a harsh glare when his pupils were so distended. But, yes—it was Bancroft, all right, and there was an empty booth adjoining his.

Dalgetty relaxed his eyes to normal perception. Even in the short moment of dilation the fluoros had given him a headache. He blocked it off from consciousness and started across the floor.

A hostess stopped him with a touch on the arm as he was about to enter the vacant cavern. She was young, an iridescent mantrap in her brief uniform. With all the money flowing into Pacific Colony, they could afford decorative help here.

"I'm sorry, sir," she said. "Those are kept for parties. Would you like a table?"

"I'm a party," he answered. "or can soon become one." He moved aside a trifle, so that none of the Bancroft group should happen to look out and see him. "If you could arrange some company for me . . ." He fumbled out a C-note, wondering just how such things could be done gracefully.

"Why, of course, sir." She took it with a smoothness he envied and handed him a stunning smile in return. "Just make yourself comfortable."

Dalgetty stepped into the grotto with a fast movement.

This wasn't going to be simple. The rough red walls closed in on top of him, forming a space big enough for twenty people or so. A few strategically placed fluoros gave an eerie undersea light, just enough to see by—but no one could look in. A heavy curtain could be drawn if one wanted to be absolutely secluded. Privacy—*uh*-huh!

He sat down at the driftwood table and leaned back against the coral. Closing his eyes, he made an effort of will. His nerves were already keyed up to such a tautness that it seemed they must break, and it took only seconds to twist his mind along the paths required.

The noise of the tavern rose from a tiny mumble to a clattering surf to a huge and saw-edged wave. Voices dinned in his head, shrill and deep, hard and soft, a senseless stream of talking jumbled together into words, words, words. Somebody dropped a glass, and it was like a bomb going off.

Dalgetty winced, straining his ear against the grotto side. Surely enough of their speech would come to him, even through all that rock! The noise level was high, but the human mind, if trained in concentration, is an efficient filter. The outside racket receded from Dalgetty's awareness, and slowly he gathered in the trickle of sound.

First man: "—no matter. What can they do?"

Second man: "Complain to the government. Do you want the FBI on our trail? I don't."

First man: "Take it easy. They haven't yet done so, and it's been a good week now since—"

Second man: "How do you know they haven't?"

Third man—heavy, authoritative voice. Yes, Dalgetty remembered it now from TV speeches—it was Bancroft himself: "*I* know. I've got enough connections to be sure of that."

Second man: "Okay, so they haven't reported it. But why not?"

Bancroft: "You know why. They don't want the government mixing into this any more than we do."

Woman: "Well, then, are they just going to sit and take it? No, they'll find some way to—"

"HELLO, THERE, MISTER!!!"

Dalgetty jumped and whirled around. His heart began to race until he felt his ribs tremble, and he cursed his own tension.

"WHY, WHAT'S THE MATTER, MISTER? YOU LOOK—"

Effort again, forcing the volume down, grasping the thunderous heart in fingers of command and dragging it toward rest. He focused his eyes on the girl who had entered. It was the rec girl, the one he had asked for because he had to sit in this booth.

Her voice was speaking on an endurable level now. Another pretty little bit of fluff. He smiled shakily. "Sit down, sweet. I'm sorry. My nerves are shot. What'll you have?"

"A daiquiri, please." She smiled and placed herself beside him. He dialed on the dispenser—the cocktail for her, a scotch and soda for himself.

"You're new here," she said. "Have you just been hired, or are you a visitor?" Again the smile. "My name's Glenna."

"Call me Joe," said Dalgetty. His first name was actually Simon. "No, I'll only be here a short while."

"Where you from?" she asked. "I'm clear from New Jersey myself."

"Proving that nobody is ever born in California." He grinned. The control was asserting itself, his racing emotions were checked, and he could think clearly again. "I'm—uh—just a floater. Don't have any real address right now."

The dispenser ejected the drinks on a tray and flashed the charge—$20. Not bad, considering everything. He gave the machine a fifty and it made change, a five-buck coin and a bill.

"Well," said Glenna, "here's to you."

"And you." He touched glasses, wondering how to say what he had to say. Damn it, he couldn't sit here just talking or necking, he'd come to listen but . . . A sardonic montage of all the detective shows he had ever seen winked through his mind. The amateur who rushes in and solves the case, *heigh-ho*. He had never appreciated all the detail involved till now.

There was hesitation in him. He decided that a straightforward approach was his best bet. Deliberately then he created a cool confidence. Subconsciously he feared this girl, alien as she was to his class. All right, force the reaction to the surface, recognize it, suppress it. Under the table his hands moved in the intricate symbolic pattern which aided such emotion-harnessing.

"Glenna," he said, "I'm afraid I'll be rather dull company. The fact is I'm doing some research in psychology, learning how to concentrate under different conditions. I wanted to try it in a place like this, you understand." He slipped out a 2-C bill and laid it before her. "If you'd just sit here quietly. It won't be for more than an hour, I guess."

"Huh!" Her brows lifted. Then, with a shrug and a wry smile, "Okay, you're paying for it." She took a cigarette from the flat case at her sash, lit it, and relaxed. Dalgetty leaned against the wall and closed his eyes again.

The girl watched him curiously. He was of medium height, stockily built, inconspicuously dressed in a blue short-sleeved tunic, gray slacks, and sandals. His square snub-nosed face was lightly freckled, with hazel eyes and a rather pleasant shy smile. The rusty hair was close-cropped. A young man, she guessed, about twenty-five, quite ordinary and uninteresting, except for the wrestler's muscles and, of course, his behavior.

Oh, well, it took all kinds.

Dalgetty had a moment of worry. Not because the yarn he had handed her was thin but because it brushed too close to the truth. He thrust the unsureness out of him. Chances were she hadn't understood any of it, wouldn't even mention it. At least not to the people he was hunting.

Or who were hunting him?

Concentration, and the voices slowly came again: "—maybe. But I think they'll be more stubborn than that."

Bancroft: "Yes. The issues are too large for a few lives to matter. Still, Michael Tighe is only human. He'll talk."

The woman: "He can be made to talk, you mean?" She had one of the coldest voices Dalgetty had ever heard.

Bancroft: "Yes. Though I hate to use extreme measures."

Man: "What other possibilities have we got? He won't say anything unless he's forced to. And meanwhile his people will be scouring the planet to find him. They're a shrewd bunch."

Bancroft, sardonically: "What can they do, please? It takes more than an amateur to locate a missing man. It calls for all the resources of a large police organization. And the last thing they want, as I've said before, is to bring the goverment in on this."

The woman: "I'm not so sure of that, Tom. After all, the Institute is a legal group. It's government sponsored, and its influence is something tremendous. Its graduates—"

Bancroft: "It educates a dozen different kinds of psychotechnicians, yes. It does research. It gives advice. It publishes findings and theories. But believe me, the Psychotechnic Institute is like an iceberg. Its real nature and purpose are hidden way under water. No, it isn't doing anything illegal that I know of. Its aims are so large that they transcend law altogether."

Man: "What aims?"

Bancroft: "I wish I knew. We've only got hints and guesses, you know. One of the reasons we've snatched

Tighe is to find out more. I suspect that their real work requires secrecy."

The woman, thoughtfully: "Y-y-yes. I can see how that might be. If the world at large were aware of being—manipulated—then manipulation might become impossible. But just where does Tighe's group want to lead us?"

Bancroft: "I don't know, I tell you. I'm not even sure that they do want to—take over. Something even bigger than that." A sight. "Let's face it, Tighe is a crusader too. In his own way he's a very sincere idealist. He just happens to have the wrong ideals. That's one reason why I'd hate to see him harmed."

Man: "But if it turns out that we've got to—"

Bancroft: "Why, then we've got to, that's all. But I won't enjoy it."

Man: "Okay, you're the leader, you say when. But I warn you not to wait too long. I tell you, the Institute is more than a collection of unworldly scientists. They've got *someone* out searching for Tighe, and if they should locate him, there could be real trouble."

Bancroft, mildly: "Well, these are troubled times, or will be shortly. We might as well get used to that."

The conversation drifted away into idle chatter. Dalgetty groaned to himself. Not once had they spoken of the place where their prisoner was kept.

All right, little man, what next? Thomas Bancroft was big game. His law firm was famous. He had been in Congress and the Cabinet. Even with the Labor Party in power he was a respected elder statesman. He had friends in government, business, unions, guilds and clubs and leagues from Maine to Hawaii. He had only to say the word, and Dalgetty's teeth would be kicked in some dark night. Or, if he proved squeamish, Dalgetty might find himself arrested on a charge like conspiracy and tied up in court for the next six months.

By listening in he had confirmed the suspicion of

Ulrich at the Institute that Thomas Bancroft was Tighe's kidnapper—but that was no help. If he went to the police with that story they would (a) laugh, long and loud—(b) lock him up for pyschiatric investigation—(c) worst of all, pass the story on to Bancroft, who would thereby know what the Institute's children could do and would take appropriate countermeasures.

II

Of course, this was just the beginning. The trail was long. But time was hideously short before they began turning Tighe's brain inside out. And there were wolves along the trail.

For a shivering instant, Simon Dalgetty realized what he had let himself in for.

It seemed like forever before the Bancroft crowd left. Dalgetty's eyes followed them out of the bar—four men and the woman. They were all quiet, mannerly, distinguished-looking, in rich dark slack suits. Even the hulking bodyguard was probably a college graduate, Third Class. You wouldn't take them for murderers and kidnappers and the servants of those who would bring back political gangsterism. But then, reflected Dalgetty, they probably didn't think of themselves in that light either.

The enemy—the old and protean enemy, who had been fought down as Fascist, Nazi, Shintoist, Communist, Atomist, Americanist, and God knew what else for a bloody century—had grown craftier with time. Now he could fool even himself.

Dalgetty's senses went back to normal. It was a sudden immense relief to be merely sitting in a dimly lit booth with a pretty girl, to be no more than human for a while. But his sense of mission was still dark within him.

"Sorry I was so long," he said. "Have another drink."

"I just had one." She smiled.

He noticed the $10-figure glowing on the dispenser and fed it two coins. Then, his nerves still vibrating, he dialed another whiskey for himself.

"You know those people in the next grotto?" asked Glenna. "I saw you watching them leave."

"Well, I know Mr. Bancroft by reputation," he said. "He lives here, doesn't he?"

"He's got a place over on Gull Station," she said, "but he's not here very much, mostly on the mainland, I guess."

Dalgetty nodded. He had come to Pacific Colony two days before, had been hanging around in the hope of getting close enough to Bancroft to pick up a clue. Now he had done so and his findings were worth little. He had merely confirmed what the Institute already considered highly probable without getting any new information.

He needed to think over his next move. He drained his drink. "I'd better jet off," he said.

"We can have dinner in here if you want," said Glenna.

"Thanks, I'm not hungry." That was true enough. The nervous tension incidental to the use of his powers raised the devil with appetite. Nor could he be too lavish with his funds. "Maybe later."

"Okay, Joe, I might be seeing you." She smiled. "You're a funny one. But kind of nice." Her lips brushed his, and then she got up and left. Dalgetty went out the door and punched for a topside elevator.

It took him past many levels. The tavern was under the station's caissons near the main anchor cable, looking out into deep water. Above it were storehouses, machine rooms, kitchens, all the paraphernalia of modern existence. He stepped out of a kiosk onto an upper deck, thirty feet above the surface. Nobody else was there, and he walked over to the railing and leaned on it, looking across the water and savoring loneliness.

Below him the tiers dropped away to the main deck, flowing lines and curves, broad sheets of clear plastic, animated signs, the grass and flowerbeds of a small park, people walking swiftly or idly. The huge gyro-stabilized bulk did not move noticeably to the long Pacific swell. Pelican Station was the colony's "downtown," its shops and theaters and restaurants, service and entertainment.

Around it the water was indigo blue in the evening light, streaked with arabesques of foam, and he could hear waves rumble against the sheer walls. Overhead the sky was tall with a few clouds in the west turning aureate. The hovering gulls seemed cast in gold. A haziness in the darkened east betokened the southern California coastline. He breathed deeply, letting nerves and muscles and viscera relax, shutting off his mind and turning for a while into an organism that merely lived and was glad to live.

Dalgetty's view in all directions was cut off by the other stations, the rising streamlined bulks which were Pacific Colony. A few airy flex-strung bridges had been completed to link them, but there was still an extensive boat traffic. To the south he could see a blackness on the water that was a sea ranch. His trained memory told him, in answer to a fleeting question, that according to the latest figures, eighteen-point-three percent of the world's food supply was now being derived from modified strains of seaweed. The percentage would increase rapidly, he knew.

Elsewhere were mineral-extracting plants, fishery bases, experimental and pure research stations. Below the floating city, digging into the continental shelf, was the underwater settlement—oil wells to supplement the industrial synthesizing process, mining, exploration in tanks to find new resources, a slow growth outward as men learned how to go deeper into cold and darkness and pressure. It was expensive, but an overcrowded world had little choice.

Venus was already visible, low and pure on the dusking horizon. Dalgetty breathed the wet pungent sea air into his lungs and thought with some pity of the men out there—and on the Moon, on Mars, between worlds. They were doing a huge and heartbreaking job; but he wondered if it were bigger and more meaningful than this work here in Earth's oceans.

Or a few pages of scribbled equations, tossed into a desk drawer at the Institute. Enough. Dalgetty brought his mind to heel like a harshly trained dog. He was also here to work.

The forces he must encounter seemed monstrous. He was one man, alone against he knew not what kind of organization. He had to rescue one other man before—well, before history was changed and spun off on the wrong course, the long downward path. He had his knowledge and abilities, but they wouldn't stop a bullet. Nor did they include education for this kind of warfare. War that was not war, politics that was not politics but a handful of scrawled equations and a bookful of slowly gathered data and a brainful of dreams.

Bancroft had Tighe—somewhere. The Institute could not ask the government for help, even if to a large degree the Institute was the government. It could, perhaps, send Dalgetty a few men, but it had no goon squads. And time was like a hound on his heels.

The sensitive man turned, suddenly aware of someone else. This was a middle-aged fellow, gaunt and gray-haired, with an intellectual cast of feature. He leaned on the rail and said quietly, "Nice evening, isn't it?"

"Yes," said Dalgetty. "Very nice."

"It gives me a feeling of real accomplishment, this place," said the stranger.

"How so?" asked Dalgetty, not unwilling to make

conversation.

The man looked out over the sea and spoke softly as if to himself. "I'm fifty years old. I was born during World War Three and grew up with the famines and the mass insanities that followed. I saw fighting myself in Asia. I worried about a senselessly expanding population pressing on senselessly diminished resources. I saw an America that seemed equally divided between decadence and madness.

"And yet I can stand now and watch a world where we've got a functioning United Nations, where population increase is leveling off and democratic government spreading to country after country, where we're conquering the seas and even going out to other planets. Things have changed since I was a boy, but on the whole it's been for the better."

"Ah," said Dalgetty, "a kindred spirit. Though I'm afraid it's not quite that simple."

The man arched his brows. "So you vote Conservative?"

"The Labor Party *is* conservative," said Dalgetty. "As proof of which it's in coalition with the Republicans and the Neofederalists as well as some splinter groups. No, I don't care if it stays in, or if the Conservatives prosper, or the Liberals take over. The question is—who shall control the group in power?"

"Its membership, I suppose," said the man.

"But just who is its membership? You know as well as I do that the great failing of the American people has always been their lack of interest in politics."

"What? Why, they vote, don't they? What was the last percentage?"

"Eight-eight-point-three-seven. Sure they vote—once the ticket has been presented to them. But how many of them have anything to do with nominating the candidates or writing the platforms? How many will actually take time out to *work* at it—or even write their Congressmen? 'Ward heeler' is still a term of contempt.

"All too often in our history the vote has been simply a matter of choosing between two well-oiled machines. A sufficiently clever and determined group can take over a party, keep the name and the slogans, and in a few years do a complete behind-the-scenes *volte-face.*" Dalgetty's words came fast; this was one facet of a task to which he had given his life.

"Two machines," said the stranger, "or four or five as we've got now, are at least better than one."

"Not if the same crowd controls all of them," Dalgetty said grimly.

"But—"

" 'If you can't lick 'em, join 'em.' Better yet, join all sides. Then you *can't* lose."

"I don't think that's happened yet," said the man.

"No, it hasn't," said Dalgetty, "not in the United States, though in some other countries—never mind. It's still in the process of happening, that's all. The lines today are drawn not by nations or parties, but by—philosophies, if you wish. Two views of man's destiny cutting across all national political, racial, and religious lines."

"And what are those two views?" asked the stranger quietly.

"You might call them libertarian and totalitarian, though the latter don't necessarily think of themselves as such. The peak of rampant individualism was reached in the nineteenth century, legally speaking. Though, in point of fact, social pressure and custom were more straitjacketing than most people today realize.

"In the twentieth century that social rigidity—in manners, morals, habits of thought—broke down. The emancipation of women, for instance, or the easy divorce or the laws about privacy. But at the same time legal control began tightening up again. Government took over more and more functions, taxes got steeper, the individual's life got more and more bound by regulations saying 'thou shalt' and 'thou shalt not.'

"Well, it looks as if war is going out as an institution. That takes off a lot of pressure. Such hampering restrictions as conscription to fight or work, or rationing, have been removed. What we're slowly attaining is a society where the individual has maximum freedom, both from law *and* custom. It's perhaps farthest advanced in America, Canada, and Brazil, but it's growing the world over.

"But there are elements which don't like the consequences of genuine libertarianism. And the new science of human behavior, mass and individual, is achieving rigorous formulation. It's becoming the most powerful tool man has ever had—for whoever controls the human mind will also control all that man can do. That science can be used by anyone, mind you. If you'll read between the lines, you'll see what a hidden struggle is shaping up for control of it as soon as it reaches maturity and empirical usability."

"Ah, yes," said the man. "The Psychotechnic Institute."

Dalgetty nodded, wondering why he had jumped into such a lecture. Well, the more people who had some idea of the truth the better—though it wouldn't do for them to know the whole truth either. Not yet.

"The Institute trains so many for governmental posts and does so much advisory work," said the man, "that sometimes it looks almost as if it were quietly taking over the whole show."

Dalgetty shivered a little in the sunset breeze and wished he'd brought his cloak. He thought wearily, *Here it is again. Here is the story they are spreading, not in the blatant accusations, not all at once, but slowly and subtly, a whisper here, a hint there, a slanted news story, a supposedly dispassionate article . . . Oh, yes, they know their applied semantics.*

"Too many people fear such an outcome," he declared. "It just isn't true. The Institute is a private research organization with a Federal grant. Its records are open to anyone."

"All the records?" The man's face was vague in the gathering twilight.

Dalgetty thought he could make out a skeptically lifted brow. He didn't reply directly but said, "There's a foggy notion in the public mind that a group equipped with a complete science of man — which the Institute hasn't got by a long shot — could 'take over' at once and, by manipulations of some unspecified but frightfully subtle sort, rule the world. The theory is that if you know just what buttons to push and so on, men will do precisely as you wish without knowing that they're being guided. The theory happens to be pure jetwash."

"Oh, I don't know," said the man. "In general terms it sounds pretty plausible."

Dalgetty shook his head. "Suppose I were an engineer," he said, "and suppose I saw an avalanche coming down on me. I might know exactly what to do to stop it — where to plant my dynamite, where to build my concrete wall, and so on. Only the knowledge wouldn't help me. I'd have neither the time nor the strength to use it.

"The situation is similar with regard to human dynamics, both mass and individual. It takes months or years to change a man's convictions, and when you have hundreds of millions of men . . ." He shrugged. "Social currents are too large for all but the slightest, most gradual control. In fact, perhaps the most valuable results obtained to date are not those which show what can be done but what cannot."

"You speak with the voice of authority," said the man.

"I'm a psychologist," said Dalgetty truthfully enough. He didn't add that he was also a subject, observer, and guinea pig in one. "And I'm afraid I talk too much. Go from bad to voice."

"Ouch," said the man. He leaned his back against the rail and his shadowy hand extended a pack. "Smoke?"

"No, thanks, I don't."

"You're a rarity." The brief lighter-flare etched the stranger's face against the dusk.

"I've found other ways of relaxing."

"Good for you. By the way, I'm a professor myself. English Lit at Colorado."

"Afraid I'm rather a roughneck in that respect," said Dalgetty. For a moment he had a sense of loss. His thought processes had become too far removed from the ordinary human for him to find much in fiction or poetry. But music, scultpure, painting—there was something else. He looked over the broad glimmering water, at the stations dark against the first stars, and savored the many symmetries and harmonies with a real pleasure. You needed senses like his before you could know what a lovely world this was.

"I'm on vacation now," said the man. Dalgetty did not reply in kind. After a moment— "You are too, I suppose?"

Dalgetty felt a slight shock. A personal question from a stranger—well, you didn't expect otherwise from someone like the girl Glenna, but a professor should be better conditioned to privacy customs.

"Yes," he said shortly. "Just visiting."

"By the way, my name is Tyler, Harmon Tyler."

"Joe Thomson." Dalgetty shook hands with him.

"We might continue our conversation if you're going to be around for a while," said Tyler. "You raised some interesting points."

Dalgetty considered. It would be worthwhile staying as long as Bancroft did, in the hope of learning some more. "I may be here a couple of days yet," he said.

"Good," said Tyler. He looked up at the sky. It was beginning to fill with stars. The deck was still empty. It ran around the dim upthrusting bulk of a weather-observation tower which was turned over to its automatics for the night, and there was no one else to be seen. A few fluoros cast wan puddles of luminence on the plastic flooring.

Glancing at his watch, Tyler said casually, "It's about nineteen-thirty hours now. If you don't mind waiting till twenty hundred, I can show you something interesting."

"What's that?"

"Ah, you'll be surprised." Tyler chuckled. "Not many people know about it. Now, getting back to that point you raised earlier . . ."

The half hour passed swiftly. Dalgetty did most of the talking.

"—and mass action. Look, to a rather crude first approximation, a state of semantic equilibrium on a worldwide scale, which of course has never existed, would be represented by an equation of the form—"

"Excuse me." Tyler consulted the shining dial again. "If you don't mind stopping for a few minutes I'll show you that odd sight I was talking about."

"Eh? Oh—oh, sure."

Tyler threw away his cigarette. It was a tiny meteor in the gloom. He took Dalgetty's arm. They walked slowly around the weather tower.

The men came from the opposite side and met them halfway. Dalgetty had hardly seen them before he felt the sting in his chest.

A needle gun!

The world roared about him. He took a step forward, trying to scream, but his throat locked. The deck lifted up and hit him, and his mind whirled toward darkness.

From somewhere, will rose within him, trained reflexes worked, he summoned all that was left of his draining strength and fought the anesthetic. His wrestling with it as a groping in fog. Again and again he spiraled into unconsciousness and rose strangling. Dimly, through nightmare, he was aware of being carried. Once someone stopped the group in a corridor and asked what was wrong. The answer seemed to come from immensely far away. "I dunno. He passed out—just like that. We're taking him to a doctor."

There was a century spent going down some elevator. The boathouse walls trembled liquidly around him. He was carried aboard a large vessel; it was not visible through the gray mist. Some dulled portion of himself thought that this was obviously a private boathouse, since no one was trying to stop—trying to stop—trying to stop . . .

III

He woke slowly, with a dry retch, and blinked his eyes open. Noise of air, he was flying, it must have been a triphibian they took him on to. He tried to force recovery, but his mind was still to paralyzed.

"Here. Drink this."

Dalgetty took the glass and gulped thirstily. It was coolness and steadiness spreading through him. The vibrato within him faded, and the headache dulled enough to be endurable. Slowly he looked around, and felt the first crawl of panic.

No! He suppressed the emotion with an almost physical thrust. Now was the time for calm and quick wit and—

A big man near him nodded and stuck his head out the door. "He's okay now, I guess," he called. "Want to talk to him?"

Dalgetty's eyes roved the compartment. It was a rear cabin in a large airboat, luxuriously furnished with reclining seats and an inlaid table. A broad window looked out on the stairs.

Caught! It was pure bitterness, an impotent rage at

himself. *Walked right into their arms!*

Tyler came into the room, followed by a pair of burly stone-faced men. He smiled. "Sorry," he murmured, "but you're playing out of your league, you know."

"Yeah." Dalgetty shook his head. Wryness twisted his mouth. "I don't league it much either."

Tyler grinned. It was a sympathetic expression. "You punsters are incurable," he said. "I'm glad you're taking it so well. We don't intend any harm to you."

Skepticism was dark in Dalgetty, but he managed to relax. "How'd you get on to me?" he asked.

"Oh, various ways. You were pretty clumsy, I'm afraid." Tyler sat down across the table. The guards remained standing. "We were sure the Institute would attempt a counterblow, and we've studied it and its personnel thoroughly. You were so recognized, Dalgetty—and you're known to be very close to Tighe. So you walked after us without even a face-mask."

"At any rate, you were noticed hanging around the colony. We checked back on your movements. One of the rec girls had some interesting things to tell of you. We decided you'd better be questioned. I sounded you out as much as a casual acquaintance could and then took you to the rendezvous." Tyler spread his hands. "That's all."

Dalgetty sighed, and his shoulders slumped under a sudden enormous burden of discouragement. Yes, they were right. He was out of his orbit. "Well," he said, "what now?"

"Now we have you *and* Tighe," said the other. He took out a cigarette. "I hope you're somewhat more willing to talk than he is."

"Suppose I'm not?"

"Understand this," Tyler frowned. "There are reasons for going slow with Tighe. He has hostage value, for one thing. But you're nobody. And while we aren't monsters, I for one have little sympathy to spare for your kind of fanatic."

"Now there," said Dalgetty with a lift of sardonicism, "is an interesting example of semantic evolution. This being, on the whole, an easygoing tolerant period, the word 'fanatic' has come to be simply an epithet — a fellow on the other side."

"That will do," snapped Tyler. "You won't be allowed to stall. We want a lot of questions answered." He ticked the points off on his fingers. "What are the Institute's ultimate aims? How is it going about attaining them? How far has it gotten? Precisely what has it learned, in a scientific way, that it hasn't published? How much does it know about us?" He smiled thinly. "You've always been so close to Tighe. He raised you, didn't he? You should know just as much as he."

Yes, thought Dalgetty, *Tighe raised me. He was all the father I ever had, really. I was an orphan, and he took me in, and he was good.*

Sharp in his mind rose the image of the old house. It had lain on broad wooded grounds in the fair hills of Maine, with a little river running down to a bay winged with sailboats. There had been neighbors — quiet-spoken folk with something more real about them than most of today's rootless world knew. And there had been many visitors, men and women with minds like flickering sword blades.

He had grown up among intellects aimed at the future. He and Tighe had traveled widely. They had often been in the huge pylon of the main Institute building. They had gone over to Tighe's native England once a year at least. But always the old house had been dear to them.

It stood on a ridge, long and low and weathered gray like a part of the earth. By day it had rested in a green sun-dazzle of trees or a glistening purity of snow. By night you heard the boards creaking and the lonesome sound of wind talking down the chimney. Yes, it had been good.

And there had been the wonder of it. He loved his training. The horizonless world within himself was a glorious thing to explore. And that had oriented him outward to the real world — he had felt wind and rain and sunlight, the pride of high buildings and the surge of a galloping horse, thresh of waves and laughter of women and smooth mysterious purr of great machines, with a fullness that made him pity those deaf and dumb and blind around him.

Oh yes, he loved those things. He was in love with the whole turning planet and the big skies overhead. It was a world of light and strength and swift winds, and it would be bitter to leave it. But Tighe was locked in darkness.

He said slowly, "All we ever were was a research and educational center, a sort of informal university specializing in the scientific study of man. We're not any kind of political organization. You'd be surprised how much we differ in our individual opinions."

"What of it?" shrugged Tyler. "This is something larger than politics. Your work, if fully developed, would change our whole society, perhaps the whole nature of man. We *know* you've learned more things that you've made public. Therefore you're reserving that information for uses of your own."

"And you want it for your purposes?"

"Yes," said Tyler. After a moment, "I despise melodrama, but if you don't cooperate, you're going to get the works. And we've got Tighe too, never forget that. One of you ought to break down if he watches the other being questioned."

We're going to the same place! We're going to Tighe!

The effort to hold face and voice steady was monstrous. "Just where are we bound?"

"An island. We should be there soon. I'll be going back again myself, but Mr. Bancroft is coming shortly. That should convince you just how important this is to us."

Dalgetty nodded. "Can I think it over for a while? It isn't an easy decision for me."

"Sure. I hope you decide right."

Tyler got up and left with his guards. The big man who had handed him the drink earlier sat where he had been all the time. Slowly the psychologist began to tighten himself. The faint drone of turbines and whistles of jets and sundered air began to enlarge.

"Where are we going?" he asked.

"CAN'T TELL YOU THAT. SHUDDUP, WILL YOU?"

"But surely . . ."

The guard didn't answer. But he was thinking. *Ree-vil-la-ghee-gay-doe—never could p'rnounce that damn Spig name . . . cripes, what a God-forsaken hole! . . . Mebbe I can work a trip over to Mexico . . . That little gal in Guada . . .*

Dalgetty concentrated. Revilla—he had it now. Islas de Revillagigedo, a small group some 350 or 400 miles off the Mexican coast, little visited, with very few inhabitants. His eidetic memory went to work, conjuring an image of a large-scale map he had once studied. Closing his eyes he laid off the exact distance, latitude and longitude, individual islands.

Wait, there was one farther west, belonging to the group. And—he riffled through all the facts he had ever learned pertaining to Bancroft. Wait now, Bertrand Meade, who seemed to be the kingpin of the whole movement—yes, Meade owned that tiny island.

So that's where we're going! He sank back, letting weariness overrun him. It would be awhile yet before they arrrived.

Dalgetty sighed and looked out at the stars. Why had men arranged such clumsy constellations when the total pattern of the sky was a big and lovely harmony? He knew his personal danger would be enormous once he was on the ground. Torture, mutilation, even death.

Dalgetty closed his eyes again. Almost at once he was asleep.

IV

They landed on a small field while it was still dark. Hustled out into a glare of lights, Dalgetty did not have much chance to study his surroundings. There were men standing on guard with magnum rifles, tough-looking professional goons in loose gray uniforms. Dalgetty followed obediently across the concrete, along a walk, and through a garden to the looming curved bulk of a house.

He paused just a second as the door opened for them and stood looking out into the darkness. The sea rolled and hissed there on the wide beach. He caught the clean salt smell of it and filled his lungs. It might be the last time he ever breathed such air.

"Get along with you." An arm jerked him into motion again.

Down a bare coldly lit hallway, down an escalator, into the guts of the island. Another door, a room beyond it, an ungentle shove. The door clashed to behind him.

Dalgetty looked around. The cell was small, bleakly furnished with bunk, toilet, and washstand, had a ventilator grille in one wall. Nothing else. He tried listening with maximum sensitivity, but he caught only remote confused murmurs.

Dad! he thought. *You're here somewhere too.*

He flopped on the bunk and spent a moment analyzing the aesthetics of the layout. It had a certain pleasing severity, the unconscious balance of complete functionalism. Soon Dalgetty went back to sleep.

A guard with a breakfast tray woke him. Dalgetty tried to read the man's thoughts, but there weren't any to speak of. He ate ravenously under a gun muzzle, gave the tray back, and returned to sleep. It was the same at lunchtime.

His time-sense told him that it was 1435 hours when he

was roused again. There were three men this time, husky specimens. "Come on," said one of them. "Never saw such a guy for pounding his ear."

Dalgetty stood up, running a hand through his hair. The red bristles were scratchy on his palm. It was a cover-up, a substitute symbol to bring his nervous system back under full control. The process felt as if he were being tumbled through a huge gulf.

"Just how many of your fellows are there here?" he asked.

"Enough. Now get going!"

He caught the whisper of thought—*fifty of us guards, is it? Yeah, fifty, I guess.*

Fifty! Dalgetty felt taut as he walked out between two of them. Fifty goons. And they were trained, he knew that. The Institute had learned that Bertrand Meade's private army was well drilled. Nothing obtrusive about it—officially they were only servants and bodyguards—but they knew how to shoot.

And he was alone in midocean with them. He was alone, and no one knew where he was, and anything could be done to him. He felt cold, walking down the corridor.

There was a room beyond with benches and a desk. One of the guards gestured to a chair at one end. "Sit," he grunted.

Dalgetty submitted. The straps went around his wrists and ankles, holding him to the arms and legs of the heavy chair. Another buckled about his waist. He looked down and saw that the chair was bolted to the floor. One of the guards crossed to the desk and started up a tape recorder.

A door opened in the far end of the room. Thomas Bancroft came in. He was a big man, fleshy but in well-scrubbed health, his clothes designed with quiet good taste. The head was white-maned, leonine, with handsome florid features and sharp blue eyes. He smiled ever so faintly and sat down behind the desk.

The woman was with him—Dalgetty looked harder at her. She was new to him. She was medium tall, a little on the compact side, her blonde hair cut too short, no makeup on her broad Slavic features. Young, in hard condition, moving with a firm masculine stride. With those tilted gray eyes, that delicately curved nose and a wide sullen mouth, she could have been a beauty had she wanted to be.

One of the modern type, thought Dalgetty. *A flesh-and-blood machine, trying to outmale men, frustrated and unhappy without knowing it, and all the more bitter for that.*

Briefly there was sorrow in him, an enormous pity for the millions of mankind. They did not know themselves, they fought themselves like wild beasts, tied up in knots, locked in nightmare. Man could be so much if he had the chance.

He glanced at Bancroft. "I know you," he said, "but I'm afraid the lady has the advantage of me."

"My secretary and general assistant, Miss Casimir." The politician's voice was sonorous, a beautifully controlled instrument. He leaned across the desk. The recorder by his elbow whirred in the flat soundproofed stillness.

"Mr. Dalgetty," he said, "I want you to understand that we aren't fiends. Some things are too important for ordinary rules, though. Wars have been fought over them in the past and may well be fought again. It will be easier for all concerned if you cooperate with us now. No one need ever know that you have done so."

"Suppose I answer your questions," said Dalgetty. "How do you know I'm telling the truth?"

"Neoscopolamine, of course. I don't think you've been immunized. It confuses the mind too much for us to interrogate you about these complex matters under its influence, but we will surely find out if you have been answering our present questions correctly."

"And what then? Do you just let me go?"

Bancroft shrugged. "Why shouldn't we? We may have to keep you here for a while, but soon you will have ceased to matter and can safely be released."

Dalgetty considered. Not even he could do much against truth drugs. And there were still more radical procedures, prefrontal lobotomy for instance. He shivered The leatherite straps felt damp against his thin clothing.

He looked at Bancroft. "What do you really want?" he asked. "Why are you working for Bertrand Meade?"

Bancroft's heavy mouth lifted in a smile. "I thought you were supposed to answer the questions," he said.

"Whether I do or not depends on whose questions they are," said Dalgetty. *Stall for time! Put it off, the moment of terror, put it off!* "Frankly, what I know of Meade doesn't make me friendly. But I could be wrong."

"Mr. Meade is a distinguished executive."

"Uh-huh. He's also the power behind a hell of a lot of political figures, including you. He's the real boss of the Actionist movement."

"What do you know of that?" asked the woman sharply.

"It's a complicated story," said Dalgetty, "but essentially Actionism is a — a *Weltanschauung*. We're still recovering from the World Wars and their aftermath. People everywhere are swinging away from the great vague capitalized Causes toward a cooler and clearer view of life.

"It's analogous to the eighteenth-century Enlightenment, which also followed a period of turmoil between conflicting fanatacisms. A belief in reason is growing up even in the popular mind, a spirit of moderation and tolerance. There's a wait-and-see attitude toward everything, including the sciences and particularly the new half-finished science of psychodynamics. The world wants to rest for a while.

"Well, such a state of mind has its own drawbacks. It

produces wonderful structures of thought, but they've something cold about them. There is so little real passion, so much caution—the arts, for instance, are becoming ever more stylized. Old symbols like religion and the sovereign state and a particular form of government, for which men once died, are openly jeered at. We can formulate the semantic condition at the Institute in a very neat equation.

"And you don't like it. Your kind of man needs something big. And mere concrete bigness isn't enough. You could give your lives to the sciences or to interplanetary colonization or to social correction, as many people are cheerfully doing—but those aren't for you. Down underneath, you miss the universal father-image.

"You want an almighty Church or an almighty State or an almighty *anything*, a huge misty symbol which demands everything you've got and gives in return only a feeling of belonging." Dalgetty's voice was harsh. "In short, you can't stand on your own psychic feet. You can't face the truth that man is a lonely creature and that his purpose must come from within himself."

Bancroft scowled. "I didn't come here to be lectured," he said.

"Have it your way," answered Dalgetty. "I thought you wanted to know what I knew of Actionism. That's it in unprecise verbal language. Essentially you want to be a Leader in a Cause. Your men, such as aren't merely hired, want to be Followers. Only there isn't a Cause around, these days, except the common-sense one of improving human life."

The woman, Casimir, leaned over the desk. She bore a curious intensity in her eyes. "You just pointed out the drawbacks yourself," she said. "This *is* a decadent period."

"No," said Dalgetty. "Unless you insist on loaded connotations. It's a necessary period of rest. Recoil time for a whole society—well, it all works out nicely in Tighe's formulation. The present state of affairs should continue for about seventy-five years, we feel at the Institute. In that time, reason can—we hope—be so firmly implanted in the basic structure of society that when the next great wave of passion comes, it won't turn men against each other.

"The present is, well, analytic. While we catch our breath we can begin to understand ourselves. When the next synthetic—or creative or crusading period, if you wish—comes, it will be saner than all which have gone before. And man can't afford to go insane again. Not in the same world as the lithium bomb."

Bancroft nodded. "And you in the Institute are trying to control this process," he said. "You're trying to stretch out the period of—damn it, decadence! Oh, I've studied the modern school system too, Dalgetty. I know how subtly the rising generation is being indoctrinated—through policies formulated by *your* men in the government."

"Indoctrinated? Trained, I would say. Trained in self-restraint and critical thinking." Dalgetty grinned with one side of his mouth. "Well, we aren't here to argue generalities. Specifically, Meade feels he has a mission. He is the natural leader of America—ultimately, through the U.N., in which we are still powerful, the world. He wants to restore what he calls 'ancestral virtues'—you see, I've listened to his speeches and yours, Bancroft.

"These virtues consist of obedience, physical *and* mental, to 'constituted authority'—of 'dynamism,' which operationally speaking means people ought to jump when he gives an order—of . . . Oh, why go on? It's the old story. Power hunger, the recreation of the Absolute State, this time on a planetary scale.

"With psychological appeals to some and with promises of reward to others, he's built up quite a following. But he's shrewd enough to know that he can't just stage a revolution. He has to make people want him. He has to reverse the social current until it swings back to authoritarianism—with him riding the crest.

"And that of course is where the Institute comes in. Yes, we have developed theories which make at least a beginning at explaining the facts of history. It was a matter not so much of gathering data as of inventing a rigorous self-correcting symbology, and our paramathematics seems to be just that. We haven't published all of our findings, because of the uses to which they could be put. If you know exactly how to go about it, you can shape world society into almost any image you want—in fifty years or less! You want that knowledge of ours for your purposes."

Dalgetty fell silent. There was a long quietness. His own breathing seemed unnaturally loud.

"All right." Bancroft nodded again, slowly. "You haven't told us anything we don't know."

"I'm well aware of that," said Dalgetty.

"Your phrasing was rather unfriendly," said Bancroft. "What you don't appreciate is the revolting stagnation and cynicism of this age."

"Now you're using the loaded words," said Dalgetty. "Facts just *are*. There's no use passing moral judgments on reality; the only thing you can do is try to change it."

"Yes," said Bancroft. "All right then, we're trying. Do you want to help us?"

"You could beat the hell out of me," said Dalgetty, "but it wouldn't teach you a science that it takes years to learn."

"No, but we'd know just what you have and where to find it. We have some good brains on our side. Given your data and equations, they can figure it out." The pale eyes grew wholly chill. "You don't seem to appreciate your situation. You're a prisoner, understand?"

Dalgetty braced his muscles. He didn't reply.

Bancroft sighed. "Bring him in," he said.

One of the guards went out. Dalgetty's heart stumbled.

Dad, he thought. It was anguish in him. Casimir walked over to stand in front of him. Her eyes searched his.

"Don't be a fool," she said. "It hurts worse than you know. Tell us."

He looked up at her. *I'm afraid,* he thought. *God knows I'm afraid.* His own sweat was acrid in his nostrils. "No," he said.

"I tell you they'll do everything!" She had a nice voice, low and soft, but it roughened now. Her face was colorless with strain. "Go on, man, don't condemn yourself to—mindlessness!"

There was something strange here. Dalgetty's senses began to reach out. She was leaning close, and he knew the signs of horror, even if she tried to hide them. *She's not so hard as she makes out—but then why is she with them?*

He threw a bluff. "I know who you are," he said. "Shall I tell your friends?"

"No, you don't!" She stepped back, rigid, and his whetted senses caught the fear-smell. In a moment there was control, and she said, "All right then, have it your way."

And, underneath, she thought, slowed by the gluiness of panic, *Does he know I'm FBI?*

FBI! He jerked against the straps. Ye Gods!

Calmness returned to him as she walked to her chief, but his mind whirred. Yes, why not? Institute men had little connection with the Federal detectives, who, since the abolition of a discredited Security, had resumed a broad function. They might easily have become dubious about Bertrand Meade on their own, have planted operatives with him. They had women among them too, and a woman was always less conspicuous than a man.

He felt a chill. The last thing he wanted was a Federal agent here.

The door opened again. A quartet of guards brought in Michael Tighe. The Briton halted, staring before him.

"*Simon!*" It was a harsh sound, full of pain.

"Have they hurt you, Dad?" asked Dalgetty very gently.

"No, no—not till now." The gray head shook. "But you . . ."

"Take it easy, Dad," said Dalgetty.

The guards hustled Tighe over to a front-row bench and sat him down. Old man and young locked eyes across the bare space.

Tighe spoke to him in the hidden way. *What are you going to do? I can't sit and let them—*

Dalgetty could not reply unheard, but he shook his head. "I'll be okay," he answered aloud.

Do you think you can make a break? I'll try to help you.

"No," said Dalgetty. "Whatever happens, you lie low. That's an order."

He blocked off sensitivity as Bancroft snapped, "Enough. One of you is going to yield. If Dr. Tighe won't, then we'll work on him and see if Mr. Dalgetty can hold out."

He waved his hand as he took out a cigar. Two of the goons stepped up to the chair. They had rubberite hoses in their hands.

The first blow thudded against Dalgetty's ribs. He didn't feel it—he had thrown up a nerve bloc—but it rattled his teeth together. And while he was insensitive he'd be unable to listen in on . . .

Another thud, and another. Dalgetty clenched his fists. What to do, what to do? He looked over to the desk. Bancroft was smoking and watching as dispassionately as if it were some mildly interesting experiment. Casimir had turned her back.

"Something funny here, chief." One of the goons straightened. "I don't think he's feeling nothing."

"Doped?" Bancroft frowned. "No, that's hardly possible." He rubbed his chin, regarding Dalgetty with wondering eyes. Casimir wheeled around to stare. Sweat filmed Michael Tighe's face, glistening in the chill white light.

"He can still be hurt," said the guard.

Bancroft winced. "I don't like outright mutilation," he said. "But still—I've warned you, Dalgetty."

"Get out Simon," whispered Tighe. *"Get out of here."*

Dalgetty's red head lifted. Decision cyrstallized within him. He would be no use to anyone with broken arms, a crushed foot, an eye knocked out, seared lungs—and Casimir was FBI, she might be able to do something at this end in spite of all.

He tested the straps. A quarter inch of leatherite—he could snap them, but would he break his bones doing it?

Only one way to find out, he thought bleakly.

"I'll get a blowtorch," said one of the guards in the rear of the room. His face was wholly impassive. Most of these goons must be moronic, thought Dalgetty. Most of the guards in the twentieth-century extermination camps had been. No inconvenient empathy with the human flesh they broke and flayed and burned.

He gathered himself. This time it was rage, a cloud of fury rising in his mind, a ragged red haze across his vision. That they would *dare!*

He snarled as the strength surged up in him. He didn't even feel the straps as they popped across. The same movement hurtled him across the room toward the door.

Someone yelled. A guard leaped in his path, a giant of a man. Dalgetty's fist sprang before him, there was a cracking sound, and the goon's head snapped back against his own spine. Dalgetty was already past him. The door was shut in his face. Wood crashed as he went through it.

A bullet wailed after him. He dodged down the corridor, up the nearest steps, the walls blurred with his own speed. Another slug smacked into the paneling beside him. He rounded a corner, saw a window, and covered his eyes with an arm as he leaped.

The plastic was tough, but a hundred and seventy pounds hit it at fifteen feet per second. Dalgetty went through!

Sunlight flamed in his eyes as he hit the ground. Rolling over and bouncing to his feet, he set out across lawn and garden. As he ran his vision swept the landscape. In that state of fear and wrath, he could not command much thought, but his memory stored the data for reexamination.

V

The house was a rambling, two-story affair, all curves and planes between palm trees, the island sloping swiftly from its front to a beach and dock. On one side was the airfield, on another the guard barracks. To the rear, in the direction of Dalgetty's movement, the ground became rough and wild, stones and sand and saw grass and clumps of eucalyptus, climbing upward for a good two miles. On every side, he could see the infinite blue sparkle of ocean. Where could he hide?

He didn't notice the vicious cholla through which he raced, and the dry gulping of his lungs was something dreadfully remote. But when a bullet went past one ear, he heard that and drew more speed from some unknown depth. A glance behind revealed his pursuers boiling out of the house, men in gray with the hot sunlight blinking off their guns.

He ducked around a thicket, flopped, and belly-crawled over a rise of land. On the farther side, he straightened again and ran up the long slope. Another slug and another. They were almost a mile behind now, but their guns had a long reach. He bent low, zigzagging as he ran. The bullets kicked up spurts of sand around him.

A six-foot bluff loomed in his path, black volcanic rock shining like wet glass. He hit it at full speed. He almost *walked* up its face and in the instant when his momentum was gone caught a root and yanked himself to the top. Again he was out of their sight. He sprang around another hulk of stone and skidded to a halt. At his feet, a sheer cliff nearly a hundred feet to a white smother of surf.

Dalgetty gulped air, working his lungs like a bellows. A long jump down, he thought dizzily. If he didn't crack his skull open on a reef, he might well be clawed under by the sea. But there was no other place for him to go.

He made a swift estimate. He had run the upward two miles in a little over nine minutes, surely a record for such terrain. It would take the pursuit another ten or fifteen to reach him. But he couldn't double back without being seen, and this time they'd be close enough to fill him with lead.

Okay, son, he told himself. *You're going to duck now, in more than one sense.*

His light waterproof clothes, tattered by the island growth, would be no hindrance down there, but he took off his sandals and stuck them in his belt pouch. Praise all gods, the physical side of his training had included water sports. He moved along the cliff edge, looking for a place to dive. The wind whined at his feet.

There—down there. No visible rocks, though the surf boiled and smoked. He willed full energy back into himself, bent his knees, jackknifed into the sky.

The sea was a hammer blow against his body. He came up threshing and tumbling, gasped a mouthful of air that was half salt spray, was pulled under again. A rock scraped his ribs. He took long strokes, always upward to the blind white shimmer of light. He got to the crest of one wave and rode it in, surfing over a razorback reef.

Shallow water. Blinded by the steady rain of salt mist, deafened by the roar and crash of the sea, he groped toward shore. A narrow pebbly beach ran along the foot of the cliff. He moved along it, hunting a place to hide.

There—a seaworn cave, some ten feet inward, with a yard or so of fairly quiet water covering its bottom. He splashed inside and lay down, exhaustion clamping a hand on him.

It was noisy. The hollow resonance of sound filled the cave like the inside of a drum, but he didn't notice. He lay on the rocks and sand, his mind spiraling toward unconsciousness, and let his body make its own recovery.

Presently he regained awareness and looked about him. The cave was dim, with only a filtered greenish light to pick out black walls and slowly swirling water. Nobody could see much below the surface—good. He studied himself. Lacerated clothes, bruised flesh, and a long bleeding gash in one side. That was not good. A stain of blood on the water would give him away like a shout.

Grimacing, he pressed the edges of the wound together and willed that the bleeding stop. By the time a good enough clot was formed for him to relax his concentration, the guards were scrambling down to find him. He didn't have many minutes left. Now he had to do the opposite of energizing. He had to slow metabolism down, ease his heartbeat, lower his body temperature, dull his racing brain.

He began to move his hands, swaying back and forth, muttering the autohypnotic formulas. His incantations, Tighe had called them. But they were only stylized gestures leading to conditioned reflexes deep in the medulla. *Now I lay me down to sleep . . .*

Heavy, heavy—his eyelids were drooping, the wet walls receding into a great darkness, a hand cradling his head. The noise of surf dimmed, became a rustle, the skirts of the mother he had never known, come in to bid him good night. Coolness stole over him like veils dropping one by one inside his head. There was winter outside, and his bed was snug.

When Dalgetty heard the nearing rattle of boots—just barely through the ocean and his own drowsiness—he almost forgot what he had to do. No, yes, now he knew. Take several long, deep breaths, oxygenate the bloodstream, then fill the lungs once and slide down under the surface.

He lay there in darkness, hardly conscious of the voices, dimly perceived.

"A cave here—a place for him to hide."

"Nah, I don't see nothing."

Scrunch of feet on stone. "Ouch! Stubbed my damn toe. Nah, it's a closed cave. He ain't in here."

"Hm? Look at this, then. Bloodstains on this rock, right? He's *been* here, at least."

"Under water?" Rifle butts probed but could not sound the inlet.

The woman's voice. "If he is hiding down below, he'll have to come up for air."

"When? We gotta search this whole damn beach. Here, I'll just give the water a burst."

Casimir, sharply— "Don't be a fool. You won't even know if you hit him. Nobody can hold his breath more than three minutes."

"Yeah, that's right, Joe. How long we been in here?"

"One minute, I guess. Give him a couple more. Cripes! D'ja see how he ran? He ain't human!"

"He's killable, though. Me, I think he's just rolling around in the surf out there. This could be fish blood. A shark chased another fish in here and bit it."

Casimir: "Or, if his body drifted in, it's safely under. Got a cigarette?"

"Here y'are, miss. But say, I never thought to ask. How come you came with us?"

Casimir: "I'm as good a shot as you are, buster, and I want to be sure this job's done right."

Pause.

Casimir: "Almost five minutes. If he can come up now, he's a seal. Especially with his body oxygen-starved after all that running."

In the slowness of Dalgetty's brain, there was a chill wonder about the woman. He had read her thought, she was FBI, but she seemed strangely eager to hunt him down.

"Okay, let's get outta here."

Casimir: "You go on. I'll wait here just in case and come up to the house pretty soon. I'm tired of following you around."

"Okay. Le's go, Joe."

It was another four minutes or so before the pain and tension in his lungs became unendurable. Dalgetty knew he would be helpless as he rose, still in his semihibernating state, but his body was shrieking for air. Slowly he broke the surface.

The woman gasped. Then the automatic jumped into her hand and leveled between his eyes. "All right, friend. Come on out." Her voice was very low and shook a trifle, but there was grimness in it.

Dalgetty climbed onto the ledge beside her and sat with his legs dangling, hunched in the misery of returning strength. When full wakefulness was achieved, he looked at her and found she had moved to the farther end of the cave.

"Don't try to jump," she said. Her eyes caught the vague light in a wide glimmer, half frightened. "I don't know what to make of you."

Dalgetty drew a long breath and sat upright, bracing himself on the cold slippery stone. "I know who you are," he said.

"Who, then?" she challenged.

"You're an FBI agent planted on Bancroft."

Her gaze narrowed, her lips compressed. "What makes you think so?"

"Never mind—you are. That gives me a certain hold on you, whatever your purposes."

The blonde head nodded. "I wondered about that. That remark you made to me down in the cell sug-

gested—well, I couldn't take chances. Especially when
you showed you were something extraordinary by snap-
ping those straps and bursting the door open. I came
along with the search party in hope of finding you."

He had to admire the quick mind behind the wide
smooth brow. "You damn near did—for them," he accused her.

"I couldn't do anything suspicious," she answered.
"But I figured you hadn't leapt off the cliff in sheer
desperation. You must have had some hiding place in
mind, and under water seemed the most probable. In
view of what you'd already done, I was pretty sure you
could hold your breath abnormally long." Her smile was
a little shaky. "Though I didn't think it would be *in-
humanly* long."

"You've got brains," he said, "but how much heart?"

"What do you mean?"

"I mean, are you going to throw Dr. Tighe and me to
the wolves now? Or will you help us?"

"That depends," she answered slowly. "What are you
here for?"

His mouth twisted ruefully. "I'm not here on purpose
at all," Delgatty confessed. "I was just trying to get a clue
to Dr. Tighe's whereabouts. They outsmarted me and
brought me here. Now I *have* to rescue him." His eyes
held hers. "Kidnapping is a Federal offense. It's your duty
to help me."

"I may have higher duties," she countered. Leaning
forward, tautly, "But how do you expect to do this?"

"I'm damned if I know," Dalgetty looked moodily out
at the beach and the waves and the smoking spindrift.
"But that gun of yours would be a big help."

She stood for a moment, scowling with thought. "If I
don't come back soon, they'll be out hunting for me."

"We've got to find another hiding place," he agreed.
"Then they will assume I survived after all and grabbed
you. They'll be scouring the whole island for us. If we

haven't been located before dark, they'll be spread thin enough to give us a chance."

"It makes more sense for me to go back now," she said. "Then I can be on the inside to help you."

He shook his head. "Uh-huh. Quit making like a stereo-show detective. If you leave me your gun, claiming you lost it, that's sure to bring suspicion on you, the way they're excited right now. If you don't, I'll still be on the outside and unarmed—and what could you do, one woman alone in that nest? Now we're two with a shooting iron between us. I think that's a better bet."

After a while, she nodded. "Okay, you win. Assuming"—the half-lowered gun was raised again with a jerking motion—"that I will aid you. Who are you? *What* are you, Dalgetty?"

He shrugged. "Let's say I'm Dr. Tighe's assistant and have some unusual powers. You know the Institute well enough to realize this isn't just a feud between two gangster groups."

"I wonder . . ." Suddenly she clashed the automatic back in its holster. "All right. For the time being only, though!"

Relief was a wave rushing through him. "Thank you," he whispered. Then, "Where can we go?"

"I've been swimming around here in the quieter spots," she said. "I know a place. Wait here."

She stepped across the cave and peered out its mouth. Someone must have hailed her, for she waved back. She stood leaning against the rock, and Dalgetty saw how the seaspray gleamed in her hair. After a long five minutes, she turned to him again.

"All right," she said. "The last one just went up the path. Let's go." They walked along the beach. It trembled underfoot with the rage of the sea. There was a grinding under the snort and roar of surf, as if the world's teeth ate rock.

The beach curved inward, forming a small bay

sheltered by outlying skerries. A narrow path ran upward from it, but it was toward the sea that the woman gestured. "Out there," she said. "Follow me." She took off her shoes as he had done and checked her holster: the gun was waterproof, but it wouldn't do to have it fall out. She waded into the sea and struck out with a powerful crawl.

VI

They climbed up on one of the hogback rocks some ten yards from shore. This one rose a good dozen feet above the surface. It was cleft in the middle, forming a little hollow hidden from land and water alike. They crawled into this and sat down, breathing hard. The sea was loud at their backs, and the air felt cold on their wet skins.

Dalgetty leaned back against the smooth stone, looking at the woman, who was unemotionally counting how many clips she had in her pouch. The thin drenched tunic and slacks showed a very nice figure. "What's your name?" he asked.

"Casimir," she answered, without looking up.

"First name, I mean. Mine is Simon."

"Elena, if you must know. Four packs, a hundred rounds plus ten in the chamber now. If we have to shoot them all, we'd better be good. These aren't magnums, so you have to hit a man just right to put him out of action."

"Well," shrugged Dalgetty, "we'll just have to lumber along as best we can. I oak we don't make ashes of ourselves."

"Oh, *no!*" He couldn't tell whether it was appreciation or dismay. "At a time like this, too."

"It doesn't make me very popular," he agreed. "Everybody says to elm with me. But, as they say in France, ve are alo-o-one now, mon cherry, and tree's a crowd."

"Don't get ideas," she snapped.

"Oh, I'll get plenty of ideas, though I admit this isn't the place to carry them out." Dalgetty folded his arms behind his head and blinked up at the sky. "Man, could I use a nice tall mint julep right now."

Elena frowned. "If you're trying to convince me you're just a simple American boy, you might as well quit," she said thinly. "That sort of—of emotional control, in a situation like this, only makes you less human."

Dalgetty swore at himself. She was too damn quick, that was all. And her intelligence might be enough for her to learn . . .

Will I have to kill her?

He drove the thought from him. He could overcome his own conditioning about anything, including murder, if he wanted to, but he'd never want to. No, that was out. "How did you get here?" he asked. "How much does the FBI know?"

"Why should I tell you?"

"Well, it'd be nice to know if we can expect reinforcements."

"We can't." Her voice was bleak. "I might as well let you know. The Institute could find out anyway through its government connections—the damned octopus!" She looked into the sky. Dalgetty's gaze followed the curve of her high cheekbones. Unusual face—you didn't often see such an oddly pleasing arrangement. The slight departure from symmetry . . .

"We've wondered about Bertrand Meade for some time, as every thinking person has," she began tonelessly. "It's too bad there are so few thinking people in the country."

"Something the Institute is trying to correct," Dalgetty put in.

Elena ignored him. "It was finally decided to work agents into his various organizations. I've been with Thomas Bancroft for about two years now. My background was carefully faked, and I'm a useful assistant. But even so, it was only a short while back that I got sufficiently into his confidence to be given some inkling of what's going on. As far as I know, no other FBI operative has learned as much."

"And what have you found out?"

"Essentially the same things you were describing in the cell, plus more details on the actual work they're doing. Apparently the Institute was on to Meade's plans long before we were. It doesn't speak well for your purposes, whatever they are, that you haven't asked us for help before this."

"The decision to kidnap Dr. Tighe was taken only a couple of weeks ago. I haven't had a chance to communicate with my associates in the force. There's always someone around, watching. The setup's well arranged, so that even those not under suspicion don't have much chance to work unobserved, once they've gotten high enough to know anything important. Everybody spies on everybody else and submits periodic reports."

She gave him a harsh look. "So here I am. No official person knows my whereabouts, and if I should disappear, it would be called a deplorable accident. Nothing could be proved, and I doubt if the FBI would ever get another chance to do any effective spying."

"But you have proof enough for a raid," he ventured.

"No, we haven't. Up till the time I was told Dr. Tighe was going to be snatched, I didn't know for certain that anything illegal was going on. There's nothing in the law against like-minded people knowing each other and having a sort of club. Even if they hire tough characters and arm them, the law can't protest. The Act of Nineteen Ninety-nine effectively forbids private armies, but it would be hard to prove Meade has one."

"He doesn't really," said Dalgetty. "Those goons aren't much more than what they claim to be—bodyguards. This whole fight is primarily on a—a mental level."

"So I gather. And can a free country forbid debate or propaganda? Not to mention that Meade's people include some powerful men in the government itself. If I could get away from here alive, we'd be able to hang a kidnapping charge on Thomas Bancroft, with assorted charges of threat, mayhem, and conspiracy, but it wouldn't touch the main group." Her fists clenched. "It's like fighting shadows."

" 'You war against the sunset-glow. The judgement follows fast, my lord!' " quoted Dalgetty. *Heriot's Ford* was one of the few poems he liked. "Getting Bancroft out of the way would be something," he added. "The way to fight Meade is not to attack him physically but to change the conditions under which he must work."

"Change them to what?" Her eyes challenged his. He noticed that there were small gold flecks in the gray. "What does the Institute want?"

"A sane world," he replied.

"I've wondered," she said. "Maybe Bancroft is more nearly right than you. Maybe I should be on his side after all."

"I take it you favor libertarian government," he said. "In the past, it's always broken down sooner or later, and the main reason has been that there aren't enough people with the intelligence, alertness, and toughness to resist the inevitable encroachments of power on liberty.

"The Institute is trying to do two things—create such a citizenry and simultaneously to build up a society which itself produces men of that kind and reinforces those traits in them. It can be done, given time. Under ideal conditions, we estimate it would take about three hundred years for the whole world. Actually, it'll take longer."

"But just what kind of person is needed?" Elena asked coldly. "Who decides it? *You* do. You're just the same as all other reformers, including Meade—hell-bent to change the whole human race over to your particular ideal, whether they like it or not."

"Oh, they'll like it," he smiled. "That's part of the process."

"It's a worse tyranny than whips and barbed wire," she snapped.

"You've never experienced those, then."

"You *have* got that knowledge," she accused. "You have the data and the equations to be—sociological engineers."

"In theory," he said. "In practice, it isn't that easy. The social forces are so great that—well, we could be overwhelmed before accomplishing anything. And there are plenty of things we still don't know. It will take decades, perhaps centuries, to work out a complete dynamics of man. We're one step beyond the politican's rule of thumb, but not up to the point where we can use slide rules. We have to feel our way."

"Nevertheless," she said, "you've got the beginnings of a knowledge which reveals the true structure of society and the processes that make it. Given that knowledge, man could in time build his own world order the way he desired it, a stable culture that wouldn't know the horrors of oppression or collapse. But you've hidden away the very fact that such information exists. You're using it in secret."

"Because we have to," Dalgetty said. "If it were generally known that we're putting pressure on here and there and giving advice slanted just the way *we* desire, the whole thing would blow up in our faces. People don't like being shoved around."

"And still you're doing it!" One hand dropped to her gun. "You, a clique of maybe a hundred men . . ."

"More than that. You'd be surprised how many are with us."

"You've decided *you* are the almighty arbiters. Your superior wisdom is going to lead poor blind mankind up the road to heaven. I say it's down the road to hell! The last century saw the dictatorship of the elite and the dictatorship of the proletariat. This one seems to be birthing the dictatorship of the intellectuals. I don't like any of them!"

"Look, Elena." Dalgetty leaned on one elbow and faced her. "It isn't that simple. All right, we've got some special knowledge. When we first realized we were getting somewhere in our research, we had to decide whether to make our results public or merely give out selected, less important findings. Don't you see, no matter what we did, it would have been us, the few men, who decided? Even destroying all our information would have been a decision."

His voice grew more urgent. "So we made what I think was the right choice. History shows as conclusively as our own equations that freedom is not a 'natural' condition of man. It's a mestastable state at best, all too likely to collapse into tyranny. The tyranny can be imposed from outside by the better-organized armies of a conqueror, or it can come from within—through the will of the people themselves, surrendering their rights to the father-image, the almighty leader, the absolute state.

"What use does Bertrand Meade want to make of our findings if he can get them? To bring about the end of freedom by working on the people till they themselves desire it. And the damnable part of it is that Meade's goal is much more easily attainable than ours.

"So suppose we made our knowledge public. Suppose we educated anyone who desired it in our techniques. Can't you see what would happen? Can't you see the struggle that would be waged for control of the human mind? It could start as innocuously as a businessman planning a more effective advertising campaign. It would end in a welter of propaganda, counterpropaganda, social and economic manipulations, corruption, competition for the key offices—and so, ultimately, there would be violence.

"All the psychodynamic tensors ever written down won't stop a machine gun. Violence riding over a society thrown into chaos, enforced peace — and the peacemakers, perhaps with the best will in the world, using the Institute techniques to restore order. Then one step leads to another, power gets more and more centralized, and it isn't long before you have the total state back again. Only this total state could *never* be overthrown!"

Elena Casimir bit her lip. A stray breeze slid down the rock wall and rumpled her bright hair. After a long while she said, "Maybe you're right. But America today has, on the whole, a good government. You could let them know."

"Too risky. Sooner or later, someone, probably with very idealistic motives, would force the whole thing into the open. So we're keeping hidden even the fact that our most important equations exist — which is why we didn't ask for help when Meade's detectives finally learned what they did."

"How do you know your precious Institute won't become just such an oligarchy as you describe?"

"I don't," he replied, "but it's improbable. You see, the recruits who are eventually taught everything we know are pretty thoroughly indoctrinated with our own present-day beliefs. And we've learned enough individual psych to do some real indoctrinating! They'll pass it on to the next generation, and so on.

"Meanwhile, we hope the social structure and the mental climate is being modified in such a way that eventually it would be very difficult, if not impossible, for anyone to impose absolute control by any means. For, as I said before, even an ultimately developed psychodynamics can't do everything. Ordinary propaganda, for instance, is quite ineffective on people trained in critical thinking.

"When enough people the world over are sane, we can make the knowledge general. Meanwhile, we've got to keep it under wraps and quietly prevent anyone else from learning the same things independently. Most such prevention, by the way, consists merely of recruiting promising researchers into our own ranks."

"The world's too big," she said very softly. "You can't foresee all that'll happen. Too many things could go wrong."

"Maybe. It's a chance we've got to take." His own gaze was somber.

They sat for a while in stillness. Then she said, "It all sounds very pretty. But—what are you, Dalgetty?"

"Simon," he corrected.

"What are you?" she repeated. "You've done things I wouldn't have believed were possible. *Are you human?*"

"I'm told so." He smiled.

"Yes? I wonder! How is it possible that you—"

He wagged a finger. "Ah-ah! Right of privacy." And with swift seriousness, "You know too much already. I have to assume that you can keep it secret all your life."

"That remains to be seen," Elena said, not looking at him.

VII

Sundown burned across the waters, and the island rose like a mountain of night against the darkening sky. Dalgetty stretched cramped muscles and peered over the bay.

In the hours of waiting, there had not been much said between him and the woman. He had dropped a few questions, with the careful casualness of the skilled analyst, and gotten the expected reactions. He knew a little more about her—a child of the strangling dying cities and shadowy family life of the 1980's, forced to armor herself in harshness, finding in the long training for her work and now in the job itself an ideal to substitute for the tenderness she had never known.

He felt pity for her but there was little he could do to help just now. To her own queries he gave guarded replies. It occurred to him briefly that he was, in his way, as lonesome as she. *But of course I don't mind—or do I?*

Mostly they tried to plan their next move. For the time, at least, they were of one purpose. She described the layout of house and grounds and indicated the cell where Michael Tighe was ordinarily kept. But there was not much they could do to think out tactics. "If Bancroft gets alarmed enough," she said, "he'll have Dr. Tighe flown elsewhere."

He agreed. "That's why we'd better hit tonight, before he can get that worried." The thought was pain within him. *Dad, what are they doing to you now?*

"We have also the matter of food and drink." Her voice was husky with thirst and dull with the discouragement of hunger. "We can't stay out here like this much longer." She gave him a strange glance. "Don't you feel weak?"

"Not now," he said. He had blocked off the sensations.

"They—*Simon!*" She grabbed his arm. "A boat—hear?"

The murmur of jets drifted to him through the beating waves. "Yeah. Quick—underneath."

They scrambled over the hogback and slid down its farther side. The sea clawed at Dalgetty's feet, and foam exploded over his head. He hunched low, throwing one arm about her as she slipped. The airboat murmured overhead, hot gold in the sunset light. Dalgetty crouched, letting the breakers run coldly around him. The ledge where they clung was worn smooth, offered little to hold on to.

The boat circled, its jets thunderous at low speed. *They're worried about her now. They must be sure I'm still alive.*

White water roared above his head. He breathed a hasty gasp of air before the next comber hit him. Their bodies were wholly submerged, their faces shouldn't show in that haze of foam — but the jet was soaring down, and there would be machine guns on it.

Dalgetty's belly muscles stiffened, waiting for the tracers to burn through him.

Elena's body slipped from his grasp and went under. He hung there, not daring to follow. A stolen glance upward — yes, the jet was out of sight again, moving back toward the field. He dove off the ledge and struck into the waves. The girl's head rose over them as he neared. She twisted from him and made her own way back to the rock. But when they were in the hollow again, her teeth rattled with chill, and she pressed against him for warmth.

"Okay," he said shakily. "Okay, we're all right now. You are hereby entitled to join our Pacific wet-erans' club."

Her laugh was small under the boom of breakers and hiss of scud. "You're trying hard, aren't you?"

"I — *oh*, oh! Get *down!*"

Peering over the edge, Dalgetty saw the men descending the path. They were half a dozen, armed and wary. One had a WT radio unit on his back. In the shadow of the cliff, they were almost invisible as they began prowling the beach.

"Still hunting us!" Her voice was a groan.

"You didn't expect otherwise, did you? I'm just hoping they don't come out here. Does anybody else know of this spot?" He held his lips close to her ear.

"No, I don't believe so," she breathed. "I was the only one who cared to go swimming at this end of the island. But . . ."

Dalgetty waited, grimly. The sun was down at last, the twilight thickening. A few stars twinkled to life in the east. The goons finished their search and settled in a line along the beach.

"Oh-oh," muttered Dalgetty. "I get the idea. Bancroft's had the land beaten for me so thoroughly he's sure I must be somewhere out to sea. If I were he, I guess I'd swum far out to be picked up by a waterboat. So—he's guarding every possible approach against a landing party."

"What can we do?" whispered Elena. "Even if we can swim around their radius of sight we can't land just anywhere. Most of the island is vertical cliff. Or can you . . .?"

"No," he said. "Regardless of what you may think, I don't have vacuum cups on my feet. But how far does that gun of yours carry?"

She stole a glance over the edge. Night was sweeping in. The island was a wall of blackness, and the men at its foot were hidden. "You can't *see!*" she protested.

He squeezed her shoulder. "Oh, yes, I can, honey. But whether I'm a good enough shot to . . . We'll have to try it, that's all."

Her face was a white blur, and fear of the unknown put metal in her voice. "Part seal, part cat, part deer, part what else? I don't think you're human, Simon Dalgetty."

He didn't answer. The abnormal voluntary dilation of pupils hurt his eyes.

"What else has Dr. Tighe done?" Her tone was chill in the dark. "You can't study the human mind without studying the body too. What's he done? Are you the mutant they're always speculating about? Did Dr. Tighe create or find homo superior?"

"If I don't plug that radio com-set before they can use it," he said, "I'll be homo-genized."

"You can't laugh it off," she said through taut lips. "If you aren't of our species, I have to assume you're our enemy—till you prove otherwise!" Her fingers closed hard on his arm. "Is that what your little gang at the Institute is doing? Have they decided that mere humanity isn't good enough to be civilized? Are they preparing the way for your kind to take over?"

"Listen," he said wearily. "Right now we're two people, very mortal indeed, being hunted. So shut up!"

He took the pistol from her holster and slipped a full clip into its magazine. His vision was at high sensitivity now, her face showed white against the wet rock, with gray highlights along its strong cheekbones beneath the wide frightened eyes. Beyond the reefs, the sea was gunmetal under the stars, streaking with foam and shadow.

Ahead of him, as he rose to his feet, the line of guards stood out as paler darknesses against the vertiginous island face. They had mounted a heavy machine gun to point seaward and a self-powered spotlight, not turned on, rested nearby. Those two things could be dangerous, but first he had to find the radio set that could call the whole garrison down on them.

There! It was a small hump on the back of one man, near the middle of the beach. He was pacing restlessly up and down with a tommy gun in his hands. Dalgetty raised the pistol with slow hard-held concentration, wishing it were a rifle. *Remember your target practice now, arm loose, fingers extended, don't pull the trigger but squeeze—because you've got to be right the first time!*

He shot. The weapon was a military model, seminoiseless and with no betraying streak of light. The first bullet spun the goon on his heels and sent him lurching across sand and rock. Dalgetty worked the trigger, spraying around his victim, a storm of lead that *must* ruin the sender.

Chaos on the beach! If that spotlight went on with his eyes at their present sensitivity, he'd be blind for hours. He fired carefully, smashing lens and bulb. The machine gun opened up, stuttering wildly into the dark. If someone elsewhere on the island heard that noise—Dalgetty shot again, dropping the gunner over his weapon.

Bullets spanged around him, probing the darkness.

One down, two down, three down. A fourth was running along the upward path. Dalgetty fired and missed, fired and missed, fired and missed. He was getting out of range, carrying the alarm—*there!* He fell slowly, like a jointed doll, rolling down the trail. The two others were dashing for the shelter of a cave, offering no chance to nail them.

Dalgetty scrambled over the rock, splashed into the bay, and struck out for the shore. Shots raked the water. He wondered if they could hear his approach through the sea noise. Soon he'd be close enough for nominal night vision. He gave himself wholly to swimming.

His feet touched sand and he waded ashore, the water dragging at him. Crouching, he answered the shots coming from the cave. The shriek and yowl were everywhere around him now. It seemed impossible that they should not hear up above. He tensed his jaws and crawled toward the machine gun. A cold part of him noticed that the fire was in a random pattern. They couldn't see him, then.

The man lying by the gun was still alive but unconscious. That was enough. Dagletty crouched over the trigger. He had never handled a weapon like this, but it must be ready for action—only minutes ago it had tried to kill him. He sighted on the cave mouth and cut loose.

Recoil made the gun dance till he caught on to the trick of using it. He couldn't see anyone in the cave, but he could bounce lead off its walls. He shot for a full minute before stopping. Then he crawled away at an angle till he reached the cliff. Sliding along this, he approached the entrance and waited. No sound came from inside.

He risked a quick glance. Yes, it had done the job. He felt a little sick.

Elena was climbing out of the water when he returned. There was a strangeness in the look she gave him. "All taken care of?" she asked tonelessly.

He nodded, remembered she could hardly see the movement, said aloud, "Yes, I think so. Grab some of this hardware and let's get moving."

With his nerves already keyed for night vision it was not difficult to heighten other perceptions and catch her thinking . . . *not human. Why should he mind if he kills human beings when he isn't one himself?*

"But I do mind," he said gently. "I've never killed a man before and I don't like it."

She jerked away from him. It had been a mistake, he realized. "Come on," he said. "Here's your pistol. Better take a tommy gun too if you can handle it."

"Yes," she said. He had lowered his reception again, her voice fell quiet and hard. "Yes, I can use one."

On whom? he wondered. He picked up an automatic rifle from one of the sprawled figures. "Let's go," he said. Turning, he led the way up the path. His spine prickled with the thought of her at his back, keyed to a pitch of near-hysteria.

"We're out to rescue Michael Tighe, remember," he whispered over his shoulder. "I've had no military experience, so we'll probably make every mistake in the books. But we've got to get Dr. Tighe."

She didn't answer.

At the top of the path, Dalgetty went down on his stomach again and slithered up over the crest. Slowly he raised his head to peer in front of him. Nothing moved, nothing stirred. He stooped low as he walked forward.

The thickets fenced off vision a few yards ahead. Beyond them, at the end of the slope, he could glimpse lights. Bancroft's place must be one glare of radiance. How to get in there without being seen? He drew Elena close to him. For a moment she stiffened at his touch, then she yielded. "Any ideas?" he asked.

"No," she replied.

"I could play dead," he began tentatively. "You could claim to have been caught by me, to have gotten your gun back and killed me. They might lose suspicion then and carry me inside."

"You think you could fake *that?*" She pulled away from him again.

"Sure. Make a small cut and force it to bleed enough to look like a bullet wound—which doesn't usually bleed much, anyway. Slow down heartbeat and respiration till their ordinary senses couldn't detect them. Near-total muscular relaxation, including even those unromantic aspects of death which are so rarely mentioned. Oh, yes."

"Now I know you aren't human," she said. There was a shudder in her voice. "Are you a synthetic thing? Did they make you in a laboratory, Dalgetty?"

"I just want your opinion of the idea," he muttered with a flicker of anger.

It must have taken an effort for Elena to wrench clear of her fear of him. But then she shook her head. "Too risky. If I were one of those fellows, with all you've already done to make me wonder about you, the first thing I'd do on finding your supposed corpse would be to put a bullet through its brain—and maybe a stake through its heart. Or can you survive that too?"

"No," he admitted. "All right, it was just a thought. Let's work a bit closer to the house."

They went through brush and grass. It seemed to him that an army would make less noise. Once his straining ears caught a sound of boots, and he yanked Elena into the gloom under a eucalyptus. Two guards tramped by, circling the land on patrol. Their forms loomed huge and black against the stars.

Near the edge of the grounds, Dalgetty and Elena crouched in the long stiff grass and looked at the place they must enter. The man had had to lower his visual sensitivity as they approached the light. There were floodlights harsh on dock, airfield, barracks, and lawn, with parties of guards moving around each section. Light showed in only one window of the house, on the second story. Bancroft must be there, pacing and peering out into the night where his enemy stirred. Had he called by radio for reinforcements?

At least no airboat had arrived or left. Dalgetty knew he would have seen one in the sky. Dr. Tighe was here yet—if he lived.

Decision grew in the man. There was a wild chance. "Are you much of an actress, Elena?" he whispered.

"After two years as a spy I'd better be." Her face bore a hint of puzzlement under the tension as she looked at him. He could guess her thought— *For a superman, he asks some simpleminded questions. But then what is he? Or is he only dissembling?*

He explained his idea. She scowled. "I know it's crazy," he told her, "but have you anything better to offer?"

"No. If you can handle your part . . ."

"And you yours." He gave her a bleak look, but there was an appeal in it. Suddenly his half-glimpsed face looked strangely young and helpless. "I'll be putting my life in your hands. If you don't trust me, you can shoot. But you'll be killing a lot more than me."

"Tell me what you are," she said. "How can I know what the ends of the Institute are when they're using such means as you? Mutant or android or"—she caught her breath—"or actually a creature from outer space, the stars. Simon Dalgetty, what are you?"

"If I answered that," he said with desolation in his voice, "I'd probably be lying anyway. You've got to trust me this far."

She sighed. "All right." He didn't know if she was lying too.

He laid the rifle down and folded his hands on top of his head. She walked behind him, down the slope toward the light, her submachine gun at his back.

As he walked, he was building up a strength and speed no human ought to possess.

One of the sentries pacing through the garden came to

a halt. His rifle swung up, and the voice was a hysterical yammer: "Who goes?"

"It's me, Buck," cried Elena. "Don't get trigger-happy. I'm bringing in the prisoner."

"Huh?"

Dalgetty shuffled into the light and stood slumped, letting his jaw hang slack, as if he were near falling with weariness.

"You *got* him!" The goon sprang forward.

"Don't holler," said Elena. "I got this one, all right, but there are others. You keep on your beat. I got his weapons from him. He's harmless now. Is Mr. Bancroft in the house?"

"Yeah, yeah—sure." The heavy face peered at Dalgetty with more than a tinge of fear. "But lemme go along. Yuh know what he done last time."

"Stay on your post!" she snapped. "You've got your orders. I can handle him."

VIII

It might not have worked on most men, but these goons were not very bright. The guard nodded, gulped, and resumed his pacing. Dalgetty walked on up the path toward the house.

A man at the door lifted his rifle. "Halt, there! I'll have to call Mr. Bancroft first." The sentry went inside and thumbed an intercom switch.

Dalgetty, poised in a nervous tautness that could explode into physical strength, felt a clutch of fear. The whole thing was so fiendishly uncertain—anything could happen.

Bancroft's voice drifted out. "That you, Elena? Good work, girl! How'd you do it?" The warmth in his tone,

under the excitement, made Dalgetty wonder briefly just
what the relationship between those two had been.

"I'll tell you upstairs, Tom," she answered. "This is too
big for anyone else to hear. But keep the patrols going.
There are more like this creature around the island."

Dalgetty could imagine the primitive shudder in
Thomas Bancroft, instinct from ages when the night was
prowling terror about a tiny circle of fire. "All right. If
you're sure he won't—"

"I've got him well covered."

"I'll send over half a dozen guards just the same. Hold
it."

The men came running from barracks, where they
must have been waiting for a call to arms, and closed in.
It was a ring of tight faces and wary eyes and pointing
guns. They feared him, and the fear made them deadly.
Elena's countenance was wholly blank.

"Let's go," she said.

A man walked some feet ahead of the prisoner, casting
glances behind him all the time. One followed on either
side, the rest were at the rear. Elena walked among them,
her weapon never wavering from his back. They went
down the long handsome corridor and stood on
the purring escalator. Dalgetty's eyes roved with a
yearning in them—how much longer, he wondered,
would he be able to see anything at all?

The door to Bancroft's study was ajar, and Tighe's
voice drifted out. It was a quiet drawl, unshaken despite
the blow it must have been to hear of Dalgetty's recapture.
Apparently he was continuing a conversation begun
earlier:

". . . science goes back a long way, actually. Francis
Bacon speculated about a genuine science of man. Boole
did some work along those lines as well as inventing the
symbolic logic which was to be such a major tool in
solving the problem.

"In the last century, a number of lines of attack were

developed. There was already the psychology of Freud and his successors, of course, which gave the first real notion of human semantics. There were the biological, chemical, and physical approaches to man as a mechanism. Comparative historians like Spengler, Pareto, and Toynbee realized that history did not merely happen but had some kind of pattern.

"Cybernetics developed such concepts as homeostasis and feedback, concepts which were applicable to individual man and to society as a whole. Games theory, the principle of least effort, and Haeml's generalized epistemology pointed toward basic laws and the analytical approach.

"The new symbologies in logic and mathematics suggested formulations—for the problem was no longer one of gathering data so much as of finding a rigorous symbolism to handle them and indicate new data. A great deal of the Institute's work has lain simply in collecting and synthesizing all these earlier findings."

Dalgetty felt a rush of admiration. Trapped and helpless among enemies made ruthless by ambition and fear, Michael Tighe could still play with them. He must have been stalling for hours, staving off drugs and torture by revealing first one thing and then another—but subtly, so that his captors probably didn't realize he was only telling them what they could find in any library.

The party entered a large room, furnished with wealth and taste, lined with bookshelves. Dalgetty noticed an intricate Chinese chess set on the desk. So Bancroft or Meade played chess—that was something they had in common, at least, on this night of murder.

Tighe looked up from the armchair. A couple of guards stood behind him, their arms folded, but he ignored them. "Hello, son," he murmured. Pain flickered in his eyes. "Are you all right?"

Dalgetty nodded mutely. There was no way to signal

the Englishman, no way to let him hope.

Bancroft stepped over to the door and locked it. He gestured at the guards, who spread themselves around the walls, their guns aimed inward. He was shaking ever so faintly, and his eyes glittered as with fever. "Sit down," he said. *There!*"

Dalgetty took the indicated armchair. It was deep and soft. It would be hard to spring out of quickly. Elena took a seat opposite him, poised on its edge, the tommy gun in her lap. It was suddenly very still in the room.

Bancroft went over to the desk and fumbled with a humidor. He didn't look up. "So you caught him," he said.

"Yes," replied Elena. "After he caught me first."

"How did you—turn the tables?" Bancroft took out a cigar and bit the end off savagely. "What happened?"

"I was in a cave, resting," she said tonelessly. "He rose out of the water and grabbed me. He'd been hiding underneath longer than anybody would have thought possible. He forced me out to a rock in the bay there—you know it? We hid till sundown, when he opened up on your men on that beach. He killed them all.

"I'd been tied, but I'd managed to rub the strips loose. It was just a piece off his shirt he tied me with. While he was shooting I grabbed a stone and clipped him behind the ear. I dragged him to shore while he was still out, took one of the guns lying there, and marched him here."

"Good work." Bancroft inhaled raggedly. "I'll see that you get a proper bonus for this, Elena. But what else? You said . . ."

"Yes." Her gaze was steady on him. "We talked, out there in the bay. He wanted to convince me I should help him. Tom—he isn't human."

"Eh?" Bancroft's heavy form jerked. With an effort he steadied himself. "What do you mean?"

"That muscular strength and speed and telepathy. He can see in the dark and hold his breath longer than any man. No, he isn't human."

Bancroft looked at Dalgetty's motionless form. The prisoner's eyes clashed with his, and it was he who looked away again. "A telepath, did you say?"

"Yes," she answered. "Do you want to prove it, Dalgetty?"

There was stillness in the room. After a moment, Dalgetty spoke. "You were thinking, Bancroft, 'All right, damn you, can you read my mind? Go ahead and try it, and you'll know what I'm thinking about you.' The rest was obscenities."

"A guess," said Bancroft. Sweat trickled down his cheeks. "Just a good guess. Try again."

Another pause, then, "Ten, nine, seven, A, B, M, Z, Z . . .' Shall I keep on?" Dalgetty asked quietly.

"No," muttered Bancroft. "No, that's enough. What are you?"

"He told me," put in Elena. "You're going to have trouble believing it. I'm not sure if I believe it myself. But he's from another star."

Bancroft opened his lips and shut them again. The massive head shook in denial.

"He is—from Tau Ceti," said Elena. "They're way beyond us. It's the thing people have been speculating about for the last hundred years."

"Longer, my girl," said Tighe. There was no emotion in his face or voice save a dry humor, but Dalgetty knew what a flame must suddenly be leaping up inside him. "Read Voltaire's *Micromégas*."

"I've read such fiction," said Bancroft harshly. "Who hasn't? All right, why are they here, what do they want?"

"You could say," spoke Dalgetty, "that we favor the Institute."

"But you've been raised from childhood . . ."

"Oh yes. My people have been on Earth a long time. Many of them are born here. Our first spaceship arrived in nineteen sixty-five." He leaned forward in his chair. "I

expected Casimir to be reasonable and help me rescue
Dr. Tighe. Since she hasn't done so, I must appeal to your
own common sense. We have crews on Earth. We know
where all our people are at any given time. If necessary, I
can die to preserve the secret of our presence, but in that
case you will die too, Bancroft. The island will be
bombed."

"I . . ." The chief looked out the window into the enor-
mity of night. "You can't expect me to—to accept this as
if . . ."

"I've some things to tell you which may change your
mind," said Dalgetty. "They will certainly prove my
story. Send your men out, though. This is only for your
ears."

"And have you jump me!" snapped Bancroft.

"Casimir can stay," said Dalgetty, "and anyone else you
are absolutely certain can keep a secret and control his
own greed."

Bancroft paced once around the room. His eyes flickered back and forth over the watching men. Frightened
faces, bewildered faces, ambitious faces—it was a hard
decision, and Dalgetty knew grimly that his life rested on
his and Elena's estimate of Thomas Bancroft's character.

"All right! Dumason, Zimmerman, O'Brien, stay in
here. If that bird moves, shoot him. The rest of you wait
just outside." They filed out. The door closed behind
them. The three guards left posted themselves with
smooth efficiency, one at the window and one at either
adjoining wall. There was a long quiet.

Elena had to improvise the scheme and think it at Dalgetty. He nodded. Bancroft planted himself before the
chair, legs spread wide as if braced for a blow, fists on
hips.

"All right," he said. "What do you want to tell me?"

"You've caught me," said Dalgetty, "so I'm prepared to
bargain for my life and Dr. Tighe's freedom. Let me
show you—" He began to rise, gripping both arms of his

chair.

"Stay where you are!" snapped Bancroft, and three guns swiveled around to point at the prisoner. Elena backed away until she stood beside the one near the desk.

"As you will." Dalgetty leaned back again, casually shoving his chair a couple of feet. He was now facing the window and, as far as he could tell, sitting exactly on a line between the man there and the man at the farther wall. "The Union of Tau Ceti is interested in seeing that the right kind of civilizations develop on other planets. You could be of value to us, Thomas Bancroft, if you can be persuaded to our side, and the rewards are considerable." His glance went for a moment to the girl, and she nodded imperceptibly. "For example . . ."

The power rushed up in him. Elena clubbed her gun butt and struck the man next to her behind the ear. In the fractional second before the others could understand and react, Dalgetty was moving.

The impetus which launched him from the chair sent that heavy padded piece of furniture sliding across the floor to hit the man behind him with a muffled thud. His left fist took Bancroft on the jaw as he went by. The guard at the window had no time to swing his gun back from Elena and squeeze the trigger before Dalgetty's hand was on his throat. His neck snapped.

Elena stood over her victim even as he toppled and aimed at the man across the room. The armchair had knocked his rifle aside. "Drop that or I shoot," she said.

Dalgetty snatched up a gun for himself, leveling it at the door. He more than half expected those outside to come rushing in, expected hell would explode. But the thick oak panels must have choked off sound.

Slowly, the man behind the chair let his rifle fall to the floor. His mouth was stretched wide with supernatural fear.

"My God!" Tighe's long form was erect, shaking, his calm broken into horror. "Simon, the risk . . ."

"We didn't have anything to lose, did we?" Dalgetty's voice was thick, but the abnormal energy was receding from him. He felt a surge of weariness and knew that soon the payment must be made for the way he had abused his body. He looked down at the corpse before him. "I didn't mean to do that," he whispered.

Tighe collected himself with an effort of disciplined will and stepped over to Bancroft. "He's alive, at least," he said. "Oh, my God, Simon! You could have been killed so easily."

"I may yet. We aren't out of the woods by any means. Find something to tie those two others up with, will you, Dad?"

The Englishman nodded. Elena's slugged guard was stirring and groaning. Tighe bound and gagged him with strips torn from his tunic. Under the submachine gun, the other submitted meekly enough. Dalgetty rolled them behind a sofa with the one he had slain.

Bancroft was wakening too. Dalgetty located a flask of bourbon and gave it to him. Clearing eyes looked up with the same terror. "Now what?" mumbled Bancroft. "You can't get away—"

"We can damn well try. If it had come to fighting with the rest of your gang, we'd have used you as a hostage, but now there's a neater way. On your feet! Here, straighten your tunic, comb your hair. Okay, you'll do just as you're told, because if anything goes wrong, we'll have nothing at all to lose by shooting you." Dalgetty rapped out his orders.

Bancroft looked at Elena, and there was more than physical hurt in his eyes. "Why did you do it?"

"FBI," she said.

He shook his head, still stunned, and shuffled over to the desk visiphone and called the hangar. "I've got to get to the mainland in a hurry. Have the speedster ready in ten minutes. No, just the regular pilot, nobody else. I'll have Dalgetty with me, but it's okay. He's on our side now."

They went out the door. Elena cradled her tommy gun under one arm. "You can go back to the barracks, boys," said Bancroft wearily to the men outside. "It's all been settled."

A quarter hour later, Bancroft's private jet was in the air. Five minutes after that, he and the pilot were bound and locked in a rear compartment. Michael Tighe took the controls. "This boat has legs," he said. "Nothing can catch us between here and California."

"All right." Dalgetty's tones were flat with exhaustion. "I'm going back to rest, Dad." Briefly his hand rested on the older man's shoulder. "It's good to have you back," he said.

"Thank you, son," said Michael Tighe. "I can't tell you more. I haven't the words."

IX

Dalgetty found a reclining seat and eased himself into it. One by one, he began releasing the controls over himself—sensitivities, nerve blocs, glandular stimulation. Fatigue and pain mounted within him. He looked out at the stars and listened to the dark whistle of air with merely human senses.

Elena Casimir came to sit beside him, and he realized that his job wasn't done. He studied the long lines of her face. She could be a hard foe but just as stubborn a friend.

"What do you have in mind for Bancroft?" he asked.

"Kidnapping charges for him and the whole gang," she said. "He won't wriggle out of it, I can guarantee you." Her eyes rested on him, unsure, a little frightened. "Federal prison psychiatrists have Institute training," she murmured. "You'll see that his personality is reshaped *your* way, won't you?"

"As far as possible," Simon said. "Though it doesn't matter much. Bancroft is finished as a factor to be reckoned with. There's still Bertrand Meade himself, of course. Even if Bancroft made a full confession, I doubt that we could touch him. But the Institute has now learned to take precautions against extralegal methods—and within the framework of the law, we can give him cards and spades and still defeat him."

"With some help from my department," Elena said. There was a touch of steel in her voice. "But the whole story of this rescue will have to be played down. It wouldn't do to have too many ideas floating around in the public mind, would it?"

"That's right," he admitted. His head felt heavy, he wanted to rest it on her shoulder and sleep for a century. "It's up to you, really. If you submit the right kind of report to your superiors, it can all be worked out. Everything else will just be detail. But otherwise, you'll ruin everything."

"I don't know." She looked at him for a long while. "I don't know if I should or not. You may be correct about the Institute and the justice of its aims and methods. But how can I be sure, when I don't know what's behind it? How do I know there wasn't more truth than fiction in that Tau Ceti story, that you aren't really the agent of some nonhuman power quietly taking over all our race?"

At another time Dalgetty might have argued, tried to veil it from her, tried to trick her once again. But now he was too weary. There was a great surrender in him. "I'll tell you if you wish," he said, "and after that it's in your hands. You can make us or break us."

"Go on, then." Her tone withdrew into wariness.

"I'm human," he said. "I'm as human as you are. Only I've had rather special training, that's all. It's another discovery of the Institute for which we don't feel the world is ready. It'd be too big a temptation for too many people, to create followers like me." He looked away, into the windy dark. "The scientist is also a member of the society and has a responsibility toward it. This—restraint—of ours is one way in which we meet that obligation."

She didn't speak, but suddenly one hand reached over and rested on his. The impulsive gesture brought warmth flooding through him.

"Dad's work was mostly in mass-action psych," he said, making his tone try to cover what he felt, "but he has plenty of associates trying to understand the individual human being as a functioning mechanism. A lot's been learned since Freud, both from the psychiatric and the neurological angle. Ultimately, those two are interchangeable.

"Some thirty years ago, one of the teams which founded the Institute learned enough about the relationship between the conscious, subconscious, and involuntary minds to begin practical tests. Along with a few others, I was a guinea pig. And their theories worked.

"I needn't go into the details of my training. It involved physical exercises, mental practice, some hypnotism, diet, and so on. It went considerably beyond the important Synthesis education, which is the most advanced thing known to the general public. But its aim—only partially realized as yet—its aim was simply to produce the completely integrated human being."

Dalgetty paused. The wind flowed and muttered beyond the wall.

"There is no sharp division between conscious and subconscious or even between those and the centers controlling involuntary functions," he said. "The brain is a continuous structure. Suppose, for instance, that you become aware of a runaway car bearing down on you.

"Your heartbeat speeds up, your adrenalin output increses, your sight sharpens, your sensitivity to pain drops—it's all preparation for fight or flight. Even without obvious physical necessity, the same thing can happen on a lesser scale—for example, when you read an exciting story. And psychotics, especially hysterics, can produce some of the damnedest physiological symptoms you ever saw."

"I begin to understand," she whispered.

"Rage or fear brings abnormal strength and fast reaction. But the psychotic can do more than that. He can show physical symptoms like burns, stigmata or—if female—false pregnancy. Sometimes he becomes wholly insensitive in some part of his body via a nerve bloc. Bleeding can start or stop without apparent cause. He can go into a coma, or he can stay awake for days without getting sleepy. He can—"

"Read minds?" It was a defiance.

"Not that I know of." Simon chuckled. "But human sense organs are amazingly good. It only takes three or four quanta to stimulate the visual purple—a little more actually, because of absorption by the eyeball itself. There have been hysterics who could hear a watch ticking twenty feet away that the normal person could not hear at one foot. And so on.

"There are excellent reasons why the threshold of perception is relatively high in ordinary people—the stimuli of usual conditions would be blinding and deafening, unendurable, if there weren't a defense." He grimaced. "I *know!*"

"But the telepathy?" Elena persisted.

"It's been done before," he said. "Some apparent cases of mind reading in the last century were shown to be due to extremely acute hearing. Most people subvocalize their surface thoughts. With a little practice, a person who can hear those vibrations can learn to interpret them. That's all. " He smiled with one side of his mouth. "If you want to hide your thoughts from me, just break that habit, Elena."

She looked at him with an emotion he could not quite recognize. "I see," she breathed. "And your memory must be perfect too, if you can pull any datum out of the subconscious. And you can—do everything, can't you?"

"No," he said. "I'm only a test case. They've learned a great deal by observing me, but the only thing that makes me unusual is that I have conscious control of certain normally subconscious and involuntary functions. Not all of them, by a long shot. And I don't use that control any more than necessary.

"There are sound biological reasons why man's mind is so divided and plenty of penalties attached to a case like mine. It'll take me a couple of months to get back in shape after this bout. I'm due for a good old-fashioned nervous breakdown, and while it won't last long, it won't be much fine while it does last."

The appeal rose in his eyes as he watched Elena. "All right," he said. "Now you have the story. What are you going to do about it?"

For the first time she gave him a real smile. "Don't worry," she said. "Don't worry, Simon."

"Will you come hold my hand while I'm recuperating?" he asked.

"I'm holding it now, you fool," Elena answered.

Dalgetty chuckled happily. Then he went to sleep.

Although the Institute continued to claim disinterested good intentions, abuse was inherent in psychodynamics. The debate between Dalgetty and Casimir was carried on by others with increasing vehemence and violence. The new planetary settlements offered broader battlefields for contending movements. In midcentury Venus withdrew from the United Nations following the Second Conference of Rio. Later events demonstrated that it was simpler to remodel a world than to remake mankind.

THE BIG RAIN

I

The room was small and bare, nothing but a ventilator grill to relieve the drabness of its plastic walls, no furniture except a table and a couple of benches. It was hot, and the cold light of fluoros glistened off the sweat which covered the face of the man who sat there alone.

He was a big man, with hard bony features under close-cropped reddish-brown hair; his eyes were gray, with something chilly in them, and moved restlessly about the chamber to assess its crude homemade look. The coverall which draped his lean body was a bit too colorful. He had fumbled a cigarette out of his belt pouch and it smoldered between his fingers, now and then he took a heavy drag on it. But he sat quietly enough, waiting.

The door opened and another man came in. This one was smaller, with bleak features. He wore only shorts to whose waistband was pinned a star-shaped badge, and a needle gun holstered at his side, but somehow he had a military look.

"Simon Hollister?" he asked unnecessarily.

"That's me," said the other, rising. He loomed over the newcomer, but he was unarmed; they had searched him thoroughly the minute he disembarked.

"I am Captain Karsov, Guardian Corps." The English was fluent, with only a trace of accent. "Sit down." He lowered himself to a bench. "I am only here to talk to you."

Hollister grimaced. "How about some lunch?" he complained. "I haven't eaten for"—he paused a second—"thirteen hours, twenty-eight minutes."

His precision didn't get by Karsov, but the officer ignored it for the time being. "Presently," he said. "There isn't much time to lose, you know. The last ferry leaves in forty hours, and we have to find out before then if you are acceptable or must go back on it."

"Hell of a way to treat a guest," grumbled Hollister.

"We did not ask you to come," said Karsov coldly. "If you wish to stay on Venus, you had better conform to the regulations. Now, what do you think qualifies you?"

"To live here? I'm an engineer. Construction experience in the Amazon basin and on Luna. I've got papers to prove it, and letters of recommendation, if you'd let me get at my baggage."

"Eventually. What is your reason for emigrating?"

Hollister looked sullen. "I didn't like Earth."

"Be more specific. You are going to be narcoquizzed later, and the whole truth will come out. These questions are just to guide the interrogators, and the better you answer me now the quicker and easier the quiz will be for all of us."

Hollister bristled. "That's an invasion of privacy."

"Venus isn't Earth," said Karsov with an attempt at patience. "Before you were even allowed to land, you signed a waiver which puts you completely under our jurisdiction as long as you are on this planet. I could kill you, and the U.N. would not have a word to say. But we do need skilled men, and I would rather O.K. you for citizenship. Do not make it too hard for me."

"All right." Hollister shrugged heavy shoulders. "I got in a fight with a man. He died. I covered up the traces pretty well, but I could never be sure—sooner or later the police might get on to the truth, and I don't like the idea of corrective treatment. So I figured I'd better blow out while I was still unsuspected."

"Venus is no place for the rugged individualist, Hollister. Men have to work together, and be very tolerant of each other, if they are to survive at all."

"Yes, I know. This was a special case. The man had it coming." Hollister's face twisted. "I have a daughter—Never mind. I'd rather tell it under narco than consciously. But I just couldn't see letting a snake like that get 'corrected' and then walk around free again." Defensively: "I've always been a rough sort, I suppose, but you've got to admit this was extreme provocation."

"That is all right," said Karsov, "if you are telling the truth. But if you have family ties back on Earth, it might lessen your usefulness here."

"None," said Hollister bitterly. "Not any more."

The interview went on. Karsov extracted the facts skillfully: Hollister, Simon James; born Frisco Unit, U.S.A., of good stock; chronological age, thirty-eight Earth-years; physiological age, thanks to taking intelligent advantage of biomedics, about twenty-five; Second-class education, major in civil engineering with emphasis on nuclear-powered construction machines; work record; psych rating at last checkup; et cetera, et cetera, et cetera. Somewhere a recorder took sound and visual impressions of every nuance for later analysis and filing.

At the end, the Guardian rose and stretched. "I think you will do," he said. "Come along now for the narco-quiz. It will take about three hours, and you will need another hour to recover, and then I will see that you get something to eat."

The city crouched on a mountainside in a blast of eternal wind. Overhead roiled the poisonous gray clouds; sometimes a sleet of paraformaldehyde hid the grim red slopes around, and always the scudding dust veiled men's eyes so they could not see the alkali desert below.

Fantastically storm-gnawed crags loomed over the city, and often there was the nearby rumble of an avalanche, but the ledge on which it stood had been carefully checked for stability.

The city was one armored unit of metal and concrete, low and rounded as if it hunched its back against the shrieking steady gale. From its shell protruded the stacks of hundreds of outsize Hilsch tubes, swivel-mounted so that they always faced into the wind. It blew past filters which caught the flying dust and sand and tossed them down a series of chutes to the cement factory. The tubes grabbed the rushing air and separated fast and slow molecules; the cooler part went into a refrigeration system which kept the city at a temperature men could stand—outside, it hovered around the boiling point of water; the smaller volume of super-heated air was conducted to the maintenance plant where it helped run the city's pumps and generators. There were also nearly a thousand windmills, turning furiously and drinking the force of the storm.

None of this air was for breathing. It was thick with carbon dioxide; the rest was nitrogen, inert gases, formaldehyde vapor, a little methane and ammonia. The city devoted many hectacres of space to hydroponic plants which renewed its oxygen and supplied some of the food, as well as to chemical purifiers, pumps, and blowers. "Free as air" was a joke on Venus.

Near the shell was the spaceport where ferries from the satellite station and the big interplanetary ships landed. Pilots had to be good to bring down a vessel, or even take one up, under such conditions as prevailed here. Except for the landing cradles, the radio mast, and the GCA shack in the main shell, everything was underground, as most of the city was.

Some twenty thousand colonists lived there. They were miners, engineers, laborers, technicians in the food and maintenance centers. There were three doctors, a scattering of teachers and librarians and similar personnel, a handful of police and administrators. Exactly fifteen people were employed in brewing, distilling, tavern-running, movie operation, and the other non-essential occupations which men required as they did food and air.

This was New America, chief city of Venus in 2051 A.D.

Hollister didn't enjoy his meal. He got it, cafeteria style, in one of the big plain messhalls, after a temporary ration book had been issued him. It consisted of a few vegetables, a lot of potato, a piece of the soggy yeast synthetic which was the closest to meat Venus offered—all liberally loaded with a tasteless basic food concentrate—a vitamin capsule, and a glass of flavored water. When he took out one of his remaining cigarettes, a score of eyes watched it hungrily. Not much tobacco here either. He inhaled savagely, feeling the obscure guilt of the have confronted with the have-not.

There were a number of people in the room with him, eating their own rations. Men and women were represented about equally. All wore coveralls or the standard shorts, and most looked young, but hard too, somehow—even the women. Hollister was used to female engineers and technicians at home, but here *everybody* worked.

For the time being, he stuck to his Earthside garments.

He sat alone at one end of a long table, wondering why nobody talked to him. You'd think they would be starved for a new face and word from Earth. Prejudice? Yes, a little of that, considering the political situation; but Hollister thought something more was involved.

Fear. They were all afraid of something.

When Karsov strolled in, the multilingual hum of conversation died, and Hollister guessed shrewdly at the fear. The Guardian made his way directly to the Earthling's place. He had a blocky, bearded man with a round smiling face in tow.

"Simon Hollister . . . Heinrich Gebhardt," the policeman introduced them. They shook hands, sizing each other up. Karsov sat down. "Get me the usual," he said, handing over his ration book.

Gebhardt nodded and went over to the automat. It scanned the books and punched them when he had dialed his orders. Then it gave him two trays, which he carried back.

Karsov didn't bother to thank him. "I have been looking for you," he told Hollister. "Where have you been?"

"Just wandering around," said the Earthling cautiously. Inside, he felt muscles tightening, and his mind seemed to tilt forward, as if sliding off the hypnotically imposed pseudo-personality which had been meant as camouflage in the narcoquiz. "It's quite a labyrinth here."

"You should have stayed in the barracks," said Karsov. There was no expression in his smooth-boned face; there never seemed to be. "Oh, well. I wanted to say you have been found acceptable."

"Good," said Hollister, striving for imperturbability.

"I will administer the oath after lunch," said Karsov. "Then you will be a full citizen of the Venusian Federation. We do not hold with formalities, you see — no time." He reached into a pocket and got out a booklet which he gave to Hollister. "But I advise you to study this carefully. It is a resumé of the most important laws, insofar as they differ from Earth's. Punishment for infraction is severe."

Gebhardt looked apologetic. "It hass to be," he added. His bass voice had a slight blur and hiss of German accent, but he was good at the English which was becoming the common language of Venus. "This planet vas made in hell. If ve do not all work together, ve all die."

"And then, of course, there is the trouble with Earth," said Karsov. His narrow eyes studied Hollister for a long moment. "Just how do people back there feel about our declaration of independence?"

"Well—" Hollister paused. Best to tell the unvarnished truth, he decided. "Some resentment, of course. After all the money we . . . they . . . put into developing the colonies—"

"And all the resources they took out," said Gebhardt. "Men vere planted on Venus back in the last century to mine fissionables, vich vere getting short efen then. The colonies vere made self-supporting because that vas cheaper than hauling supplies for them, vich vould haff been an impossible task anyvay. Some of the colonies vere penal, some vere manned by arbitrarily assigned personnel; the so-called democracies often relied on broken men, who could not find vork at home or who had been displaced by var. No, ve owe them notting."

Hollister shrugged. "I'm not arguing. But people do wonder why, if you wanted national status, you didn't at least stay with the U.N. That's what Mars is doing."

"Because we are . . . necessarily . . . developing a whole new civilization here, something altogether remote from anything Earth has ever seen," snapped Karsov. "We will still trade our fissionables for things we need, until the day we can make everything here ourselves, but we want as little to do with Earth as possible. Never mind, you will understand in time."

Hollister's mouth lifted in a crooked grin. There hadn't been much Earth could do about it; in the present state of astronautics, a military expedition to suppress the nationalists would cost more than anyone could hope to gain even from the crudest imperialism. Also, as long as no clear danger was known to exist, it wouldn't have sat well with a planet sick of war; the dissension produced might well have torn the young world government which still had only limited powers, apart.

But astronautics was going to progress, he thought

grimly. Spaceships wouldn't have to improve much to carry, cheaply, loads of soldiers in cold sleep, ready to land when thermonuclear bombardment from the skies had smashed a world's civilization. And however peaceful Earth might be, she was still a shining temptation to the rest of the System, and it look very much as if something was brewing here on Venus which could become ugly before the century was past.

Well—

"Your first assignment is already arranged," said Karsov. Hollister jerked out of his reverie and tried to keep his fists unclenched. "Gebhardt will be your boss. If you do well, you can look for speedy promotion. Meanwhile,"—he flipped a voucher across—"here is the equivalent of the dollars you had along, in our currency."

Hollister stuck the sheet in his pouch. It was highway robbery, he knew, but he was in no position to complain and the Venusian government wanted the foreign exchange. And he could only buy trifles with it anyway; the essentials were issued without payment, the size of the ration depending on rank. Incentive bonuses were money, though, permitting you to amuse yourself but not to consume more of the scarce food or textiles or living space.

He reflected that the communist countries before World War Three had never gone this far. Here, everything was government property. The system didn't call itself communism, naturally, but it was, and probably there was no choice. Private enterprise demanded a fairly large economic surplus, which simply did not exist on Venus.

Well, it wasn't his business to criticize their internal arrangements. He had never been among the few fanatics left on Earth who still made a god of a particular economic set-up.

Gebhardt cleared his throat. "I am in charge of the atmosphere detail in this district," he said. "I am here on leafe, and vill be going back later today. Very glad to haff you, Hollister, ve are alvays short of men. Ve lost two in the last rock storm."

"Cheerful news," said the Earthman. His face resumed its hard woodenness. "Well, I didn't think Venus was going to be any bed of roses."

"It vill be," said Gebhardt. Dedication glowed on the hairy face. "Some day it vill be."

II

The oath was pretty drastic: in effect, Hollister put himself completely at the mercy of the Technic Board, which for all practical purposes was the city government. Each colony, he gathered, had such a body, and there was a federal board in this town which decided policy for the entire planet.

Anyone who wished to enter the government had to pass a series of rigid test, after which there were years of apprenticeship and study, gradual promotion on the recommendations of seniors. The study was an exhausting course of history, psycho-technics, and physical science: in principle, thought Hollister, remembering some of the blubberheads who still got themselves elected at home, a good idea. The governing boards combined legislative, executive, and judicial functions, and totaled only a couple of thousand people for the whole world. It didn't seem like much for a nation of nearly two million, and the minimal paperwork surprised him—he had expected an omnipresent bureaucracy.

But of course they had the machines to serve them, recording everything in electronic files whose computers could find and correlate any data and were always checking up. And he was told pridefully that the schools were inculcating the rising generation with a tight ethic of obedience.

Hollister had supper, and returned to the Casual barracks to sleep. There were only a few men in there with him, most of them here on business from some other town. He was wakened by the alarm, whose photocells singled him out and shot forth a supersonic beam; it was a carrier wave for the harsh ringing in his head which brought him to his feet.

Gebhardt met him at an agreed-on locker room. There was a wiry, tough-looking Mongoloid with him who was introduced as Henry Yamashita. "Stow your fancy clothes, boy," boomed the chief, "and get on some TBI's." He handed over a drab, close-fitting coverall.

Hollister checked his own garments and donned the new suit wordlessly. After that there was a heavy plasticord outfit which, with boots and gloves, decked his whole body. Yamashita helped him strap on the oxygen bottles and plug in the Hilsch cooler. The helmet came last, its shoulder-piece buckled to the airsuit, but all of them kept theirs hinged back to leave their heads free.

"If somet'ing happens to our tank," said Gebhardt, "you slap that helmet down fast. Or maybe you like being embalmed. Haw!" His cheerfulness was more evident when Karsov wasn't around.

Hollister checked the valves with the caution taught him on Luna — his engineering experience was not faked. Gebhardt grunted approvingly. Then they slipped on the packs containing toilet kits, change of clothes, and emergency rations; clipped ropes, batteries, and canteens to their belts — the latter with the standard sucker tubes by which a man could drink directly even in his suit; and clumped out of the room.

A descending ramp brought them to a garage where the tanks were stored. These looked not unlike the sandcats of Mars, but were built lower and heavier, with a refrigerating tube above and a grapple in the nose. A mechanic gestured at one dragging a covered steel wagon full of supplies, and the three men squeezed into the tiny transparent cab.

Gebhardt gunned the engine, nodding as it roared. "O.K.," he said. "On ve go."

"What's the power source?" asked Hollister above the racket.

"Alcohol," answerd Yamashita. "We get it from the formaldehyde. Bottled oxygen. A compressor and cooling system to keep the oxy tanks from blowing up on us — not that they don't once in a while. Some of the newer models use a peroxide system."

"And I suppose you save the water vapor and CO_2 to get the oxygen back," ventured Hollister.

"Just the water. There's always plenty of carbon dioxide." Yamashita looked out, and his face set in tight lines.

The tank waddled through the great air lock and up a long tunnel toward the surface. When they emerged, the wind was like a blow in the face. Hollister felt the machine shudder, and the demon howl drowned out the engine. He accepted the earplugs Yamashita handed him with a grateful smile.

There was dust and sand scudding by them, making it hard to see the mountainside down which they crawled. Hollister caught glimpses of naked fanglike peaks, raw slashes of ocher and blue where minerals veined the land, the steady march of dunes across the lower ledges. Overhead, the sky was an unholy tide of ragged, flying clouds, black and gray and sulfurous yellow. He could not see the sun, but the light around him was a weird hard brass color, like the light on Earth just before a thunderstorm.

The wind hooted and screamed, banging on the tank walls, yelling and rattling and groaning. Now and then a dull quiver ran through the land and trembled in Hollister's bones, somewhere an avalanche was ripping out a mountain's flanks. Briefly, a veil of dust fell so thick around them that they were blind, grinding through an elemental night with hell and the furies loose outside. The control board's lights were wan on Gebhardt's intent face, most of the time he was steering by instruments.

Once the tank lurched into a gully. Hollister, watching the pilot's lips, thought he muttered. "Damn! That vasn't here before!" He extended the grapple, clutching rock and pulling the tank and its load upward.

Yamashita clipped two small disks to his larynx and gestured at the same equipment hanging on Hollister's suit. His voice came thin but fairly clear: "Put on your talkie unit if you want to say anything." Hollister obeyed, guessing that the earplugs had a transistor arrangement powered by a piece of isotope 'which reproduced the vibrations in the throat. It took concentration to understand the language as they distorted it, but he supposed he'd catch on fast enough.

"How many hours till nightfall?" he asked.

"About twenty." Yamashita pointed to the clock on the board, it was calibrated to Venus' seventy-two hour day. "It's around one hundred thirty kilometers to the camp, so we should just about make it by sunset."

"That isn't very fast," said Hollister. "Why not fly, or at least build roads?"

"The aircraft are all needed for speed travel and impassable terrain, and the roads will come later," said Yamashita. "These tanks can go it all right—most of the time."

"But why have the camp so far from the city?"

"It's the best location from a supply standpoint. We get most of our food from Little Moscow, and water from Hellfire, and chemicals from New America and Roger's Landing. The cities more or less specialize, you know. They have to: there isn't enough iron ore and whatnot handy to any one spot to build a city big enough to do everything by itself. So the air camps are set up at points which minimize the total distance over which supplies have to be hauled."

"You mean action distance, don't you? The product of the energy and time required for hauling."

Yamashita nodded, with a new respect in his eyes. "You'll do," he said.

The wind roared about them. It was more than just the slow rotation of the planet and its nearness to the sun which created such an incessant storm; if that had been all, there would never have been any chance of making it habitable. It was the high carbon dioxide content of the air, and its greenhouse effect; and in the long night, naked arid rock cooled off considerably. With plenty of water and vegetation, and an atmosphere similar to Earth's, Venus would have a warm but rather gentle climate on the whole, the hurricanes moderated to trade winds; indeed, with the lower Coriolos force, the destructive cyclones of Earth would be unknown.

Such, at least, was the dream of the Venusians. But looking out, Hollister realized that a fraction of the time and effort they were expending would have made the Sahara desert bloom. They had been sent here once as miners, but there was no longer any compulsion on them to stay; if they asked to come back to Earth, their appeal could not be denied however expensive it would be to ship them all home.

Then why didn't they?

Well, why go back to a rotten civilization like—Hollister caught himself. Sometimes his pseudo-memories were real enough in him to drown out the genuine ones, rage and grief could nearly overwhelm him till he recalled that the sorrow was for people who had never existed. The anger had had to be planted deep, to get by a narcoquiz, but he wondered if it might not interfere with his mission, come the day.

He grinned sardonically at himself. One man, caught on a planet at the gates of the Inferno, watched by a powerful and ruthless government embracing that entire world, and he was setting himself against it!

Most likely he would die here, and the economical Venusians would process his body for its chemicals as they did other corpses, and that would be the end of it as far as he was concerned.

Well, he quoted to himself, *a man might try.*

Gebhardt's camp was a small shell, a radio mast, and a shed sticking out of a rolling landscape of rock and sand; the rest was underground. The sun was down on a ragged horizon, dimly visible as a huge blood-red disk, when he arrived. Yamashita and Hollister had taken their turns piloting; the Earthman found it exhausting work, and his head rang with the noise when he finally stepped out into the subterranean garage.

Yamashita led him to the barracks. "We're about fifty here," he explained. "All men." He grinned. "That makes a system of minor rewards and punishments based on leaves to a city *very* effective."

The barracks was a long room with triple rows of bunks and a few tables and chairs; only Gebhardt rated a chamber of his own, though curtains on the bunks did permit some privacy. An effort had been made to brighten the place up with murals, some of which weren't bad at all, and the men sat about reading, writing letters, talking, playing games. They were the usual conglomerate of races and nationalities, with some interesting half-breeds; hard work and a parsimonious diet had made them smaller than the average American or European, but they looked healthy enough.

"Simon Hollister, our new sub-engineer," called Yamashita as they entered. "Just got in from Earth. Now you know as much as I do." He flopped onto a bunk while the others drifted over. "Go ahead. Tell all. Birth, education, hobbies, religion, sex life, interests, prejudices—they'll find it out anyway, and God knows we could use a little variety around here."

A stocky blond man paused suspiciously. "From Earth?" he asked slowly. "We've had no new people from Earth for thirty years. What did you want to come here for?"

"I felt like it," snapped Hollister. "That's enough!"

"So, a jetheading snob, huh? We're too good for you, I guess."

"Take it easy, Sam," said someone else.

"Yeah," a Negro grinned, "he might be bossin' you, you know."

"That's just it," said the blond man. "I was born here. I've been studying, and I've been on air detail for twenty years, and this bull walks right in and takes my promotion the first day."

Part of Hollister checked off the fact that the Venusians used the terms "year" and "day" to mean those periods for their own world, one shorter and one longer than Earth's. The rest of him tightened up for trouble, but others intervened. He found a vacant bunk and sat down on it, swinging his legs and trying to make friendly conversation. It wasn't easy. He felt terribly alone.

Presently someone got out a steel and plastic guitar and strummed it, and soon they were all singing. Hollister listened with half an ear.

"When the Big Rain comes, all the
    air will be good,
and the rivers all flow with beer,
with the cigarets bloomin' by the
    beefsteak bush,
and the ice-cream-bergs right here.
When the Big Rain comes, we will all
    be a-swillin'
of champagne, while the violin tree
plays love songs because all the gals
    will be willin',
and we'll all have a Big Rain
    spree!—"

Paradise, he thought. *They can joke about it, but it's still the Paradise they work for and know they'll never see. Then why* do *they work for it? What is it that's driving them?*

After a meal, a sleep, and another meal, Hollister was given a set of blueprints to study. He bent his mind to the task, using all the powers which an arduous training had given it, and in a few hours reported to Gebhardt. "I know them," he said.

"Already?" The chief's small eyes narrowed. "It iss not vort'vile trying to bluff here, boy. Venus always calls it."

"I'm not bluffing," said Hollister angrily. "If you want me to lounge around for another day, O.K., but I know those specs by heart."

The bearded man stood up. There was muscle under his plumpness. "O.K., by damn," he said. "You go out vit me next trip."

That was only a few hours off. Gebhardt took a third man, a quiet grizzled fellow they called Johnny, and let Hollister drive. The tank hauled the usual wagonload of equipment, and the rough ground made piloting a harsh task. Hollister had used multiple transmissions before, and while the navigating instruments were complicated, he caught on to them quickly enough; it was the strain and muscular effort that wore him out.

Venus' night was not the pitchy gloom one might have expected. The clouds diffused sunlight around the planet, and there was also a steady flicker of aurora even in these middle latitudes. The headlamps were needed only when they went into a deep ravine. Wind growled around them, but Hollister was getting used to that.

The first airmaker on their tour was only a dozen kilometers from the camp. It was a dark, crouching bulk on a stony ridge, its intake funnel like the rearing neck of some archaic monster. They pulled up beside, slapped down their helmets, and went one by one through the air lock.

It was a standard midget type, barely large enough to hold one man, which meant little air to be pumped out and hence greater speed in getting through. Gebhardt had told Hollister to face the exit leeward; now the three roped themselves together and stepped around the tank, out of its shelter.

Hollister lost his footing, crashed to the ground, and went spinning away in the gale. Gebhardt and Johnny dug their cleated heels in and brought the rope up short. When they had the new man back on his feet, Hollister saw them grinning behind their faceplates. Thereafter, he paid attention to his balance, leaning against the wind.

Inspection and servicing of the unit was a slow task, and it was hard to see the finer parts even in the headlight's glare. One by one, the various sections were uncovered and checked, adjustments made, full gas bottles removed and empty one substituted.

It was no wonder Gebhardt had doubted Hollister's claim. The airmaker was one of the most complicated machines in existence. A thing meant to transform the atmosphere of a planet had to be.

The intake scooped up the wind and drove it, with the help of wind-powered compressors, through a series of chambers; some of them held catalysts, some electric arcs or heating coils maintaining temperature—the continuous storm ran a good-sized generator—and some led back into others in a maze of interconnections. The actual chemistry was simple enough. Paraform was broken down and yielded its binding water molecules; the formaldehyde, together with that taken directly from the air, reacted with ammonia and methane—or with itself—to produce a whole series of hydrocarbons, carbohydrates, and more complex compounds for food, fuel, and fertilizer; such carbon dioxide as did not enter other reactions was broken down by sheer brute force in an arc to oxygen and soot. The oxygen was bottled for industrial use; the remaining substances were partly separated by distillation—again using wind power, this time to refrigerate—and collected. Further processing would take place at the appropriate cities.

Huge as the unit loomed, it seemed pathetically small when you thought of the fantastic tonnage which was the total planetary atmosphere. But more of its kind were being built every day and scattered around the surface of the world; over a million already existed, seven million was the goal, and that number should theoretically be able to to do the job in another twenty Earth-years.

That was theory, as Gebhardt explained over the helmet radio. Other considerations entered, such as the law of diminishing returns: as the effect of the machines became noticeable, the percentage of the air they could deal with would necessarily drop; then there was stratospheric gas, some of which apparently never got down to the surface; and the chemistry of a changing atmosphere had to be taken into account. The basic time estimate for this stage of the work had to be revised upward another decade.

There was oxygen everywhere, locked into rocks and ores, enough for the needs of man if it could be gotten out. Specially mutated bacteria were doing that job, living off carbon and silicon, releasing more gas than their own metabolisms took up; their basic energy source was the sun. Some of the oxygen recombined, of course, but not enough to matter, especially since it could only act on or near the surface and most of the bacterial gnawing went on far down. Already there was a barely detectable percentage of the element in the atmosphere. By the time the airmakers were finished, the bacteria would also be.

Meanwhile giant pulverizers were reducing barren stone and sand to fine particles which would be mixed with fertilizers to yield soil; and the genetic engineers were evolving still other strains of life which could provide a balanced ecology; and the water units were under construction.

These would be the key to the whole operation. There was plenty of water on Venus, trapped down in the body of the planet, and the volcanoes brought it up as they had done long ago on Earth. Here it was quickly snatched by the polymerizing formaldehyde, except in spots like Hellfire where machinery had been built to extract it from magma and hydrated minerals. But there was less formaldehyde in the air every day.

At the right time, hydrogen bombs were to be touched off in places the geologists had already selected, and the volcanoes would all wake up. They would spume forth plenty of carbon dioxide — though by that time the amount of the free gas would be so low that this would be welcomed — but there would be water too, unthinkable tons of water. And simultaneously, aircraft would be sowing platinum catalyst in the skies, and with its help Venus' own lightning would attack the remaining poisons in the air. They would come down as carbohydrates and other compounds, washed out by the rain and leached from the sterile ground.

That would be the Big Rain. It would last an estimated ten Earth-years, and at the end there would be rivers and lakes and seas on a planet which had never known them. And the soil would be spread, the bacteria and plants and small animal life released. Venus would still be mostly desert, the rains would slacken off but remain heavy for centuries, but men could walk unclothed on this world and they could piece by piece make the desert green.

A hundred years after the airmen had finished their work, the reclaimed sections might be close to Earth conditions. In five hundred years, all of Venus might be Paradise.

To Hollister it seemed like a long time to wait.

III

He didn't need many days to catch on to the operations and be made boss of a construction gang. Then he took out twenty men and a train of supplies and machinery, to erect still another airmaker.

It was blowing hard then, too hard to set up the seal-tents which ordinarily provided a measure of comfort. Men rested in the tanks, side by side, dozing uneasily and smelling each other's sweat. They griped loudly, but endured. It was a lengthy trip to their site; eventually the whole camp was to be broken up and re-established in a better location, but meanwhile they had to accept the monotony of travel.

Hollister noticed that his men had evolved an Asian ability just to sit, without thinking hour after hour. Their conversation and humor also suggested Asia: acrid, often brutal, though maintaining a careful surface politeness most of the time. It was probably more characteristic of this particular job than of the whole planet, though, and maybe they sloughed it off again when their hitches on air detail had expired and they got more congenial assignments.

As boss, he had the privilege of sharing his tank with only one man; he chose the wizened Johnny, whom he rather liked. Steering through a yelling sandstorm, he was now able to carry on a conversation—and it was about time, he reflected, that he got on with his real job.

"Ever thought of going back to Earth?" he asked casually.

"Back?" Johnny looked surprised. "I was born here."

"Well . . . going to Earth, then."

"What'd I use for passage money?"

"Distress clause of the Space Navigation Act. They'd have to give you a berth if you applied. Not that you couldn't repay your passage, with interest, in a while. With your experience here, you could get a fine post in one of the reclamation projects on Earth."

"Look," said Johnny in a flustered voice, "I'm a good Venusian. I'm needed here and I know it."

"Forget the Guardians," snapped Hollister, irritated. "I'm not going to report you. Why you people put up with a secret police anyway, is more than I can understand."

"You've got to keep people in line," said Johnny. "We all got to work together to make a go of it."

"But haven't you ever thought it'd be nice to decide your own future and not have somebody tell you what to do next?"

"It ain't just 'somebody.' It's the Board. They know how you and me fit in best. Sure, I suppose there are subversives, but I'm not one of them."

"Why don't the malcontents just run away, if they don't dare apply for passage to Earth? They could steal materials and make their own village. Venus is a big place."

"It ain't that easy. And supposin' they could and did, what'd they do then? Just sit and wait for the Big Rain? We don't want any freeloaders on Venus, mister."

Hollister shrugged. There was something about the pyschology that baffled him. "I'm not preaching revolution," he said carefully. "I came here of my own free will, remember. I'm just trying to understand the setup."

Johnny's faded eyes were shrewd on him. "You've always had it easy compared to us, I guess. It may look hard to you here. But remember, we ain't never had it different, except that things are gettin' better little by little. The food rations gets upped every so often, and we're allowed a dress suit now as well as utility clothes, and before long there's goin' to be broadcast shows to the outposts — and some day the Big Rain is comin'. Then we can all afford to take it free and easy." He paused.

"That's why we broke with Earth. Why should we slave our guts out to make a good life for our grandchildren, if a bunch of free-loaders are gonna come from Earth and fill up the planet then? It's *ours*. It's gonna be the richest planet men ever saw, and it belongs to us what developed it.

Official propaganda line, thought Hollister. It sounded plausible enough till you stopped to analyze. For one thing, each country still had the right to set its own immigration policies. Furthermore, at the rate Earth was progressing, with reclamation, population control, and new resources from the oceans, by the time Venus was ripe there wouldn't be any motive to leave home—an emigration which would be too long and expensive anyway. For their own reasons, which he still had to discover, the rulers of Venus had not mentioned all the facts and had instead, built up a paranoid attitude in their people.

The new airmake site was the top of a ridge thrusting from a boulder-strewn plain. An eerie copper-colored light seemed to tinge the horizon with blood. A pair of bulldozers had already gone ahead and scooped out a walled hollow in which seal-tents could be erected; Hollister's gang swarmed from the tanks and got at that job. Then the real work began—blasting and carving a foundation, sinking piers, assembling the unit on top.

On the fourth day the rock storm came. It had dawned with an angry glow like sulfur, and as it progressed the wind strengthened and a dirty rack of clouds whipped low overhead. On the third shift, the gale was strong enough to lean against, and the sheet steel which made the unit's armour fought the men as if it lived.

The blond man, Sam Robbins, who had never liked Hollister, made his way up to the chief. His voice came over the helmet radio, dim beneath static and the drumming wind: "I don't like this. Better we take cover fast."

Hollister was not unwilling, but the delicate arc electrodes were being set up and he couldn't take them down again; nor could he leave them unprotected to the scouring drift of sand. "As soon as we get the shielding up," he said.

"I tell you, there's no time to shield 'em!"

"Yes, there is." Hollister turned his back. Robbins snarled something and returned to his labor.

A black wall, rust-red on the edges, was lifting to the east, the heaviest sandstorm Hollister had yet seen. He hunched his shoulder and struggled through the sleetlike dust to the unit. Tuning up his radio: "Everybody come help on this. The sooner it gets done, the sooner we can quit."

The helmeted figures swarmed around him, battling the thunderously flapping metal sheets, holding them down by main force while they were welded to the frame. Hollister saw lightning livid across the sky. Once a bolt flamed at the rod which protected the site. Thunder rolled and banged after it.

The wind slapped at them, and a sheet tore loose and went sailing down the hill. It struck a crag and wrapped itself around. "Robbins, Lewis, go get that!" cried Hollister, and returned attention to the piece he was clutching. An end ripped loose from his hands and tried to slash his suit.

The wind was so deafening that he couldn't hear it rise still higher, and in the murk of sand whirling about him he was nearly blind. But he caught the first glimpse of gale-borne gravel whipping past, and heard the terror in his earphones: "Rock storm!"

The voice shut up; orders were strict that the channel be kept clear. But the gasping man labored still more frantically, while struck metal rang and boomed.

Hollister peered through the darkness. "That's enough!" he decided. "Take cover!"

Nobody dropped his tools, but they all turned fast and

groped down toward the camp. The way led past the crag, where Robbins and Lewis had just quit wrestling with the stubborn plate.

Hollister didn't see Lewis killed, but he did see him die. Suddenly his airsuit was flayed open, and there was a spurt of blood, and he toppled. The wind took his body, rolling it out of sight in the dust. *A piece of rock,* thought Hollister wildly. *It tore his suit, and he's already embalmed—*

The storm hooted and squealed about him as he climbed the sand wall. Even the blown dust was audible, hissing against his helmet. He fumbled through utter blackness, fell over the top and into the comparative shelter of the camp ground. On hands and knees, he crawled toward the biggest of the self-sealing tents.

There was no time for niceties. They sacrificed the atmosphere within, letting the air lock stand open while they pushed inside. Had everybody made it to some tent or other? Hollister wasn't sure, but sand was coming in, filling the shelter. He went over and closed the lock. Somebody else started the pump, using bottled nitrogen to maintain air pressure and flush out the poisons. It seemed like a long time before the oxygen containers could be opened.

Hollister took off his helmet and looked around. The tent was half filled by seven white-faced men standing in the dust. The single fluorotube threw a cold light on their sweating bodies and barred the place with shadows. Outside, the wind bellowed.

."Might as well be comfortable," said Johnny in a small voice, and began shucking his airsuit. "If the tent goes, we're all done for anyhow." He sat down on the ground and checked his equipment methodically. Then he took a curved stone and spat on it and began scouring his faceplate to remove the accumulated scratches in its hard plastic. One by one the others imitated him.

"You there!"

Hollister looked up from his own suit. Sam Robbins stood before him. The man's eyes were red and his mouth worked.

"You killed Jim Lewis."

There was murder here. Hollister raised himself till he looked down at the Venusian. "I'm sorry he's dead," he replied, trying for quietness. "He was a good man. But those things will happen."

Robbins shuddered. "You sent him down there where the gravel got him. I was there, too. Was it meant for me?"

"Nobody could tell where that chunk was going to hit," said Hollister mildly. "I could just as easily have been killed."

"I *told* you to quit half an hour before the things started."

"We couldn't quit then without ruining all our work. Sit down, Robbins. You're overtired and scared."

The men were very still sitting and watching in the thick damp heat of the tent. Thunder crashed outside.

"You rotten Earthling—" Robbins fist lashed out. It caught Hollister on the cheekbone and he stumbled back, shaking a dazed head. Robbins advanced grinning.

Hollister felt a cold viciousness of rage. It was his pseudopersonality he realized dimly but no time to think of that now. As Robbins closed in, he crouched and punched for the stomach.

Hard muscle met him. Robbins clipped him on the jaw. Hollister tried an uppercut, but it was skillfully blocked. This man knew how to fight.

Hollister gave him another fusillade in the belly. Robbins grunted and rabbit-punched. Hollister caught it on his shoulder, reached up, grabbed an arm, and whirled his enemy over his head. Robbins hit a bunk-frame that buckled under him.

He came back, dizzy but game. Hollister was well

trained in combat. But it took him a good ten minutes to stretch his man bleeding on the ground.

Panting, he looked about him. There was no expression on the faces that ringed him in. "Anybody else?" he asked hoarsely.

"No, boss," said Johnny. "You're right, o' course. I don't think nobody else here wants twenty lashes back at base."

"Who said—" Hollister straightened, blinking. "Lashes?"

"Why, sure. This was mutiny, you know. It's gotta be punished."

Hollister shook his head. "Too barbaric. Correction—"

"Look, boss," said Johnny, "you're a good engineer but you don't seem to understand much about Venus yet. We ain't got the time or the manpower or the materials to spend on them there corrective jails. A bull what don't keep his nose clean gets the whip or the sweatbox, and then back to the job. The really hard cases go to the uranium mines at Lucifer." He shivered, even in the dense heat.

Hollister frowned. "Not a bad system," he said, to stay in character. "But I think Robbins here has had enough. I'm not going to report him if he behaves himself from now on, and I'll trust the rest of you to cooperate."

They mumbled assent. He wasn't sure whether they respected him for it or not, but the boss was boss. Privately, he suspected that the Boards must frame a lot of men, or at least sentence them arbitrarily for minor crimes to keep the mines going; there didn't seem to be enough rebellion in the Venusian character to supply them otherwise.

Chalk up another point for the government. The score to settle was getting rather big.

IV

Time was hard to estimate on Venus; it wasn't only that they had their own calendar here, but one day was so much like another. Insensibly and despite himself, Hollister began sliding into the intellectual lethargy of the camp. He had read the few books—and with his trained memory, he could only read a book once—and he knew every man there inside out, and he had no family in one of the cities to write to and think about. The job itself presented a daily challenge, no two situations were ever quite the same and occasionally he came near death, but outside of it there was a tendency to stagnate.

The other two engineers, Gebhardt and Yamashita, were pleasant company. The first was from Hörselberg, which had been a German settlement and still retained some character of its own, and he had interesting stories to tell of it; the second, though of old Venus-American stock, was mentally agile for a colonist, had read more than most and had a lively interest in the larger world of the Solar System. But even the stimulation they offered wore a little thin in six months or so.

The region spun through a "winter' that was hardly different from summer except in having longer nights, and the sterile spring returned, and the work went on. Hollister's time sense ticked off days with an accuracy falling within a few seconds, and he wondered how long he would be kept here and when he would get a chance to report to his home office. That would be in letters ostensibly to friends, which one of the spaceships would carry back; he knew censors would read them first, but his code was keyed to an obscure eighteenth-century book he was certain no one on Venus had ever heard of.

Already he knew more about this planet than anyone on Earth. It had always seemed too expensive to send correspondents here, and the last couple of U.N. representatives hadn't found much to tell. That secretiveness toward Earthmen might be an old habit, going back to the ultra-nationalistic days of the last century. Colony A and Colony B, of two countries which at home might not be on speaking terms, were not supposed to give aid and comfort to each other; but on Venus such artificial barriers had to go if anyone was to survive. Yamashita told with relish how prospectors from Little Moscow and Trollen had worked together and divided up their finds. But of course, you couldn't let your nominal rulers know—

Hollister was beginning to realize that the essential ethos of Venus was, indeed, different from anything which existed on Earth. It had to be, the landscape had made it so. Man was necessarily a more collective creature than at home. That helped explain the evolution of the peculiar governmental forms and the patience of the citizenry toward the most outrageous demands. Even the dullest laborer seemed to live in the future.

Our children and grandchildren will build the temples, read the books, write the music. Ours is only to lay the foundation.

And was that why they stuck here, instead of shipping back and turning the whole job over to automatic machinery and a few paid volunteers? They had been the lonely, the rejected, the dwellers in outer darkness, for a long time; now they could not let go of their fierce and angry pride, even when there was no more need for it. Hollister thought about Ireland. Man is not a logical animal.

Still, there were features of Venusian society that struck him as unnecessary and menacing. Something would have to be done about them, though as yet he wasn't sure what it would be.

He worked, and he gathered impressions and filed them away, and he waited. And at last the orders came through. This camp had served its purpose, it was to be broken up and replanted elsewhere, but first its personnel were to report to New America and get a furlough. Hollister swung almost gaily into the work of dismantling everything portable and loading it in the wagons. Maybe he finally was going to get somewhere.

He reported at the Air Control office with Gebhardt and Yamashita, to get his pay and quarters assignment. The official handed him a small card. "You've been raised to chief engineer's rank," he said. "You'll probably get a camp of your own next time."

Gebhardt pounded him on the back. *Ach, sehr gut!* I recommended you, boy, you did fine, but I am going to miss you."

"Oh . . . we'll both be around for a while, won't we?" asked Hollister uncomfortably.

"Not I! I haff vife and kids, I hop the next rocket to Hörselberg."

Yamashita had his own family in town, and Hollister didn't want to intrude too much on them. He wandered off, feeling rather lonesome.

His new rating entitled him to private quarters, a tiny room with minimal furniture, though he still had to wash and eat publicly like everyone else except the very top. He sat down in it and began composing the planned letters.

There was a knock on the door. He fumbled briefly, being used to scanners at home and not used to doors on Venus, and finally said: "Come in."

A woman entered. She was young, quite good-looking, with a supple tread and spectacularly red hair. Cool green eyes swept up and down his height. "My name is Barbara Brandon," she said. "Administrative assistant in Air Control."

"Oh . . . hello." He offered her the chair. "You're here on business?"

Amusement tinged her impersonal voice. "In a way.

I'm going to marry you."

Hollister's jaw did not drop, but it tried. "Come again?" he asked weakly.

She sat down. "It's simple enough. I'm thirty-seven years old, which is almost the maximum permissible age of celibacy except in special cases." With a brief, unexpectedly feminine touch: "That's Venus years, of course! I've seen you around, and looked at your record; good heredity there. I think. Pops O.K.'d it genetically—that's Population Control—and the Guardians cleared it, too."

"Um-m-m . . . look here." Hollister wished there were room to pace. He settled for sitting on the table and swinging his legs. "Don't I get any say in the matter?"

"You can file any objections, of course, and probably they'd be heeded; but you'll have to have children by someone pretty soon. We need them. Frankly, I think a match between us would be ideal. You'll be out in the field so much that we won't get in each other's hair, and we'd probably get along well enough while we are together."

Hollister scowled. It wasn't the morality of it—much. He was a bachelor on Earth, secret service Un-men really had no business getting married; and in any case the law would wink at what he had done on Venus if he ever got home. But something about the whole approach annoyed him.

"I can't see where you need rules to make people breed," he said coldly. "They'll do that anyway. You don't realize what a struggle it is on Earth to bring the population back down toward a sensible figure."

"Things are different here," answered Barbara Brandon in a dry tone. "We're going to need plenty of people for a long time to come, and they have to be of the right stock. The congenitally handicapped can't produce enough to justify their own existence; there's been a program of euthanasia here, as you may know. But the new people are also needed in the right places. This town, for instance, can only accommodate so much population increase per year. We can't send surplus children off to a special crèche because there aren't enough teachers or doctors or anything, so the mothers have to take care of all their own kids; or the fathers, if they happen to have a job in town and the mother is a field worker. The whole process has *got* to be regulated."

"Regulations!" Hollister threw up his hands. "Behold the bold frontiersman!"

The girl looked worried. "Careful what you say." She smiled at him with a touch of wistfulness. "It needn't be such a hindrance to you. Things are . . . pretty free except where the production of children is involved."

"I—This is kind of sudden." Hollister tried to smile back. "Don't think I don't appreciate the compliment. But I need time to think, adjust myself—Look, are you busy right now?"

"No, I'm off."

"All right. Put on your party clothes and we'll go out and have some drinks and talk the matter over."

She glanced shyly at the thin, colored coverall she wore. "These are my party clothes," she said.

Hollister's present rank let him visit another bar than the long, crowded room where plain laborers caroused. This one had private tables, decorations, music in the dim dusky air. It was quiet, the engineer aristocracy had their own code of manners. A few couples danced on a small floor.

He found an unoccupied table by the curving wall, sat down, and dialed for drinks and cigarettes. Neither were good enough to justify their fantastic cost, but it had been a long time since he had enjoyed any luxuries at all. He felt more relaxed with them. The girl looked quite beautiful in the muted light.

"You were born here, weren't you, Barbara?" he asked

after a while.

"Of course," she said. "You're the first immigrant in a long time. Used to be some deportees coming in every once in a while, but—"

"I know. 'Sentence suspended on condition you leave Earth.' That was before all countries had adopted the new penal code. Never mind. I was just wondering if you wouldn't like to see Earth—sometime."

"Maybe. But I'm needed here, not there. And I like it." There was a hint of defiance in the last remark.

He didn't press her. The luminous murals showed a soft unreal landscape of lakes and forests, artificial stars twinkled gently in the ceiling. "Is this what you expect Venus to become?" he asked.

"Something like this. Probably not the stars, it'll always be cloudy here, but they'll be honest rain clouds. We should live to see the beginning of it."

"Barbara," he asked, "do you believe in God?"

"Why, no. Some of the men are priests and rabbis and whatnot in their spare time, but—No, not I. What about it?"

"You're wrong," he said. "Venus is your god. This is a religious movement you have here, with a slide rule in its hand."

"So—?" She seemed less assured, he had her off balance and the green eyes were wide and a little frightened.

"An Old Testament god," he pursued, "merciless, all-powerful, all-demanding. Get hold of a Bible if you can, and read Job and Ecclesiastes. You'll see what I mean. When is the New Testament coming . . . or even the prophet Micah?"

"You're a funny one," she said uncertainly. Frowning, trying to answer him on his own terms. "After the Big Rain, things will be easier. It'll be—" She struggled through vague memories. "It'll be the Promised Land."

"You've got this one life," he said. "Is there any sound

reason for spending it locked in these iron boxes, with death outside, when you could lie on a beach on Earth and everything you're fighting for is already there?"

She grabbed his hand where it lay on the table. Her fingers were cold, and she breathed fast. "No! Don't say such things! You're here too. You came here—"

Get thee behind me, Satan.

"Sorry." He lifted his glass. "Here's freefalling."

She clinked with him smiling shakily.

"There isn't any retirement on Venus, is there?" he asked.

"Not exactly. Old people get lighter work, of course. When you get too old to do anything . . . well, wouldn't you want euthanasia?"

He nodded, quite sincerely, though his exact meaning had gone by her. "I was just thinking of . . . shall we say us . . . rose-covered cottages, sunset of life. Darby and Joan stuff."

She smiled, and reached over to stroke his cheek lightly. "Thanks," she murmured. "Maybe there will be rose-covered cottages by the time we're that old."

Hollister turned suddenly, aware with his peripheral senses of the man who approached. Or maybe it was the sudden choking off of low-voiced conversation in the bar. The man walked very softly up to their table and stood looking down on them. Then he pulled out the extra chair for himself.

"Hello, Karsov," said Hollister dully.

The Guardian nodded. There was a ghostly smile playing about his lips. "How are you?" he asked, with an air of not expecting a reply. "I am glad you did so well out there. Your chief recommended you very highly."

"Thanks," said Hollister, not hiding the chill in his voice. He didn't like the tension he could see in Barbara.

"I just happened by and thought you would like to know you will have a crew of your own next trip," said the policeman. "That is, the Air Control office has made a recommendation to me." He glanced archly at Barbara. "Did you by any chance have something to do with that, Miss Brandon? Could be!" Then his eyes fell to the cigarettes, and he regarded them pointedly till Barbara offered him one.

"Pardon me." Hollister held his temper with an effort and kept his voice urbane. "I'm still new here, lot of things I don't know. Why does your office have to pass on such a matter?"

"My office has to pass on everything," said Karsov.

"Seems like a purely technical business, as long as my own record is clean."

Karsov shook his sleek head. "You do not understand. We cannot have someone in a responsible position who is not entirely trustworthy. It is more than a matter of abstaining from criminal acts. You have to be with us all the way. No reservations. That is what Psych Control and the Guardians exist for."

He blew smoke through his nose and went on in a casual tone: "I must say your attitude has not been entirely pleasing. You have made some remarks which could be . . . misconstrued. I am ready to allow for your not being used to Venusian conditions, but you know the law about sedition."

For a moment, Hollister savored the thought of Karsov's throat between his fingers. "I'm sorry," he said.

"Remember, there are recorders everywhere, and we make spot checks directly on people, too. You could be narocquizzed again any time I ordered it. But I do not think that will be necessary just yet. A certain amount of grumbling is only natural, and if you have any genuine complaints you can file them with your local Technic Board."

Hollister weighed the factors in his mind. Karsov packed a gun, and— But too sudden a meekness could be no less suspicious. "I don't quite understand why you have to have a political police," he ventured. "It seems like an ordinary force should be enough. After all . . . where would an insurrectionist go?"

He heard Barbara's tiny gasp, but Karsov merely looked patient. "There are many factors involved," said the Guardian. "For instance, some of the colonies were not quite happy with the idea of being incorporated into the Venusian Federation. They preferred to stay with their mother countries, or even to be independent. Some fighting ensued, and they must still be watched. Then, too, it is best to keep Venusian society healthy while it is new and vulnerable to subversive radical ideas. And finally, the Guardian Corps is the nucleus of our future army and space navy."

Hollister wondered if he should ask why Venus needed military forces, but decided against it. The answer would only be some stock phrase about terrestrial imperialists, if he got any answer at all. He'd gone about far enough already.

"I see," he said. "Thanks for telling me."

"Would you like a drink, sir?" asked Barbara timidly.

"No," said Karsov. "I only stopped in on my way elsewhere. Work, always work." He got up. "I think you are making a pretty good adjustment, Hollister. Just watch your tongue . . . and your mind. Oh, by the way. Under the circumstances, it would be as well if you did not write any letters home for a while. That could be misunderstood. You may use one of the standard messages. They are much cheaper, too." He nodded and left.

Hollister's eyes followed him out. *How much does he know?*

"Come on," said Barbara. There was a little catch in her voice. "Let's dance."

Gradually they relaxed, easing into the rhythm of the music. Hollister dismissed the problem of Karsov for the time being, and bent mind and senses to his companion. She was lithe and slim in his arms, and he felt the stirrings of an old hunger in him.

The next Venus day he called on Yamashita. They had a pleasant time together, and arranged a party for later; Hollister would bring Barbara. But as he was leaving, the Venusian drew him aside.

"Be careful, Si," he whispered. "They were here a few hours after I got back, asking me up and down about you. I had to tell the truth, they know how to ask questions and if I'd hesitated too much it would have been narco. I don't think you're in any trouble, but be careful!"

Barbara had arranged her vacation to coincide with his—efficient girl! They were together most of the time. It wasn't many days before they were married. That was rushing things, but Hollister would soon be back in the field for a long stretch and—well—they had fallen in love. Under the circumstances, it was inevitable. Curious how it broke down the girl's cool self-possession, but that only made her more human and desirable.

He felt like a thorough skunk, but maybe she was right. *Carpe diem*. If he ever pulled out of this mess, he'd just have to pull her out with him; meanwhile, he accepted the additional complication of his assignment. It looked as if that would drag on for years, anyhow; maybe a lifetime.

They blew themselves to a short honeymoon at a high-class—and expensive—resort by Thunder Gorge, one of Venus' few natural beauty spots. The atmosphere at the lodge was relaxed, congenial, not a Guardian in sight and more privacy than elsewhere on the planet. Psych Control was shrewd enough to realize that people need an occasional surcease from all duty, some flight from the real world of sand and stone and steel. It helped keep them sane.

Even so, there was a rather high proportion of mental disease. It was a taboo subject, but Hollister got a doctor drunk and wormed the facts out of him. The psychotic were not sent back to Earth, as they could have been at no charge; they might talk too much. Nor were there facilities for proper treatment on Venus. If the most drastic procedures didn't restore a patient to some degree of usefulness in a short time—they had even revived the barbarism of prefontal lobotomy!—he was quietly gassed.

"But it'll all be diff'rent af'er uh Big Rain," said the doctor. "My son ull have uh real clinic, he will."

More and more, Hollister doubted it.

A few sweet crazy days, and vacation's end was there and they took the rocket back to New America. It was the first time Hollister had seen Barbara cry.

He left her sitting forlornly in the little two-room apartment they now rated, gathering herself to arrange the small heap of their personal possessions, and reported to Air Control. The assistant super gave him a thick, bound sheaf of papers.

"Here are orders and specs," he said. "You can have two days to study them." Hollister, who could memorize the lot in a few hours, felt a leap of gladness at the thought of so much free time. The official leaned back in his chair. He was a gnarled old man, retired to a desk after a lifetime of field duty. One cheek was puckered with the scars of an operation for the prevalent HR cancer; Venus had no germs, but prepared her own special death traps. "Relax for a minute and I'll give you the general idea."

He pointed to a large map on the wall. It was not very complete or highly accurate: surveying on this planet was a job to break a man's heart, and little had been done. "We're establishing your new camp out by Last Chance. You'll note that Little Moscow, Trollen, and Roger's Landing cluster around it at an average distance of two hundred kilometers, so that's where you'll be getting your supplies, sending men on leave, and so forth. I doubt if you'll have any occasion to report back here till you break camp completely in a couple of years."

And Barbara will be here alone, Barbara and our child whom I won't even see—

"You'll take your wagon train more or less along this route," went on the super, indicating a dotted line that ran from New America. "It's been gone over and is safe. Notice the eastward jog to Lucifer at the half-way point. That's to refuel and take on fresh food stores."

Hollister frowned, striving for concentration on the job. "I can't see that. Why not take a few extra wagons and omit the detour?"

"Orders," said the super.

Whose orders? Karsov's, I'll bet my air helmet—but why?

"Your crew will be . . . kind of tough," said the old man. "They're mostly from Ciudad Alcazar, which is on the other side of the world. It was one of the stubborn colonies when we declared independence, had to be put down by force, and it's still full of sedition. These spigs are all hard cases who've been assigned to this hemisphere so they won't stir up trouble at home. I saw in your dossier that you speak Spanish, among other languages, which is one reason you're being given this bunch. You'll have to treat them rough, remember. Keep them in line."

I think there was more than one reason behind this.

"The details are all in your assignment book," said the super. "Report back here in two days, this time. O.K.—have fun!" He smiled, suddenly friendly now that his business was completed.

V

Darkness and a whirl of poison sleet turned the buildings into crouching black monsters, hardly to be told from the ragged snarl of crags which ringed them in. Hollister brought his tank to a grinding halt before a tower which fixed him with a dazzling floodlight eye. "Sit tight, Diego," he said, and slapped his helmet down.

His chief assistant, Fernandez, nodded a sullen dark head. He was competent enough, and had helped keep the unruly crew behaving itself, but remained cold toward his boss. There was always a secret sworn in his eyes.

Hollister wriggled through the air lock and dropped to the ground. A man in a reinforced, armorlike suit held a tommy-gun on him, but dropped the muzzle as he advanced. The blast of white light showed a stupid face set in lines of habitual brutality.

"You the airman come for supplies?"

"Yes. Can I see your chief?"

The guard turned wordlessly and led the way. Beyond the lock of the main shell was a room where men sat with rifles. Hollister was escorted to an inner office, where a middle-aged, rather mild-looking fellow in Guardian uniform greeted him. "How do you do? We had word you were coming. The supplies were brought to our warehouse and you can load them when you wish."

Hollister accepted a chair. "I'm Captain Thomas," the other continued. "Nice to have you. We don't see many new faces at Lucifer—not men you can talk to, anyway. How are things in New America?"

He gossiped politely for a while. "It's quite a remarkable installation we have here," he ended. "Would you like to see it?"

Hollister grimaced. "No, thanks."

"Oh, I really must insist. You and your chief assistant and one or two of the foremen. They'll all be interested, and can tell the rest of your gang how it is. There's so little to talk about out in camp."

Hollister debated refusing outright and forcing Thomas to show his hand. But why bother? Karsov had given orders, and Thomas would conduct him around at gun point if necessary. "O.K., thanks," he said coldly. "Let me get my men bunked down first, though."

"Of course. We have a spare barracks for transients. I'll expect you in two hours . . . with three of your men, remember."

Diego Fernandez only nodded when Hollister gave him the news. The chief skinned his teeth in a bleak sort of grin. "Don't forget to 'oh' and 'ah', " he said. "Our genial host will be disappointed if you don't, and he's a man I'd hate to disappoint."

The smoldering eyes watched him with a quizzical expression that faded back into blankness. "I shall get Gomez and San Rafael," said Fernandez. "They have strong stomachs."

Thomas received them almost unctuously and started walking down a series of compartments. "As engineers, you will be most interested in the mine itself," he said. "I'll show you a little of it. This is the biggest uranium deposit known in the Solar System."

He led them to the great cell block, where a guard with a shock gun fell in behind them. "Have to be careful," said Thomas. "We've got some pretty desperate characters here, who don't feel they have much to lose."

"All lifers, eh?" asked Hollister.

Thomas looked surprised. "Of course! We couldn't let them go back after what the radiation does to their germ-plasm."

A man rattled the bars of his door as they passed. "I'm from New America!" His harsh scream bounded between steel walls. "Do you know my wife? Is Martha Riley all right?"

"Shut up!" snapped the guard, and fed him a shock beam. He lurched back into the darkness of his cell. His mate, whose face was disfigured by a cancer, eased him to his bunk.

Someone else yelled, far down the long white-lit rows.

A guard came running from that end. The voice pleaded: "It's a nightmare. It's just a nightmare. The stuff's got intuh muh brains and I'm always dreamin' nightmares—"

"They get twitchy after a while," said Thomas. "Stuff *will* seep through the suits and lodge in their bodies. Then they're not much good for anything but pick-and-shovel work. Don't be afraid, gentlemen, we have reinforced suits for the visitors and guards."

These were donned at the end of the cell block. Beyond the double door, a catwalk climbed steeply, till they were on the edge of an excavation which stretched farther than they could see in the gloom.

"It's rich enough yet for open pit mining," said Thomas, "though we're driving tunnels, too." He pointed to a giant scooper. Tiny shapes of convicts scurried about it. "Four-hour shifts because of the radiation down there. Don't believe those rumors that we aren't careful with our boys. Some of them live for thirty years."

Hollister's throat felt cottony. It would be so easy to rip off Thomas' air hose and kick him down into the pit! "What about women prisoners?" he asked slowly. "You must get some."

"Oh, yes. Right down there with the men. We believe in equality on Venus."

There was a strangled sound in the earphones, but Hollister wasn't sure which of his men had made it.

"Very essential work here," said Thomas proudly. "We refine the ore right on the spot too, you know. It not only supplies such nuclear power as Venus needs, but exported to Earth it buys the things we still have to have from them."

"Why operate it with convict labor?" asked Hollister absently. His imagination was wistfully concentrated on the image of himself branding his initials on Thomas' anatomy. "You could use free men, taking proper precautions, and it would be a lot more efficient and economical of manpower."

"You don't understand." Thomas seemed a bit shocked. "These are enemies of the state."

I've read that line in the history books. Some state, if it makes itself that many enemies!

"The refinery won't interest you so much," said Thomas. "Standard procedure, and it's operated by nonpolitical prisoners under shielding. They get skilled, and become too valuable to lose. But no matter who a man is, how clever he is, if he's been convicted of treason he goes to the mine."

So this was a warning—or was it a provocation?

When they were back in the office, Thomas smiled genially. "I hope you gentlemen have enjoyed the tour," he said. "Do stop in and see me again sometime." He held out his hand. Hollister turned on his heel, ignoring the gesture, and walked out.

Even in the line of duty, a man can only do so much.

Somewhat surprisingly Hollister found himself getting a little more popular with his crew after the visit to Lucifer. The three who were with him must have seen his disgust and told about it. He exerted himself to win more of their friendship, without being too obtrusive about it: addressing them politely, lending a hand himself in the task of setting up camp, listening carefully to complaints about not feeling well instead of dismissing them all as malingering. That led to some trouble. One laborer who was obviously faking a stomach-ache was ordered back to the job and made an insulting crack. Hollister knocked him to the floor with a single blow. Looking around at the others present, he said slowly: "There will be no whippings in this camp, because I do not believe men should be treated thus. But I intend to remain chief and to get this business done." Nudging the fallen man with his foot: "Well, go on back to your work. This is forgotten, also in the records I am supposed to keep."

He didn't feel proud of himself—the man had been smaller and weaker than he. But he had to have discipline, and the Venusians all seemed brutalized to a point where the only unanswerable argument was force. It was an inevitable consequence of their type of government, and boded ill for the future.

Somewhat later, his radio-electronics technie, Valdez—a soft-spoken little fellow who did not seem to have any friends in camp—found occasion to speak with him. "It seems that you have unusual ideas about running this operation, señor," he remarked.

"I'm supposed to get the airmakers installed," said Hollister. "That part of it is right on schedule."

"I mean with regard to your treatment of the men, señor. You are the mildest chief they have had. I wish to say that it is appreciated, but some of them are puzzled. If I may give you some advice which is doubtless not needed, it would be best if they knew exactly what to expect."

Hollister felt bemused. "Fairness, as long as they do their work. What is so strange about that?"

"But some of us . . . them . . . have unorthodox ideas about politics."

"That is their affair, Señnor Valdez." Hollister decided to make himself a little more human in the technie's eyes. "I have a few ideas of my own, too."

"Ah, so. Then you will permit free discussion in the barracks?"

"Of course."

"I have hidden the recorder in there very well. Do you wish to hear the tapes daily, or shall I just make a summary?"

"I don't want to hear any tapes," stated Hollister. "That machine will not be operated."

"But they might plan treason!"

Hollister laughed and swept his hand around the wall. "In the middle of *that?* Much good may their plans do them!" Gently: "All of you may say what you will among yourselves. I am an engineer, not a secret policeman."

"I see, señor. You are very generous. Believe me, it is appreciated."

Three days later, Valdez was dead.

Hollister had sent him out with a crew to run some performance tests on the first of the new airmakers. The men came back agitatedly, to report that a short, sudden rockstorm had killed the technie. Hollister frowned, to cover his pity for the poor lonely little guy. "Where is the body?" he asked.

"Out there, señor — where else?"

Hollister knew it was the usual practice to leave men who died in the field where they fell; after Venusian conditions had done their work, it wasn't worthwhile salvaging the corpse for its chemicals. But — "Have I not announced my policy?" he snapped. "I thought that you people, of all, would be glad of it. Dead men will be kept here, so we can haul them into town and have them properly buried. Does not your religion demand that?"

"But Valdez, señor — "

"Never mind! Back you go, at once, and this time bring him in." Hollister turned his attention to the problem of filling the vacancy. Control wasn't going to like him asking for another so soon; probably he couldn't get one anyway. Well, he could train Fernandez to handle the routine parts, and do the more exacting things himself.

He was sitting in his room that night, feeling acutely the isolation of a commander — too tired to add another page to his letter to Barbara, not tired enough to go to sleep. There was a knock on the door. His start told him how thin his nerves were worn. "Come in!"

Diego Fernandez entered. The chill white fluorolight showed fear in his eyes and along his mouth. "Good evening, Simón," he said tonelessly. They had gotten to the stage of first names, though they still addressed each other with the formal pronoun.

"Good evening, Diego. What is it?"

The other bit his lip and looked at the floor. Hollister did not try to hurry him. Outside, the wind was running and great jags of lightning sizzled across an angry sky, but this room was buried deep and very quiet.

Fernandez's eyes rose at last. "There is something you ought to know, Simón. Perhaps you already know it."

"And perhaps not, Diego. Say what you will. There are no recorders here."

"Well, then, Valdez was not accidentally killed. He was murdered."

Hollister sat utterly still.

"You did not look at the body very closely, did you?" went on Fernandez, word by careful word. "I have seen suits torn open by flying rocks. This was not such a one. Some instrument did it . . . a compressed-air drill, I think."

"And do you know why it was done?"

"Yes." Fernandez's face twisted. "I cannot say it was not a good deed. Valdez was a spy for the government."

Hollister felt a knot in his stomach. "How do you know this?"

"One can be sure of such things. After the . . . the Venusians had taken Alcazar, Valdez worked eagerly with their police. He had always believed in confederation and planetary independence. Then he went away, to some engineering assignment it was said. But he had a brother who was proud of the old hidalgo blood, and this brother sought to clear the shame of his family by warning that Valdez had taken a position with the Guardians. He told it secretly, for he was not supposed to, but most of Alcazar got to know it. Then men who had fought against the invaders were sent here, to the other side of the world, and it is not often we get leave to go home even for a short while. But we remembered, and we knew Valdez when he appeared on this job. So when those men with him had a chance to revenge themselves, they took it."

Hollister fixed the brown eyes with his own. "Why do you tell me this?" he asked.

"I do not—quite know. Except that you have been a good chief. It would be best for us if we could keep you and this may mean trouble for you."

I'll say! First I practically told Valdez how I feel about the government, then he must have transmitted it with the last radio report, and now he's dead. Hollister chose his words cautiously: "Have you thought that the best way I can save myself is to denounce those men?"

"They would go to Lucifer, Simón."

"I know." He weighed the factors, surprised at his own detached calm. On the one hand there were Barbara and himself, and his own mission; on the other hand were half a dozen men who would prove most valuable come the day—for it was becoming more and more clear that the sovereign state of Venus would have to be knocked down, the sooner the better.

Beyond a small ache, he did not consider the personal element; Un-man training was too strong in him for that. A melody skipped through his head. *"Here's a how-de-do—"* It was more than a few men, he decided; this whole crew, all fifty or so, had possibilities. A calculated risk was in order.

"I did not hear anything you said," he spoke aloud. "Nor did you ever have any suspicions. It is obvious that Valdez died accidentally—too obvious to question."

Fernandez's smile flashed through the sweat that covered his face. "Thank you, Simón!"

"Thanks to *you*, Diego." Hollister gave him a drink—the boss was allowed a few bottles—and sent him on his way.

The boss was also allowed a .45 magnum automatic, the only gun in camp. Hollister took it out and checked it carefully. What was that classic verdict of a coroner's jury, a century or more ago in the States? "An act of God under very suspicious circumstances." He grinned to himself. It was not a pleasant expression.

VI

The rocket landed three days later. Hollister, who had been told by radio to expect it but not told why, was waiting outside. A landing space had been smoothed off and marked, and he had his men standing by and the tanks and bulldozers parked close to hand. Ostensibly that was to give any help which might be needed; actually, he hoped they would mix in on his side if trouble started. Power-driven sand blasts and arc welders were potentially nasty weapons, and tanks and 'dozers could substitute for armored vehicles in a pinch. The gun hung at his waist.

There was a mild breeze, for Venus, but it drove a steady scud of sand across the broken plain. The angry storm-colored light was diffused by airborne dust till it seemed to pervade the land, and even through his helmet and earphones Hollister was aware of the wind-yammer and the remote banging of thunder.

A new racket grew in heaven, stabbing jets and then the downward hurtle of sleek metal. The rocket's glider wings were fully extended, braking her against the updraft, and the pilot shot brief blasts to control his yawing vessel and bring her down on the markings. Wheels struck the hard-packed sand, throwing up a wave of it; landing flaps strained, a short burst from the nose jet arched its back against the flier's momentum, and then the machine lay still.

Hollister walked up to it. Even with the small quick-type air lock, he had to wait a couple of minutes before two suited figures emerged. One was obviously the pilot; the other—

"Barbara!"

Her face had grown thin, he saw through the helmet plate, and the red hair was disordered. He pulled her to him, and felt his faceplate clank on hers. "Barbara! What brings you here? Is everything all right?"

She tried to smile. "Not so public. Let's get inside."

The pilot stayed, to direct the unloading of what little equipment had been packed along; a trip was never wasted. Fernandez could do the honors afterward. Hollister led his wife to his own room, and no words were said for a while.

Her lips and hands felt cold.

"What is it, Barbara?" he asked when he finally came up for air. "How do we rate this?"

She didn't quite meet his eyes. "Simple enough. We're not going to have a baby after all. Since you'll be in the field for a long time, and I'm required to be a mother soon, it . . . it wasn't so hard to arrange a leave for me. I'll be here for ten days."

That was almost an Earth month. The luxury was unheard-of. Hollister sat down on his bunk and began to think.

"What's the matter?" She rumpled his hair. "Aren't you glad to see me? Maybe you have a girl lined up in Trollen?"

Her tone wasn't quite right, somehow. In many ways she was still a stranger to him, but he knew she wouldn't banter him with just that inflection. Or did she really think— "I'd no such intention," he said.

"Of course not, you jethead! I trust you." Barbara stretched herself luxuriously. "Isn't this wonderful?"

Yeah . . . too wonderful. "Why do we get it?"

"I told you." She looked surprised. "We've got to have a child."

He said grimly, "I can't see that it's so all-fired urgent.

If it were, it'd be easier, and right in line with the Board's way of thing, to use artificial insemination." He stood up and gripped her shoulders and looked straight at her. "Barbara, why are you really here?"

She began to cry, and that wasn't like her either. He patted her and mumbled awkward phrases, feeling himself a louse. But something was very definitely wrong, and he had to find out what.

He almost lost his resolution as the day went on. He had to be outside most of that time, supervising and helping; he noticed that several of the men had again become frigid to him. Was that Karsov's idea — to drive a wedge between him and his crew by giving him an unheard-of privilege? Well, maybe partly, but it could not be the whole answer. When he came back, Barbara had unpacked and somehow, with a few small touches, turned his bleak little bedroom-office into a home. She was altogether gay and charming and full of hope.

The rocket had left, the camp slept, they had killed a bottle to celebrate and now they were alone in darkness. In such a moment of wonder, it was hard to keep a guard up.

"Maybe you'll appreciate the Board a little more," she sighed. "They aren't machines. They're human, and know that we are, too."

" 'Human' is a pretty broad term," he murmured, almost automatically. "The guards at Lucifer are human, I suppose."

Her hand stole out to stroke his cheek. "Things aren't perfect on Venus," she said. "Nobody claims they are. But after the Big Rain—"

"Yeah. The carrot in front and the stick behind, and on the burro trots. He doesn't stop to ask where the road is leading. I could show it by psychodynamic equations, but even an elementary reading of history is enough: once a group gets power, it *never* gives it up freely."

"There was Kemal Atatürk, back around 1920, wasn't there?"

"Uh-huh. A very exceptional case: the hard-boiled, practical man who was still an idealist, and built his structure so well that his successors — who'd grown up under him — neither could nor wanted to continue the dictatorship. It's an example which the U.N. Inspectorate on Earth has studied closely and tried to adapt, so that its own power won't some day be abused."

"The government of Venus just isn't that sort. Their tactics prove it. Venus has to be collective till the Big Rain, I suppose, but that doesn't give anyone the right to collectivize the minds of men. By the time this hell-hole is fit for human life, the government will be unshakeably in the saddle. Basic principle of psychobiology: survival with least effort. In human society, one of the easiest ways to survive and grow fat is to rule your fellow men.

"It's significant that you've learned about Atatürk. How much have they told you about the Soviet Union? The state was supposed to wither away there, too."

"Would you actually . . . conspire to revolt?" she asked.

He slammed the brakes so hard that his body jerked. *Danger! Danger! Danger! How did I get into this? What am I saying? Why is she asking me?* With a single bound, he was out of bed and had snapped on the light.

Its glare hurt his eyes, and Barbara covered her face. He drew her hands away, gently but using his strength against her resistance. The face that looked up at him was queerly distorted; the lines were still there, but they had become something not quite human.

"Who put you up to this?" he demanded.

"No one . . . what are you talking about, what's wrong?"

"The perfect spy," he said bitterly. "A man's own wife."

"What do you mean?" She sat up, staring wildly through her tousled hair. "Have you gone crazy?"

"*Could* you be a spy?"

"I'm not," she gasped. "I swear I'm not."

"I didn't ask if you were. What I want to know is could you be a spy?"

"I'm not. It's impossible. I'm not—" She was screaming now, but the thick walls would muffle that.

"Karsov is going to send me to Lucifer," he flung at her. "Isn't he?"

"I'm not, I'm not, I'm not—"

He stabbed the questions at her, one after another, slapping when she got hysterical. The first two times she fainted, he brought her around again and continued; the third time, he called it off and stood looking down on her.

There was no fear or rage left in him, not even pity. He felt strangely empty. There seemed to be a hollowness inside his skull, the hollow man went through the motions of life and his brain still clicked rustily, but there was nothing inside, he was a machine.

The perfect spy, he thought. *Except that Karsov didn't realize Un-men have advanced psych training. I know such a state as hers when I see it.*

The work had been cleverly done, using the same drugs and machines and conditioning techniques which had given him his own personality mask. (No—not quite the same. The Venusians didn't know that a mind could be so deeply verbal-conditioned as to get by a narcoquiz; that was a guarded secret of the Inspectorate. But the principles were there.) Barbara did not remember being taken to the laboratories and given the treatment. She did not know she had been conditioned; consciously, she believed everything she had said, and it had been anguish when the man she loved turned on her.

But the command had been planted, to draw his real thoughts out of him. Almost, she had succeeded. And when she went back, a quiz would get her observations out of her in detail.

It would have worked, too, on an ordinary conspirator. Even if he had come to suspect the truth, an untrained man wouldn't have known just how to throw her conscious and subconscious minds into conflict, wouldn't have recognized her symptomatic reactions for what they were.

This tears it, thought Hollister. *This rips it wide open.* He didn't have the specialized equipment to mask Barbara's mind and send her back with a lie that could get past the Guardian psychotechnics. Already she knew enough to give strong confirmation to Karsov's suspicions. After he had her account, Hollister would be arrested and they'd try to wring his secrets out of him. That might or might not be possible, but there wouldn't be anything left of Hollister.

Not sending her back at all? No, it would be every bit as much of a giveaway, and sacrifice her own life to boot. Not that she might not go to Lucifer anyhow.

Well—

The first thing was to remove her conditioning. He could do that in a couple of days by simple hypnotherapy. The medicine chest held some drugs which would be useful. After that—

First things first. Diego can take charge for me while I'm doing it. Let the men think what they want. They're going to have plenty to think about soon.

He became aware of his surroundings again and of the slim form beneath his eyes. She had curled up in a fetal position, trying to escape. Emotions came back to him, and the first was an enormous compassion for her. He would have wept, but there wasn't time.

Barbara sat up in bed, leaning against his breast. "Yes," she said tonelessly. "I remember it all now."

"There was a child coming, wasn't there?"

"Of course. They . . . removed it." Her hand sought

his. "You might have suspected something otherwise. I'm all right, though. We can have another one sometime, if we live that long."

"And did Karsov tell you what he thought about me?"

"He mentioned suspecting you were an Un-man, but not being sure. The Technic Board wouldn't let him have you unless he had good evidence. That—No, I don't remember any more. It's fuzzy in my mind, everything which happened in that room."

Hollister wondered how he had betrayed himself. Probably he hadn't; his grumblings had fitted in with his assumed personality, and there had been no overt acts. But still, it was Karsov's job to suspect everybody, and the death of Valdez must have decided him on drastic action.

"Do you feel all right, sweetheart?" asked Hollister.

She nodded, and turned around to give him a tiny smile. "Yes. Fine. A little weak, maybe, but otherwise fine. I'm only scared."

"You have a right to be," he said bleakly. "We're in a devil of a fix."

"You *are* an Un-man, aren't you?"

"Yes. I was sent to study the Venusian situation. My chiefs were worried about it. Seems they were justified, too. I've never seen a nastier mess."

"I suppose you're right," she sighed. "Only what else could we do? Do you want to bring Venus back under Earth?"

"That's a lot of comet gas, and you'd know it if the nationalist gang hadn't been censoring the books and spewing their lies out since before you were born. This whole independence movement was obviously their work from the beginning, and I must say they've done a competent job; good psychotechnies among them. It's their way to power. Not that all of them are so cynical about it—a lot must have rationalizations of one sort or another—but that's what it amounts to.

"There's no such thing as Venus being 'under' Earth. If

ready for independence—and I agree she is—she'd be made a state in her own right with full U.N. membership. It's written into the charter that she could make her own internal policy. The only restrictions on a nation concern a few matters of trade, giving up military forces and the right to make war, guaranteeing certain basic liberties, submitting to inspection, and paying her share of U.N. expenses—which are smaller than the cost of even the smallest army. That's all. Your nationalists have distorted the truth as their breed always does."

She rubbed her forehead in a puzzled way. He could sympathize: a lifetime of propaganda wasn't thrown off overnight. But as long as she was with his cause, the rest would come of itself.

"There's no excuse whatsoever for this tyranny you live under," he continued. "It's got to go."

"What would you have us do?" she asked. "This isn't Earth. We do things efficiently here, or we die."

"True. But even men under the worst conditions can afford the slight inefficiency of freedom. It's not my business to write a constitution for Venus, but you might look at how Mars operates. They also have to have requirements of professional competence for public office, but anyone can enter the schools—deadwood gets flunked out fast enough—and the graduates have to stand for election if they want policy-making posts. Periodic elections do not necessarily pick better men than an appointive system, but they keep power from concentrating in the leaders. The Martians also have to ration a lot of things, and forbid certain actions that would endanger a whole city, but they're free to choose their own residences, and families, and ways of thinking, and jobs. They're also trying to reclaim the whole planet, but they don't assign men to that work, they hire them for it."

"Why doesn't everyone just stay at home and do

nothing?" she asked innocently.

"No work, no pay; no pay, nothing to eat. It's as simple as that. And when jobs open in the field, and all the jobs in town are filled, men will take work in the field — as free men, free to quit if they wish. Not many do, because the bosses aren't little commissars.

"Don't you see, it's the *mass* that society has to regulate; a government has to set things up so that the statistics come out right. There's no reason to regulate individuals."

"What's the difference?" she inquired.

"A hell of a difference. Some day you'll see it. Meanwhile, though, something has to be done about the government of Venus — not only on principle, but because it's going to be a menace to Earth before long. Once Venus is strong, a peaceful, nearly unarmed Earth is going to be just too tempting for your dictators. The World Wars had this much value, they hammered it into our heads and left permanent memorials of destruction to keep reminding us, that the time to cut out a cancer is when it first appears. Wars start for a variety of reasons, but unlimited national sovereignty is always the necessary and sufficient condition. I wish our agents had been on the ball with respect to Venus ten years ago; a lot of good men are going to die because they weren't."

"You might not have come here then," she said shyly.

"Thanks, darling." He kissed her. His mind whirred on, scuttling through a maze that seemed to lead only to his silent, pointless death.

"If I could just get a report back to Earth! That would settle the matter. We'd have spaceships landing U.N. troops within two years. An expensive operation, of doubtful legality perhaps, a tough campaign so far from home, especially since we wouldn't want to destroy any cities — but there'd be no doubt of the outcome, and it would surely be carried through; because it would be a matter of survival for us. Of course, the rebellious cities would be helpful, a deal could be made there—and so simple a thing as seizing the food-producing towns would soon force a surrender. You see, it's not only the warning I've got to get home, it's the utterly priceless military intelligence I've got in my head. If I fail, the Guardians will be on the alert, they may very well succeed in spotting and duping every agent sent after me and flanging up something for Earth's consumption. Venus is a long ways off—"

He felt her body tightening in his arms. "So you do want to take over Venus."

"Forget that hogwash, will you? What'd we want with this forsaken desert? Nothing but a trustworthy government for it. Anyway—" His exasperation became a flat hardness: "If you and I are to stay alive much longer it has to be done."

She said nothing to that.

His mind clicked off astronomical data and the slide rule whizzed through his fingers. "The freighters come regularly on Hohmann 'A' orbits," he said. "That means the next one is due in eight Venus days. They've only got four-man crews, they come loaded with stuff and go back with uranium and thorium ingots which don't take up much room. In short, they could carry quite a few passengers in an emergency, if those had extra food supplies."

"And the ferries land at New America," she pointed out.

"Exactly. My dear, I think our only chance is to take over the whole city!"

It was hot in the barracks room, and rank with sweat. Hollister thought he could almost smell the fear, as if he were a dog. He stood on a table at one end, Barbara next to him, and looked over his assembled crew. Small, thin, swarthy, unarmed and drably clad, eyes wide with frightened waiting, they didn't look like much of an army. But they were all he had.

"Señores," he began at last, speaking very quietly, "I have called you all together to warn you of peril to your lives. I think, if you stand with me, we can escape, but it will take courage and energy. You have shown me you possess these qualities, and I hope you will use them now."

He paused, then went on: "I know many of you have been angry with me because I have had my wife here. You thought me another of these bootlickers to a rotten government,"—that brought them to full awareness!—"who was being rewarded for some Judas act. It is not true. We all owe our lives to this gallant woman. It was I who was suspected of being hostile to the rulers, and she was sent to spy on me for them. Instead, she told me the truth, and now I am telling it to you.

"You must know that I am an agent from Earth. No, no, I am not an Imperialist. As a matter of fact, the Central American countries were worried about their joint colony, Ciudad Alcazar, your city. It was suspected she had not freely joined this confederation. There are other countries, too, which are worried. I came to investigate for them; what I have seen convinces me they were right."

He went on, quickly and not very truthfully. He had to deal with their anti-U.N. conditioning, appeal to the nationalism he despised. (At that, it wouldn't make any practical difference if some countries on Earth retained nominal ownership of certain tracts on Venus; a democratic confederation would re-absorb those within a generation, quite peacefully.) He had to convince them that the whole gang was scheduled to go to Lucifer; all were suspected, and the death of Valdez confirmed the suspcion, and there was always a labor shortage in the mines. His psych training stood him in good stead, before long he had them rising and shouting. *I should'a been a politician,* he thought sardonically.

". . . And are we going to take this outrage? Are we going to rot alive in that hell, and let our wives and children suffer, forever? Or shall we strike back, to save our own lives and liberate Venus?"

When the uproar had subsided a little, he sketched his plan: a march on Lucifer itself, to seize weapons and gain some recruits, then an attack on New America. If it was timed right, they could grab the city just before the ferries landed, and hold it while all of them were embarked on the freighter—then off to Earth, and in a year or two a triumphant return with the army of liberation!

"If anyone does not wish to come with us, let him stay here. I shall compel no man. I can only use those who will be brave, and will obey orders like soldiers, and will set lives which are already forfeit at hazard for the freedom of their homes. Are you with me? Let those who will follow me stand up and shout 'Yes!' "

Not a man stayed in his seat; the timid ones, if any, dared not do so while their comrades were rising and whooping about the table. The din roared and rolled, bunkframes rattled, eyes gleamed murder from a whirlpool of faces. The first stage of Hollister's gamble had paid off well indeed, he thought; now for the tough part.

He appointed Fernandez his second in command and organized the men into a rough corps; engineering discipline was valuable here. It was late before he and Barbara and Fernandez could get away to discuss concrete plans.

"We will leave two men here," said Hollister. "They will send the usual radio reports, which I shall write in advance for them, so no one will suspect; they will also take care of the rocket when it comes for Barbara, and I *hope* the police will assume it crashed. We will send for them when we hold New America. I think we can take Lucifer by surprise, but we can't count on the second place not being warned by the time we get there."

Fernandez looked steadily at him. "And will all of us

leave with the spaceship?" he asked.

"Of course. It would be death to stay. And Earth will need their knowledge of Venus."

"Simón, you know the ship cannot carry fifty men — or a hundred, if we pick up some others at Lucifer."

Hollister's face was wintry. "I do not think fifty will survive," he said.

Fernandez crossed himself, then nodded gravely. "I see. Well, about the supply problem —"

When he had gone, Barbara faced her husband and he saw a vague fright in her eyes. "You weren't very truthful out there, were you?" she asked. "I don't know much Spanish, but I got the drift, and —"

"All right!" he snapped wearily. "There wasn't time to use sweet reasonableness. I had to whip them up fast."

"They aren't scheduled for Lucifer at all. They have no personal reason to fight."

"They're committed now," he said in a harsh tone. "It's fifty or a hundred lives today against maybe a hundred million in the future. That's an attitude which was drilled into me at the Academy, and I'll never get rid of it. If you want to live with me, you'll have to accept that."

"I'll try," she said.

VII

The towers bulked black through a whirl of dust, under a sky the color of clotted blood. Hollister steered his tank close, speaking into its radio: "Hello, Lucifer. Hello, Lucifer. Come in."

"Lucifer," said a voice in his earphones. "Who are you and what do you want?"

"Emergency. We need help. Get me your captain."

Hollister ground between two high gun towers. They had been built and manned against the remote possibility that a convict outbreak might succeed in grabbing some tanks; he was hoping their personnel had grown lazy with uneventful years. Edging around the main shell of the prison, he lumbered toward the landing field and the nearby radio mast. One by one, the twenty tanks of his command rolled into the compound and scattered themselves about it.

Barbara sat next to him, muffled in airsuit and closed helmet. Her gauntleted hand squeezed his shoulder, he could just barely feel the pressure. Glancing around to her stiffened face, he essayed a smile.

"Hello, there! Captain Thomas speaking. What are you doing?"

"This is Hollister, from the Last Chance air camp. Remember me? We're in trouble and need help. Landslip damn near wiped our place out." The Earthman drove his machine onto the field.

"Well, what are you horsing around like that for? Assemble your tanks in front of the main lock."

"All right, all right, gimme a chance to give some orders. The boys don't seem to know where to roost."

Now! Hollister slapped down the drive switch and his tank surged forward. "Hang on!" he yelled. "Thomas, this thing has gone out of control—Help."

It might have gained him the extra minute he needed. He wasn't sure what was happening behind him. The tank smashed into the radio mast and he was hurled forward against his safety webbing. His hands flew—extend the grapple, snatch that buckling strut, drag it aside, and *push!*

The frame wobbled crazily. The tank stalled. Hollister yanked off his harness, picked up the cutting torch whose fuel containers were already on his back, and went through the air lock without stopping to conserve atmosphere. Blue flame stabbed before him, he slid down the darkened extra faceplate and concentrated on his job. Get this beast down before it sent a call for help!

Barbara got the bull-like machine going again and urged it ahead, straining at the weakened skeleton. The mast had been built for flexibility in the high winds, not for impact strength. Hollister's torch roared, slicing a main support. A piece of steel clanged within a meter of him.

He dropped the torch and dove under the tank, just as the whole structure caved in.

"Barbara!" He picked himself out of the wreckage, looking wildly into the hurricane that blew around him. "Barbara, are you all right?"

She crawled from the battered tank and into his arms. "Our car won't go any more," she said shakily. The engine hood was split open by a falling beam and oil hissed from the cracked block.

"No matter. Let's see how the boys are doing—"

He led a run across the field, staggering in the wind. A chunk of concrete whizzed by his head and he dropped as one of the guard towers went by. Good boys! They'd gone out and dynamited it!

Ignoring the ramp leading down to the garage, Fernandez had brought his tank up to the shell's main air lock for humans. It was sturdily built, but his snorting monster walked through it. Breathable air gasped out. It sleeted a little as formaldehyde took up water vapor and became solid.

No time to check on the rest of the battle outside, you could only hope the men assigned to that task were doing their job properly. Hollister saw one of his tanks go up under a direct hit. All the towers weren't disabled yet. But he had to get into the shell.

"Stay here, Barbara!" he ordered. Men were swarming from their vehicles. He led the way inside. A group of uniformed corpses waited for him, drying and shriveling even as he watched. He snatched the carbines from then and handed them out to the nearest of his followers. The rest would have to make do with their tools till more weapons could be recovered.

Automatic bulkheads had sealed off the rest of the shell. Hollister blasted through the first one. A hail of bullets from the smoking hole told him that the guards within had had time to put on their suits.

He waved an arm. "Bring up Maria Larga!"

It took a while, and he fumed and fretted. Six partisans trundled the weapon forth. It was a standard man-drawn cart for semiportable field equipment, and Long Mary squatted on it: a motor-driven blower connected with six meters of hose, an air blast. This one had had an oxygen bottle and a good-sized fuel tank hastily attached to make a super flame thrower. Fernandez got behind the steel plate which had been welded in front as armor, and guided it into the hole. The man behind whooped savagely and turned a handle. Fire blew forth, and the compartment was flushed out.

There were other quarters around the cell block, which came next, but Hollister ignored them for the time being. The air lock in this bulkhead had to be opened the regular way, only two men could go through at a time, and there might be guards on the other side. He squeezed in with San Rafael and waited while the pump cleaned out the chamber. Then he opened the inner door a crack, tossed a homemade shrapnel grenade, and came through firing.

He stumbled over two dead men beyond. San Rafael choked and fell as a gun spat farther down the corridor. Hollister's .45 bucked in his hand. Picking himself up, he looked warily down the cruelly bright length of the block. No one else. The convicts were yammering like wild animals.

He went back, telling off a few men to cut the prisoners out of their cells, issue airsuits from the lockers, and explain the situation. Then he returned to the job of cleaning out the rest of the place.

It was a dirty and bloody business. He lost ten men in all. There were no wounded: if a missile tore open a suit, that was the end of the one inside. A small hole would have given time to slap on an emergency path, but the guards were using magnum slugs.

Fernandez sought him out to report that an attempt to get away by rocket had been stopped, but that an indeterminate number of holdouts were in the refinery, which was a separate building. Hollister walked across the field, dust whirling about smashed machines, and stood before the smaller shell.

Thomas' voice crackled in his earphone: "You there! What is the meaning of this?"

That was too much. Hollister began to laugh. He laughed so long he thought perhaps he was going crazy.

Sobering, he replied in a chill tone: "We're taking over. You're trapped in there with nothing but small arms. We can blast you out if we must, but you'd do better to surrender."

Thomas, threateningly: "This place is full of radioactivity, you know. If you break in, you'll smash down the shielding—or we'll do it for you—and scatter the stuff everywhere. You won't live a week."

It might be a bluff, but— "All right," said Hollister with a cheerful note, "you're sealed in without food or water. We can wait. But I thought you'd rather save your own lives."

"You're insane. You'll be wiped out—"

"That's our affair. Any time you want out, pick up the phone and call the office. You'll be locked in the cells with supplies enough for a while when we leave." Hollister turned and walked away.

He spent the next few hours reorganizing; he had to whip the convicts into line, though when their first exuberance had faded they were for the most part ready to join him. Suddenly his army had swelled to more than two hundred. The barracks were patched up and made habitable, munitions were found and passed about, the transport and supply inventoried. Then word came that Thomas' handful were ready to surrender. Hollister marched them into the cell block and assigned some convicts to stand watch.

He had had every intention of abiding by his agreement, but when he was later wakened from sleep with the news that his guards had literally torn the prisoners apart, he didn't have the heart to give them more than a dressing down.

"Now," he said to his council of war, "we'd better get rolling again. Apparently we were lucky enough so that no word of this has leaked out, but it's a long way yet to New America."

"We have not transportation for more than a hundred," said Fernandez.

"I know. We'll take the best of the convicts; the rest will just have to stay behind. They *may* be able to pull the same trick on the next supply train that our boys in Last Chance have ready for the rocket—or they may not. In any event, I don't really hope they can last out, or that we'll be able to take the next objective unawares—but don't tell anyone that."

"I suppose not," said Fernandez somberly, "but it is a dirty business."

"War is always a dirty business," said Hollister.

He lost a whole day organizing his new force. Few if any of the men knew how to shoot, but the guns were mostly recoilless and automatic so he hoped some damage could be done; doctrine was to revert to construction equipment, which they did know how to use, in any emergency. His forty Latins were a cadre of sorts, distributed among the sixty convicts in a relationship equivalent to that between sergeant and private. The whole unit was enough to make any military man break out in a cold sweat, but it was all he had.

Supply wagons were reloaded and machine guns

mounted on a few of the tanks He had four Venusian days to get to New America and take over—and if the rebels arrived too soon, police reinforcements would pry them out agian, and if the radio-control systems were ruined in the fighting, the ferries couldn't land.

It was not exactly a pleasant situation.

The first rocket was sighted on the fifth day of the campaign. It ripped over, crossing from horizon to horizon, in a couple of minutes, but there was little doubt that it had spotted them. Hollister led his carvan off the plain, into broken country which offered more cover but would slow them considerably. Well, they'd just have to keep going day and night.

The next day it was an armored, atomic-powered monster which lumbered overhead, supplied with enough energy to go slowly and even to hover for a while. In an atmosphere without oxygen and always driven by storms, the aircraft of Earth weren't possible—no helicopters, no leisurely airboats; but a few things like this one had been built as emergency substitutes. Hollister tuned in his radio, sure it was calling to them.

"Identify yourselves! This is the Guardian Corps."

Hollister adapted his earlier lie, not expecting belief—but every minute he stalled, his tank lurched forward another hundred meters or so.

The voice was sarcastic: "And, of course, you had nothing to do with the attack on Lucifer."

"What attack?"

"That will do! Go out on the plain and set up camp till we can check on you."

"Of course," said Hollister meekly. "Signing off."

From now on, it was strict radio silence in his army. He'd gained a good hour, though, since the watchers wouldn't be sure till then that he was disobeying—and a lovely dust storm was blowing up.

Following plan, the tanks scattered in pairs, each

couple for itself till they converged on New America at
the agreed time. Some would break down, some would be
destroyed en route, some would come late—a few might
even arrive disastrously early—but there was no choice.
Hollister was reasonably sure none would desert him; they
were all committed past that point.

He looked at Barbara. Her face was tired and drawn,
the red hair hung lusterless and tangled to her shoulders,
dust and sweat streaked her face, but he thought she was
very beautiful. "I'm sorry to have dragged you into this,"
he said.

"It's all right, dear. Of course I'm scared, but I'm still
glad."

He kissed her for a long while and then slapped his
helmet down with a savage gesture.

The first bombs fell toward sunset. Hollister saw them
as flashes through the dust, and felt their concussion
rumble in the frame of his tank. He steered in a narrow,
overhung gulch, his companion vehicle nosing close
behind. There were two convicts in it—Johnson and
Waskowicz—pretty good men, he thought, considering
all they had been through.

Dust and sand were his friends, hiding him even from
the infrared 'scopes above which made nothing of mere
darkness. The rough country would help a lot, too. It was
simply a matter of driving day and night, sticking close to
bluffs and gullies, hiding under attack and then driving
some more. He was going to lose a number of his units,
but thought the harassing would remain aerial till they
got close to New America. The Guardians wouldn't risk
their heavy stuff unnecessarily at any great distance from
home.

VIII

The tank growled around a high pinnacle and faced him without warning. It was a military vehicle, and cannons swiveled to cover his approach.

Hollister gunned his machine and drove directly up the pitted road at the enemy. A shell burst alongside him, steel splinters rang on armor. Coldly, he noted for possible future reference the relatively primitive type of Venusian war equipment: no tracker shells, no rovers. He had already planned out what to do in an encounter like this, and told his men the idea—now it had happened to him.

The Guardian tank backed, snarling. It was not as fast or as maneuverable as his, it was meant for work close to cities where ground had been cleared. A blast of high-caliber machine-gun bullets ripped through the cab, just over his head. Then he struck. The shock jammed him forward even as his grapple closed jaws on the enemy's nearest tread.

"Out!" he yelled. Barbara snatched open the air lock and fell to the stones below. Hollister was after her. He flung a glance behind. His other tank was an exploded ruin, canted to one side, but a single figure was crawling from it, rising, zigzagging toward him. There was a sheaf of dynamite sticks in one hand. The man flopped as the machine gun sought him and wormed the last few meters. Waskowicz. "They got Sam," he reported, huddling against the steel giant with his companions. "Shall we blast her?"

Hollister reflected briefly. The adversary was immobilized by the transport vehicle that clutched it bulldog fashion. He himself was perfectly safe this instant, just beneath the guns. "I've got a better notion. Gimme a boost."

He crawled up on top, to the turret lock. "O.K., hand me that torch. I'm going to cut my way in!"

The flame roared, biting into metal. Hollister saw the lock's outer door move. So—just as he had expected—the lads inside wanted out! He paused. A suited arm emerged with a grenade. Hollister's torch slashed down. Barbara made a grab for the tumbling missile and failed. Waskowicz tackled her, landing on top. The thing went off.

Was she still alive—? Hollister crouched so that the antenna of his suit radio pocked into the lock. "Come out if you want to live. Otherwise I'll burn you out."

Sullenly, the remaining three men appeared, hands in the air. Hollister watched them slide to the ground, covering them with his pistol. His heart leaped within him when he saw Barbara standing erect. Waskowicz was putting an adhesive patch on his suit where a splinter had ripped it.

"You O.K.?" asked Hollister.

"Yeah," grunted the convict. "Pure dumb luck. Now what?"

"Now we got us one of their own tanks. Somebody get inside and find some wire or something to tie up the Terrible Three here. And toss out the fourth."

"That's murder!" cried one of the police. "We've only got enough oxy for four hours in these suits—"

"Then you'll just have to hope the battle is over by then," said Hollister unsympathetically. He went over and disentangled the two machines.

The controls of the captured tank were enough like those of the ordinary sort for Barbara to handle. Hollister gave Waskowicz a short lecture on the care and feeding of machine guns, and sat up by the 40 mm. cannon himself; perforce, they ignored the 20. They closed the locks but didn't bother to replenish the air inside; however, as Hollister drove up the mountainside, Waskowicz recharged their oxygen bottles from the stores inside the vehicle.

The battle was already popping when they nosed up onto the ledge and saw the great sweep of the city. Drifting dust limited his vision, but Hollister saw a few engagements between his own machines and the enemy's. Doctrine was to ram and grapple the military tank, get out and use dynamite or torches, and then worm toward the colony's main air lock. It might have to be blown open, but bulkheads should protect the civilians within.

An engineer tank made a pass at Hollister's. He turned aside, realizing that his new scheme had its own drawbacks. Another police machine came out of the dust; its guns spoke, the engineers went up in a flash and a bang, and then it had been hit from behind. Hollister set his teeth and went on. It was the first time he had seen anything like war; he had an almost holy sense of his mission to prevent this from striking Earth again.

The whole operation depended on his guess that there wouldn't be many of the enemy. There were only a few Guardians in each town, who wouldn't have had time or reserves enough to bring in a lot of reinforcements; and tanks couldn't be flown in. But against their perhaps lesser number was the fact that they would fight with tenacity and skill. Disciplined as engineers and convicts were, they simply did not have the training—even the psychological part of it which turns frightened individuals into a single selfless unit. They would tend to make wild attacks and to panic when the going got rough—which it was already.

He went on past the combat, toward the main air lock. Dim shapes began to appear through scudding dust. Half a dozen mobile cannon were drawn up in a semicircle to defend the gate. That meant—all the enemy tanks, not more than six or seven, out on the ledge fighting the attackers.

"All right," Hollister's voice vibrated in their earphones. "We'll shoot from here. Barbara, move her in a zigzag at 10 KPH, keeping about this distance; let out a yell if you think you have to take other evasive action.

Otherwise I might hit the city."

He jammed his faceplate into the rubberite viewscope and his hands and feet sought the gun controls. Crosshairs—range—*fire one!* The nearest cannon blew up.

Fire two! Fire three! His 40 reloaded itself. Second gun broken down, third a clean miss—*Fire four! Gotcha!*

A rank of infantry appeared, their suits marked with the Guardian symbol. They must have been flown here. Waskowicz blazed at them and they broke, falling like rag dolls, reforming to crawl in. They were good soliders. Now the other three enemy mobiles were swiveling about, shooting through the dust. "Get us out of here, Barbara!"

The racket became deafening as they backed into the concealing murk. Another enemy tank loomed before them. Hollister fed it two shells almost point blank.

If he could divert the enemy artillery long enough for his men to storm the gate—

He saw a police tank locked with an attacker, broken and dead. Hollister doubted if there were any left in action now. He saw none of his own vehicles moving, though he passed by the remnants of several. And where were his men?

Shock threw him against his webbing. The echoes rolled and banged and shivered for a long time. His head swam. The motors still turned, but—

"I think they crippled us," said Barbara in a small voice.

"O.K. Let's get out of here." Hollister sighed, it had been a nice try, and had really paid off better than he'd had a right to expect. He scrambled to the lock, gave Barbara a hand, and they slid to the ground as the three fieldpieces rolled into view on their self-powered carts.

The stalled tank's cannon spoke, and one of the police guns suddenly slumped. "Waskowicz!" Barbara's voice was shrill in the earphones. He stayed in there—"

"We can't save him. And if he can fight our tank long enough—Build a monument to him some day. Now come on!" Hollister led the way into curtaining gloom. The wind hooted and clawed at him.

As he neared the main lock, a spatter of rifle fire sent him to his belly. He couldn't make out who was there, but it had been a ragged volley—take a chance on their being police and nailing him— "Just us chickens, boss!" he shouted. Somewhere in a corner of his mind he realized that there was no reason for shouting over a radio system. His schooled self-control must be slipping a bit.

"Is it you, Simón?" Fernandez's voice chattered in his ears. "Come quickly, now, we're at the lock but I think they will attack soon."

Hollister wiped the dust from his faceplate and tried to count how many there were. Latins and convicts, perhaps twenty—"Are there more?" he inquired. "Are you the last?"

"I do not know, Simón," said Fernandez. "I had gathered this many, we were barricaded behind two smashed cars, and when I saw their artillery pull away I led a rush here. Maybe there are some partisans left besides us, but I doubt it."

Hollister tackled the emergency control box which opened the gate from outside. It would be nice if he didn't have to blast—Yes, by Heaven! It hadn't been locked! He jammed the whole score into the chamber, closed the outer door, and started the pumps.

"They can get in, too," said Fernandez dubiously.

"I know. Either here or by ten other entrances. But I have an idea. All of you stick by me."

The anteroom was empty. The town's civilians must be huddled in the inner compartments, and all the cops must be outside fighting. Hollister threw back his helmet, filling his lungs with air that seemed marvelously sweet, and led a quick but cautious trot down the long halls.

"The spaceship is supposed to have arrived by now," he said. "What we must do is take and hold the radio shack.

Since the police don't know exactly what our plans are, they will hesitate to destroy it just to get at us. It will seem easier merely to starve us out."

"Or use sleepy gas," said Fernandez. "Our suits' oxygen supply isn't good for more than another couple of hours."

"Yes . . . I suppose that is what they'll do. That ship had better be up there!"

The chances were that she was. Hollister knew that several days of ferrying were involved, and had timed his attack for hours after she was scheduled to arrive. For all he knew, the ferries had already come down once or twice.

He didn't know if he or anyone in his band would live to be taken out. He rather doubted it; the battle had gone worse than expected, he had not captured the city as he hoped—but the main thing was to get some kind of report back to Earth.

A startled pair of technies met the invaders as they entered. One of them began an indignant protest, but Fernandez waved a rifle to shut him up. Hollister glanced about the gleaming controls and meters. He could call the ship himself, but he didn't have the training to guide a boat down. Well—

He pulled off his gloves and sat himself at the panel. Keys clattered beneath his fingers. When were the cops coming? Any minute.

"Hello, freighter. Hello, up there. Spaceship, this is New America calling. Come in."

Static buzzed and crackled in his earphones.

"Come in spaceship. This is New America. Come in, damn it!"

Lights flashed on the board, the computer clicked, guiding the beam upward. It tore past the ionosphere and straggled weakly into the nearest of the tiny, equally spaced robot relay stations which circled the planet. Obedient to the keying signal, the robot amplified the beam and shot it to the next station, which kicked it farther along. The relayer closest to the spaceship's present position in her orbit focused the beam on her.

Or was the orbit empty?

". . . Hello, New America." The voice wavered, faint and distorted. *"Evening Star* calling New America. What's going on down there? We asked for a ferry signal three hours ago."

"Emergency," snapped Hollister. "Get me the captain—fast! Meanwhile, record this."

"But—"

"Fast, I said! And record! This is crash priority, condition red." Hollister felt sweat trickling inside his suit.

"Recording. Sending for captain now."

"Good!" Hollister leaned over the mike. "For Main Office, Earth, United Nations Inspectorate. Repeat: Main Office, U.N. Inspectorate. Urgent, confidential. This is Agent A-431-240. Repeat, Agent A-431-240. Code Watchbird. Reporting on Venusian situation as follows—" He began a swift sketch of conditions.

"I think I hear voices down the hall," whispered Barbara to Fernandez.

The Latin nodded. He had already dragged a couple of desks into the corridor to make a sort of barricade; now he motioned his men to take positions; a few outside, the rest standing by, crowded together in the room. Hollister saw what was going on and swung his gun to cover the two technies. They were scared, and looked pathetically young, but he had no time for mercy.

A voice in his earphones, bursting through static: "This is Captain Brackney. What d'you want?"

"UNI business, captain. I'm besieged in the GCA shack here with a few men. We're to be gotten out at all costs if it's humanly possible."

He could almost hear the man's mouth fall open. "God in space—is that the truth?"

Hollister praised the foresight of his office. "You have a

sealed tape aboard among your official records. All spaceships, all first-class public conveyances, do. It's changed by an Un-man every year or so. O.K., that's an ID code, secret recognition signal. It proves my right to commandeer everything you've got."

"I know that much. What's on the tape?"

"This year it will be, "Twas brillig and the slithy toves give me liberty or give me pigeons on the grass alas.' Have your radioman check that at once."

Pause. Then: "O.K., I'll take your word for it till he does. What do you want?"

"Bring two ferries down, one about fifty kilometers behind the other. No arms on board, I suppose? . . . No. Well, have just the pilots aboard, because you may have to take twenty or so back. How long will this take you? . . . Two hours? That long? . . . Yes, I realize you have to let your ship get into the right orbital position and — All right, if you can't do it in less time. Be prepared to embark anyone waiting out there and lift immediately. Meanwhile stand by for further instructions . . . Hell, yes, you can do it!"

Guns cracked outside.

"O.K. I'll start recording again in a minute. Get moving, captain!" Hollister turned back to the others.

"I have to tell Earth what I know, in case I don't make it," he said. "Also, somebody has to see that these technies get the boats down right. Diego, I'll want a few men to defend this place. The rest of you retreat down the hall and pick up some extra oxy bottles for yourselves and all the concentrated food you can carry; because that ship won't have rations enough for all of us. Barbara will show you where it is."

"And how will you get out?" she cried when he had put it into English.

"I'll come to that. You've got to go with them, dear, because you live here and know where they can get the supplies. Leave a couple of suits here for the technies, pick up others somewhere along the way. When you get outside, hide close to the dome. When the ferry lands, some of you make a rush to the shack here. It's right against the outer wall. I see you're still carrying some dynamite, Garcia. Blow a hole to let us through . . . Yes, it's risky, but what have we got to lose?"

She bent to kiss him. There wasn't time to do it properly. A tommy-gun was chattering in the corridor.

Hollister stood up and directed his two prisoners to don the extra suits. "I've no grudge against you boys," he said, "and in fact, if you're scared of what the cops might do to you, you can come along to Earth—but if those boats don't land safely, I'll shoot you both down."

Fernandez, Barbara and a dozen others slipped out past the covering fire at the barricade and disappeared. Hollister hoped they'd make it. They'd better! Otherwise, even if a few escaped, they might well starve to death on the trip home.

The food concentate would be enough. It was manufactured by the ton at Little Moscow—tasteless, but pure nourishment and bulk, normally added to the rest of the diet on Venus. It wouldn't be very palatable, but it would keep men alive for a long time.

The technies were at the board, working hard. The six remaining rebels slipped back into the room; two others lay dead behind the chewed-up barricade. Hollister picked up an auxiliary communication mike and started rattling off everything about Venus he could think of.

A Guardian stuck his head around the door. Three guns barked, and the head was withdrawn. A little later, a white cloth on a rifle barrel was waved past the edge.

Hollister laid down his mike. "I'll talk," he said. "I'll come out, with my arms. You'll have just one man in sight, unarmed." To his men he gave an order to drag the dead into the shack while the truce lasted.

Karsov met him in the hall. He stood warily, but there

was no fear on the smooth face. "What are you trying to do?" he asked in a calm voice.

"To stay out of your mines," said Hollister. It would help if he could keep up the impression this was an ordinary revolt.

"You have called that ship up there, I suppose?"

"Yes. They're sending down a ferry."

"The ferry could have an accident. We would apologize profusely, explain that a shell went wild while we were fighting you gangsters, and even pay for the boat. I tell you this so that you can see there is no hope. You had better give up."

"No hope if we do that either," said Hollister. "I'd rather take my chances back on Earth; they can't do worse than treat my mind."

"Are you still keeping up that farce?" inquired Karsov. But he wasn't sure of himself, that was plain. He couldn't understand how an Un-man could have gotten past his quiz. Hollister had no intention of enlightening him.

"What have you got to lose by letting us go?" asked the Earthman. "So we tell a horror story back home. People there already know you rule with a rough hand."

"I am not going to release you," said Karsov. "You are finished. That second party of yours will not last long, even if they make it outside as I suppose they intend—they will suffocate. I am going to call the spaceship captain on the emergency circuit and explain there is a fight going on and he had better recall his boat. That should settle the matter; if not, the boat will be shot down. As for your group, there will be sleep gas before long."

"I'll blow my brains out before I let you take me," said Hollister sullenly.

"That might save a lot of trouble," said Karsov. He turned and walked away. Hollister was tempted to kill him, but decided to save that pleasure for a while. No use goading the police into a possible use of high explosives.

He went back to the shack and called the *Evening Star* again. "Hello, Captain Brackney? UNI speaking. The bosses down here are going to radio you with a pack of lies. Pretend to believe them and say you'll recall your ferry. Remember, they think just one is coming down. Then—" He continued his orders.

"That's murder!" said the captain. "Pilot One won't have a chance—"

"Yes, he will. Call him now, use spacer code; I don't think any of these birds know it, if they should overhear you. Tell him to have his spacesuit on and be ready for a crash landing, followed by a dash to the second boat."

"It's still a long chance."

"What do you think I'm taking? These are UNI orders, captain. I'm boss till we get back to Earth, if I live so long. All right, got everything? Then I'll continue recording."

After a while he caught the first whiff and said into the mike. "The gas is coming now. I'll have to close my helmet. Hollister signing off."

His men and the technies slapped down their cover. It would be so peaceful here for a little time, with this sector sealed off while gas poured through its ventilators. Hollister tried to grin reassuringly, but it didn't come off.

"Last round," he said. "Half of us, the smallest ones, are going to go to sleep now. The rest will use their oxygen, and carry them outside when we go."

Someone protested. Hollister roared him down. "Not another word! This is the only chance for all of us. No man has oxygen for much more than an hour; we have at least an hour and a half to wait. How else can we do it?"

They submitted unwillingly, and struggled against the anaesthetic as long as they could. Hollister took one of the dead men's bottles to replace the first of his that gave out. His band was now composed of three sleeping men and three conscious but exhausted.

He was hoping the cops wouldn't assault them quickly. Probably not; they would be rallying outside, preparing to meet the ferry with a mobile canon if it should decide to land after all. The rebels trapped in here would keep.

The minutes dragged by. A man at the point of death was supposed to review his whole life, but Hollister didn't feel up to it. He was too tired. He sat watching the telescreen which showed the space field. Dust and wind and the skeleton cradles, emptiness, and a roiling gloom beyond.

One of the wakeful men, a convict, spoke into the helmet circuit: "So you are UNI. Has all this been just to get you back to Earth?"

"To get my report back," said Hollister.

"There are many dead," said one of the Latins, in English. "You have sacrificed us, played us like pawns, no? What of those two we left back at Last Chance?"

"I'm afraid they're doomed," said Hollister tonelessly, and the guilt which is always inherent in leadership was heavy on him.

"It was worth it," said the convict. "If you can smash this rotten system, it was well worth it." His eyes were haunted. They would always be haunted.

"Better not talk," said Hollister. "Save your oxygen."

One hour. The pips on the radar-scopes were high and strong now. The spaceboats weren't bothering with atmospheric braking, they were spending fuel to come almost straight down.

One hour and ten minutes. Was Barbara still alive?

One hour and twenty minutes.

One hour and thirty minutes. Any instant—

"There, señor! There!"

Hollister jumped to his feet. Up in a corner of the screen, a white wash of fire—here she came!

The ferry jetted slowly groundward, throwing up a cloud of dust as her fierce blasts tore at the field. Now and then she wobbled, caught by the high wind, but she had been built for just these conditions. Close, close—were they going to let her land after all? Yes, now she was entering the cradle, now the rockets were still.

A shellburst struck her hull amidships and burst it open. The police were cautious, they hadn't risked spilling her nuclear engine and its radioactivity on the field. She rocked in the cradle. Hollister hoped the crash-braced pilot had survived. And he hoped the second man was skillful and had been told exactly what to do.

That ferry lanced out of the clouds, descending fast. She wasn't very maneuverable, but the pilot rode her like a horseman, urging, pleading, whipping and spurring when he had to. She slewed around and fell into a shaky curve, out of screen range.

If the gods were good, her blast had incinerated the murderers of the first boat.

She came back into sight, fighting for control. Hollister howled. "Guide her into a cradle!" He waved his gun at the seated technies. "Guide her safely in if you want to live!"

She was down.

Tiny figures were running toward her, heedless of earth still smoking underfoot. Three of them veered and approached the radio shack. "O.K.!" rapped Hollister. "Back into the corridor!" He dragged one of the unconscious men himself; stooping, he sealed the fellow's suit against the poison gases outside. There would be enough air within it to last a sleeper a few minutes.

Concussion smashed at him. He saw shards of glass and wire flying out the door and ricocheting nastily about his head. Then the yell of Venus' wind came to him. He bent and picked up his man. "Let's go!"

They scrambled through the broken wall and out onto the field. The wind was at their backs, helping them for once. One of the dynamiters moved up alongside Hollister. He saw Barbara's face, dim behind the helmet.

When he reached the ferry, the others were loading the last boxes of food. A figure in space armor was clumping unsteadily toward them from the wrecked boat. Maybe their luck had turned. Sweeping the field with his eyes, Hollister saw only ruin. There were still surviving police, but they were inside the city and it would take minutes for them to get out again.

He counted the men with him and estimated the number of food boxes. Fifteen all told, including his two erstwhile captives—Barbara's party must have met opposition—but *she* still lived, God be praised! There were supplies enough, it would be a hungry trip home but they'd make it.

Fernandez peered out of the air lock. "Ready," he announced. "Come aboard. We have no seats, so we must rise at low acceleration, but the pilot says there is fuel to spare."

Hollister helped Barbara up the ladder and into the boat. "I hope you'll like Earth," he said awkwardly.

"I know I will—with you there," she told him.

Hollister looked through the closing air lock at the desolation which was Venus. Some day it would bloom, but—

"We'll come back," he said.

When the terraforming was done, would mercy and justice, as well as bounty, rain down on parched Venus? Could planets and people develop in separate ways and still remain at peace with one another? After a century's effort, the Institute's dream of a sane citizenry in a stable civilization was little closer to fulfillment. Long-term political issues within and among societies had not yet been solved. Could the Psychotechnic Institute and the Un-men it created withstand the insidious temptations of power? Watching over human destiny was their self-appointed role, but who shall watch the watchmen?

Author's Note

Science fiction is indebted to Robert A. Heinlein for many good things. Not least among them is the concept of a "future history." Other writers before him had told stories in series, but had set them in static societies or else in such short time spans that no real development occurred. Olaf Stapledon had chronicled the entire future of our species, and then of the universe, but those books of his had no characters to speak of and were on a geological rather than historical scale. Heinlein wrote vivid tales of events happening to individuals, but civilization itself became a protagonist too, ever changing as the hopefulness of the first interplanetary era was lost in corruption followed by dictatorship, regained after a revolution, shunted aside in later turmoil, eventually restored as mankind approached racial maturity.

Like most readers, I was fascinated. Rather early in my own writing career, I embarked on something similar. It would not be what I did exclusively, nor would it have a byline reserved to itself, but it would tie together a number of stories. Each of these must, of course, be comprehensible alone. Yet for those who remembered from one to the next, the interrelationships would add depth to all—or so I hoped.

Accordingly, I drew up a chart in the manner of Heinlein and, from time to time, completed a piece whose title was on it. Like him, I did not follow chronological order, but wrote whatever I felt like whenever the mood struck me. Still, the undertaking was ambitious: to tell the story of humanity from the near future on through its expansion into the galaxy.

The set of tales has been dubbed the "Psychotechnic League series." A group of them comprise this book. A few more exist, notably the novels *Virgin Planet* and *The Peregrine*.

Eventually I gave it up. That did not happen overnight; the last part, "The Pirate," appeared in 1968, though before then there had been a long hiatus. I just found myself more and more turning elsewhere, especially to a new future history quite unlike the first.

A good reason for this abandonment was that the real world had, predictably, not been behaving as I described. For example, World War Three remains ahead of us, rather than behind. No doubt I could have fudged my dates a bit. However, I could not explain away important scientific discoveries and technological advances which I had failed to foresee.

People and institutions had also changed profoundly, as had my view of them. Once I was a flaming liberal, a fact which is probably most obvious in "Un-Man." Nowadays I consider the United Nations a dangerous farce on which we ought to ring down the curtain. (In justice to it and myself, though, please remember that when I wrote this novella the U.N. had quite a different character from that it has since acquired, and looked improvable.)

Otherwise my current political opinions are irrelevant

here, because I no longer preach in my fiction, I simply tell stories. I like to think they are better stories, and better told, than formerly.

Then why resurrect these old ones?

Well, first and foremost is the hope that they will entertain you. True, they are on a time line which never came into being, but that matters little. We continue to relish the works of H. Rider Haggard and Edgar Rice Burroughs, despite everything we have learned about Africa and Mars. If you, reader, are my age, you may have encountered these yarns when they originally appeared, and they may now evoke pleasant memories of youth. If you are my daughter's age, or younger, they may be new to you—and may you enjoy them as your father or mother perhaps did!

I could even imitate Heinlein again and bail out the whole series by declaring that it shows an alternate cosmos. However, Mrs. Miesel has now done that on my behalf.

As a second justification for the book, it may prove of some small use to scholars of science fiction. These tales were not seminal like Heinlein's, but they were a noticeable part of the field a generation ago. We've all come a long way since then, but sometimes we do well to look back and see where we have been.

Poul Anderson